ASSASSIN'S MASK

ASSASSIN'S MAGIC
BOOK TWO

EVERLY FROST

Frost, Everly
Assassin's Mask

Cover design by Claire Holt with Luminescence Covers
www.luminescencecovers.com

For information on reproducing sections of this book or sales of this book,
go to
www.EverlyFrost.com
everlyfrost@gmail.com

DISCOVER THE EVER REALMS

Seven series. One world.

Suggested Reading Order:

Bright Wicked
Storm Princess
Assassin's Magic
Soul Bitten Shifter
Supernatural Legacy
Dark Magic Shifters
Kingdom of Betrayal

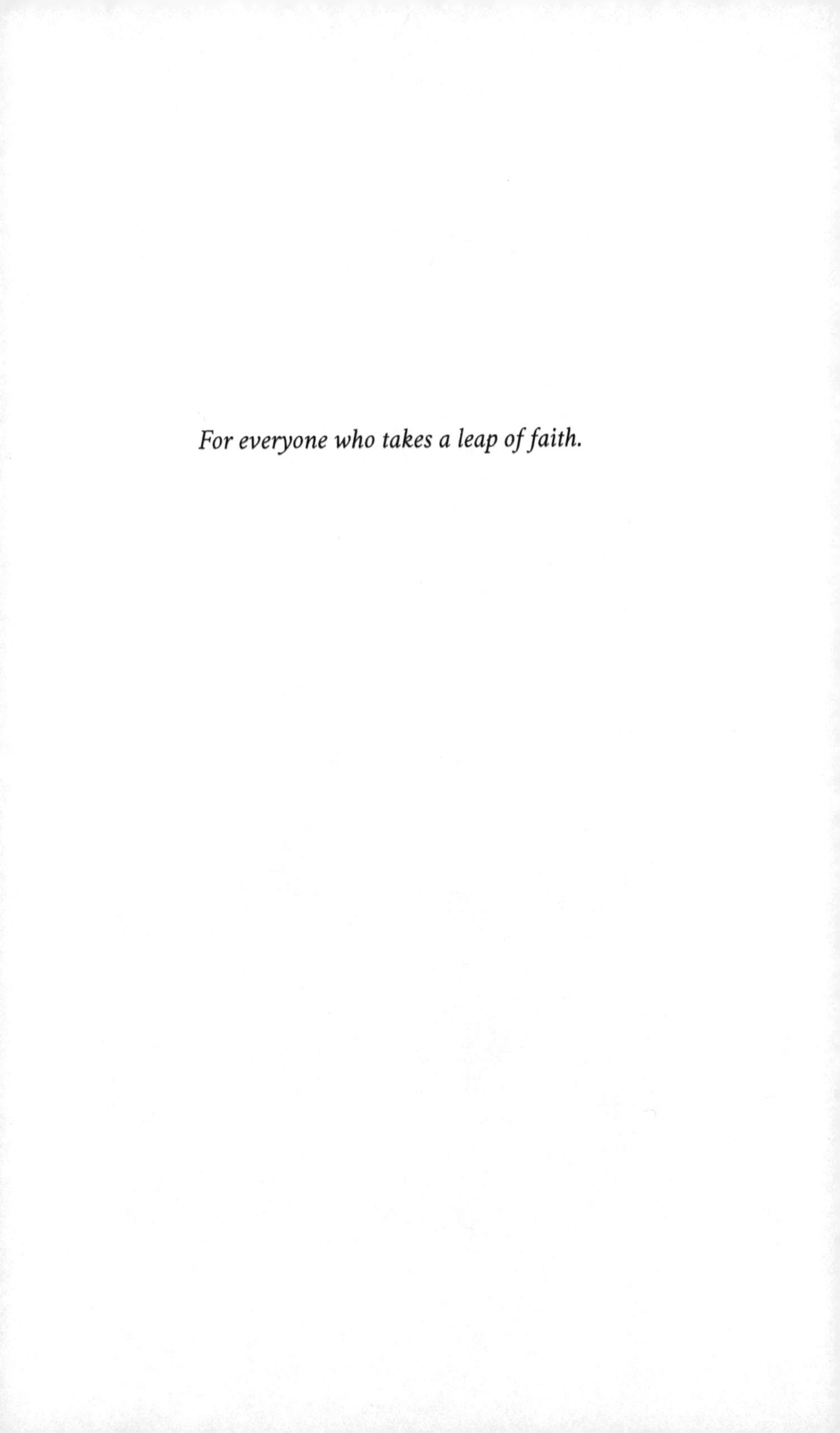

For everyone who takes a leap of faith.

CHAPTER ONE

*M*oonlight streams across the empty field as I land and fold away my wings.

I drop to the long grass, my whole body aching, my heart burning.

I flew for two days to reach this spot and now my strength is gone. Two days trying to mend the fragments of my heart.

Slade's final words echo in my mind: *She's gone.*

I force myself to stand and hurry away from the memories, all of them. I can't stay in this field while the wind whispers like his voice across my cheeks and lips. I have to get to my safe house and leave the past behind with every step.

My boots protect my calves from the sharp blades of grass but the flimsy dress I'm wearing does nothing to shield my thighs. I consider swapping the dress for my protective assassin's suit, but the dress will ensure that I don't look like a threat. I'm already a spectacle carrying a katana sword strapped to my back along with my backpack.

I don't have the energy to make myself invisible by blurring. I used up every shred of my Valkyrie power to fly non-stop, remaining within the cloud cover, staying high enough to be mistaken for a bird.

Blurring won't do me much good even if I had the strength to accomplish it right now. This is the part of my escape where I have to interact with humanity again.

Reaching the edge of the field, I head directly east along the empty road to the lone motel that squats at the edge of this secluded place. It's located west of the Platte River in Nebraska, just inside the border between the Legion and the Dominion—as far as I can get from the Legion's stronghold without crossing into Dominion territory.

I stride past the gleaming motorcycles and SUVs parked outside the building, noting how many of the vehicles contain rifles and hunting knives casually left on seats. No doubt, those are the backup weapons.

Nobody nice comes here.

Which is exactly why I picked this place.

The scent of beer and clacking from the billiard table greets me at the door. Along with about twenty male stares.

I pause, the moonlight behind me, fully aware that the dress conceals next to nothing. I may as well be standing in my underwear right now. An open invitation for trouble.

Except for the sword at my back, which will keep the wolves at bay for now. Ignoring their lewd comments and whistles, I navigate the tables, narrowly avoid a groping hand along the way, and head straight to the bartender.

Ordinarily, I'd teach the would-be groper a lesson he wouldn't soon forget but tonight I just want to find my room and crash.

The bartender is an older guy with a bunch of faded

tattoos dripping down both arms. He doesn't know my real name but he immediately recognizes me.

"Crystal," he says, since that's the name I gave him seven months ago before I entered the Legion.

The way he says my name, looking flustered and red-faced, tells me there's a problem.

I'm too tired for games. "I'm here for my room, Harry. The one I paid up for a year."

It cost me an arm and a leg to pay for a room for that long —even in this dump—but I had to be sure that the room would still be mine when I needed it. Mom left me plenty of money to live on when she died so I'll be okay. The assassin's life might be one of secrecy and danger, but her clients paid her very well.

Harry scratches his bristly chin. "Ah, well, you see... There's a problem with your room tonight."

"What problem?"

He drags out his answer. "Unfortunately, I had to give it to someone else. Just this once."

I lean across the bar, place both hands flat on it, and tap my fingernails on the enameled surface. My own tattoo is a sharp contrast to my skin. It's an intricate design in the vague shape of an 'A.' It represents my assassin's name: *Glass Arrow*, which is the name Mom wanted me to have.

Harry doesn't know what I am, but I made it clear when I booked the room that he would regret it if he breached our agreement. The room was supposed to remain vacant until I returned.

I allow a dangerous edge to enter my voice, making my threat clear. "The room that I paid for so nobody would set foot in it? You mean that room?"

"I... uh... didn't exactly have a choice. I swear nobody has touched your room until today. But he wouldn't take 'no' for an answer." Harry inhales and shudders, his jaw clenching. "I'm sorry, Crystal, but I'm more afraid of him than I am of you."

I narrow my eyes at Harry. Someone more dangerous than me? *Well, I wonder who this mystery man is?*

"I guess I'll have to kick him out. C'mon, Harry."

When he doesn't budge, I say, "You're coming upstairs with me and we're going to sort this out."

He shakes his head rapidly. "You can go up there but I'm not coming with you. Call me a coward, but I already told him the room was taken and his answer was this."

Harry tilts his neck to reveal a short, red welt. Only a blade makes a cut that precise. Whoever the mystery intruder is, he held a knife to Harry's throat. I guess Harry was telling the truth when he said he had no choice.

I snarl, "You're a coward, Harry."

"Agreed. But I'm still not going up there. Look... Why don't you come home with me after closing and crash on my couch? The missus won't mind."

"Thanks for the offer, but my things are in that room. I can't take the chance someone will mess with them. And I'm not sure what your wife would make of all my... accessories." I tap my sword meaningfully.

Harry immediately hands me the key. He probably thinks I'm about to use the sword on him, although that's the last thing I intend to do.

I prowl to the staircase at the end of the room.

There are five rooms upstairs. I chose the one at the end of the corridor with the best view of the road so I could see oncoming danger. When I reach it, I debate whether or not to knock or just barge in. Judging by the cut on Harry's neck, the intruder isn't the reasonable type. Unfortunately, kicking the door down isn't an option since I want it to remain intact.

Leaning against the wooden surface, I open my senses. There's one occupant who is possibly... asleep?

I also sense a faint wash of magic—either this guy can wield magic or he recently came into contact with it.

I'll need to proceed carefully.

I use the key to open the door and slip inside. The old wooden trunk containing all my earthly belongings rests at the side of the room beneath the window, right where I left it. It doesn't look like he has tampered with it, so that's a relief.

The curtains are closed to block out the moonlight but there's enough light to make out the bed against the wall on the far right, the bedside table beside it, and the closet against the wall at the end of the bed.

A gun and a bottle of vodka sit on the bedside table.

I quickly sum this guy up: running from his past, ended up in this dump, and if I'm right, he'll leave once he knows I won't be pushed around like Harry.

I leave his weapon where it is and stride over to the mound in the bed to shake his shoulder. "Okay, buddy, time to vacate. This room is taken."

I sense his soft inhale as he wakes up and rolls over, forcing me to jump away from him because... *Whoa...* it's like a mountain just shifted in front of me.

He slides one massive leg out of the bed, followed by the other and rises up... and up... and *up...* revealing overwhelming increments of height, one inch at a time. He clearly knows how to make a first impression, even if he is half-awake and sleepy-eyed.

Threat oozes out of him without any effort at all.

His shaved head remains half-tilted as if it wants to return to the pillow. His eyes remain half-closed. "You'd better have a good reason for disturbing my sleep, woman."

Inwardly, I sigh at the sheer size and physique of this man. I'm taller than average myself, and I often tower over guys. But not this one.

Just for once, can't I have an easy opponent?

I scowl at him. "You're in my room."

He squints at the room, then levels his gaze with mine. His eyes are gray, but not like Gareth's whose gaze is perpetually cold like metal. This guy's expression is like storm-clouds about to break.

"You weren't here when I arrived," he says.

I point to the trunk resting on the floor. "That's mine." I point to the bed. "That's mine." I wave my hand around at the room in general. "This is mine. I ask you to kindly vacate."

His answer is to leverage his big body right back onto the bed, turn his back to me, and pull up the blanket.

Um... what? Did he go straight back to sleep?

He is so still, his torso expanding and contracting with such a regular rhythm, that I can only blink at him. It makes me wonder if he was awake for any of that interaction or actually asleep the whole time.

I tap my finger against my thigh. It was impossible to miss the ring on his forefinger—jet-black with three chunky rubies set into it.

It's a ring that lacks any subtlety. A bit like him.

I can't be sure it's an assassin's ring, not from where I'm standing. I need to know what I'm dealing with. If he's an assassin, I may need to reassess my options as well as my plan of attack.

Testing my theory that he's asleep, I lean over him, avoiding contact. I swirl my hand through the space where his thick fingers curl around the edge of the blanket.

Damn. The power coming off the ring is unmistakable.

He's an assassin.

But at least it isn't a Keres ring. If it was, I'd have to run for my life. The Keres are my mortal enemy and the only creatures that can kill me. The Keres ring that Gareth tried to use against me rests in the bottom of my backpack.

As I hover over the sleeping assassin, his voice rises into the space between us. "You're starting to piss me off, woman."

Okay, not *sleeping, as it turns out.*

I lift myself very slowly away from him and retreat cautiously as he turns onto his back and, faster this time, forces himself to his feet. He rubs his hand across his eyes and growls at me, a low rumbling sound. It's startling how much he resembles an angry bear right now.

His eyes remain half-closed but he points at the gun sitting on the bedside table as if that should scare me off. "I haven't slept for forty-eight hours and you don't want to know what I was doing during that time. So I suggest you come back tomorrow. I promise, I won't touch your things. They'll be here when I'm gone."

He waits for me to skedaddle, clearly unimpressed when I don't. His dark eyebrows draw down into a dangerous scowl.

"Actually," I say, standing my ground. "It's already tomorrow and you don't have a monopoly on a bad day. I'm pretty sure whatever you've done, I can top it."

He rubs his eyes again. This time with his knuckles, dragging himself awake in a way that makes me feel sorry for him. Well, nearly. He isn't lying about being tired. The dark rings and strain on his face tell me he desperately needs to sleep.

For the first time since I hovered over him, he seems to take note of the details: my assassin-issued boots, the welts across my legs, my scanty dress, the burn marks on my hands where I touched the Keres ring while I was fighting Gareth, my glass ring, my tattoo, the sword slung over my shoulder, and finally… my face.

With every new thing he sees, his sleepy demeanor fades. By the time he focuses on my eyes, he is very much awake. He doesn't betray his intentions, but I'm certain his mind just ran to the gun on the bedside table.

I keep my tone cool and clear. "It wouldn't do either of us any good to get into it right now."

"Get into what?" he asks.

Well, for someone so blunt that was pretty obtuse.

I elaborate, "A fight."

"I've heard about you, Hunter Cassidy," he says. "It would be foolhardy for me to get into anything with you. Let alone a fight."

"I guess that gives you the advantage, because I don't know you at all."

"I'm Legion," he says. "I was sent here to make sure skirmishes with the Dominion don't break out along the border between our Factions."

I dismiss his statement with a shake of my head. "I just want my room."

"Well, I'm all out of options," he says. "This was the only vacant room for miles. I need to sleep somewhere." He takes a step toward me, a gleam in his eyes. "I heard you had no mercy, but I didn't believe it until now."

I stand my ground. "Is that my reputation? Merciless?"

"A woman who trains in the Legion can only become one of two things: a machine or a whore. I take you for the former—"

Crack.

Despite the force I put behind my fist, he doesn't go down, remaining right where he is except for turning his head in the direction of the blow. He closes his eyes and screws up his face as he processes the pain, dealing with it far quicker than I expected.

He exhales, then inhales, while I wait to see if I need to follow through with another fist.

He opens his eyes to say, "I apologize. That was intended as a compliment but it came out entirely the wrong way. I'm not at my best when I'm tired." He rubs his sore cheek where I hit him, his shoulders slumping.

Oh, boy. Now I feel sorry for him. How did he manage to do that?

Little does he know, I *am* capable of normal emotions. I'm not a machine. My emotions are the reason I'm so desperate for privacy right now. I need to cry. Wail. Scream into a pillow. I need a safe place to let out all the pain, and I need it soon, because everything that happened with Slade is quickly crashing down on me.

"May I suggest a compromise?" he asks.

I try to maintain my equilibrium. "What is that?"

"There is a pullout mattress under this bed. If you allow me to place it in the far corner of the room and get some sleep, I promise I will leave as soon as I wake. I… uh… honestly don't rate my chances of making it down the stairs right now. I'd rather not pass out on them."

"You want the merciless woman to have mercy?"

He shrugs. And then… very carefully… he says, "I would consider it a favor."

I narrow my eyes in consideration of his promise. He seems to place a lot of weight on the idea of owing me. Personally, I don't believe in favors. Superior Ridley once told me that Mom did him a favor and that turned out to be way more complicated than I ever expected.

I squeeze my eyes shut, knowing I'm going to regret this. "Okay."

"Thank you." Without any fuss, he bends to retrieve the mattress, slides it into the corner, and drops onto it. He turns to face the wall and within seconds, his rhythmic breathing tells me he's asleep again.

I lock the door to the room, since I left it slightly open in case I needed to make a quick getaway. Then I hang my head, dropping my chin to my chest.

What have I done? I have no privacy now. What are the chances I can scream into my pillow? Do I care if he hears me?

I press my hand over my mouth because everything I've been pushing down is about to force its way out. There's no stopping the tears or the cry forcing its way into my throat.

Wildly, I assess my options and land on the only one that works.

Bathroom.

I rip my boots off, dropping them to the floor along with my sword and backpack as I race to the bathroom, lock the door, and turn on the shower as well as the faucet over the sink so the running water masks any sounds I make.

To my horror, it's not tears that come out first but the contents of my stomach. It's a good thing I'm already leaning over the sink.

I feel sick. So sick.

The night on Mount Greylock replays on me in stormy flashes. Slade and I went there to fight the Furies and recover the verdan plant. When the Furies tried to kill Slade, they discovered that his blood contains Valkyrie power from the feather I used to heal him. That was when he told me that his brother was killed by a woman with silver wings. It had to be my mother, a fact that kills me, gripping my stomach like claws.

When Gareth showed up and tried to kill us, I had to reveal my wings to save us.

Now, Slade knows what I am. He knows I'm Valkyrie.

He also knows that I bonded with him, that I love him, and… he knows how to kill me. I offered him the Keres ring and he refused to take it. That was when he told me to go and never look back.

I wipe my mouth, gripping the edge of the sink so hard I'm in danger of cracking it.

To bond and then leave is agony. I need to process the pain now or it will fester and tear me apart.

Unable to scream, I wobble from one side of the small space to the next, my head in my hands. I finally sway into the stream of water inside the shower, fully clothed. The dress plasters against my skin but I let the water run cold, standing beneath the needle-sharp spray until I'm shivering.

I welcome the numbing pain. I have to forget the feeling of Slade's body next to mine, the intense need to be near him again. If I can do that, if I can block it out and bury it, then I can move on.

I'll never be the same, but I'll be able to function.

Over time, the pain will fade.

It has to.

I drag off the wet dress and my underwear, emerge from the shower, and wrap a towel around myself, creeping back into the bedroom. Retrieving the key to my trunk from a hidden compartment at the side, I quietly swing it open.

This wooden box contains everything I own—other than Mom's money, which is tucked away in multiple bank accounts. My fingertips brush the surface of Mom's ledger where it rests on top of my clothing. I can't read it—only she could—but it's my last connection with her.

Ah, my own clothes. I pull out a pair of comfortable pajamas. I'm too tired to make it back to the bathroom. I cast a furtive glance at the sleeping man in the corner before I drop the towel where I stand. I dress quickly and slide into the bed he vacated. The sharp scents of gunpowder and vodka fill my nose.

My head spins. I made it to the bed just in time.

Crying is my alcohol. I become a wobbly mess, completely uncoordinated. All I can do now is try to sleep and hope my unwelcome guest stays in his corner of the room. So far, he hasn't moved a muscle so I hope I won't have anything to worry about.

As my eyes close, I spy my dropped backpack and sword lying in the middle of the room.

Curses. I should have picked them up. I should... but... I'll just close my eyes... for a moment...

Sunlight streams across my vision.

It feels like I was asleep for two seconds but the sun tells a different story. I rub my face, squinting, dragging my blurry focus from the open curtains at the side of the room to the figure sitting on the trunk in front of the window. His big body blocks some of the light but not all of it.

He promised he would leave as soon as he woke up but he's still here.

My mystery guest leans forward, all seven foot of him, resting his elbows on his knees.

It's what he holds in his hand that kicks my heart into double time and wakes me up with cracking speed.

Of all the things I didn't want him to find…

I bolt upright. My head spins like a whirlwind. My hand slaps the wall at the head of the bed to keep myself from spinning into it.

His voice is clear and concise. Sharp. A far cry from the tired man he was in the night. "Hunter, if this is what I think it is, you're in deep trouble."

CHAPTER TWO

My response is a warbled objection.

Crying has really taken its toll on me. I hate the way my voice reveals how shattered I am. "You had no right to go through my bag."

He shrugs, unmoved by my indignation. "You left it in the middle of the floor. I almost stepped on it. When I moved it, behold, this fell out."

The Clave rests in his fingertips. It is a single, copper feather—the birth feather of the last Keres—encased in a transparent resin formed from my mother's dying blood.

He holds it carefully in his upturned palm. "I happen to know that Master Gareth cherishes this feather above every other possession. Since you have it, it means he's dead or you stole it and you're about to bring a world of trouble down on yourself."

"If I stole it, I'm not about to admit it, am I?"

My mystery guest sighs, unhappily. "So he's not dead. *Damn*. I was hoping someone finally ended him. Not you, of course, because that wouldn't be good for your health."

My eyes widen, since he's talking about his own Master. "You want Master Gareth dead?"

"Doesn't everyone?"

Wow, he's blunt. It's rare to meet someone so straight-forward, especially in the assassin's world that is full of secrets.

He continues. "Since you're here with this feather, I take it your bid for Master didn't go so well."

I scoot up the bed so I can rest against the wall to keep myself upright. Before Slade and I left the Realm, it was decided that whichever one of us returned with the verdan plant would be made Master.

Slade doesn't have the plant, but he was the only one who returned. The last I saw of him, he was binding Gareth, ready to take him back to the Realm in chains.

It is as it should be. Slade was meant to be Master. I never wanted that role.

"I was never a contender for Legion Master," I say.

"That's not what I heard." He raises his eyebrows at me when I don't respond. "Even the Dominion assassins were talking about it. The whisper is that Alexei Mason wanted to form an alliance with you."

I'm surprised. "The Dominion's Heir Apparent?"

"He's their new Master now. He was appointed a week ago."

My question is cautious. "Why would Alexei Mason want to form an alliance with me?"

"With your history—your mother being a Rogue Master who knew her own mind—and your growing reputation as someone who thinks for herself, the rumor is he thought you might finally end the feud between the Factions."

"Well, I guess that won't happen now." I remember what

Master Gareth said in his office when he didn't know I was listening—that Cain Carter and Alexei Mason don't trust each other. I trust Cain so I guess I should be wary of the new Dominion Master and, by extension, the entire Dominion, but the secrets of my own life have taught me that I should always reserve judgment for myself.

With a heavy exhale, I say, "I don't know your name."

"Call me 'Vlad.'" He continues in the same breath, "What interests me more than this feather is the plant stashed in your bag."

Great. This just gets better. The top of the verdan is visible from the open backpack lying on the floor, the plant's ruby petals a stark contrast with the black canvas.

The verdan's sap can remove the resin from the feather so I can finally reveal the weapon Mom was protecting for nearly twenty years. It's the only way I'll be free from all of the secrets in my life.

It's a small mercy that the Keres ring hasn't rolled out onto the floor. It would be difficult to explain why I have two assassin's rings and I definitely don't want anyone else getting their hands on it.

I briefly clasp the glass ring I wear on my left forefinger, finding strength in its comforting presence. It was the ring that Mom had forged so she wouldn't be exposed to the sickening magic in the assassin's rings.

"Verdan is the ultimate poison," Vlad says. "Many assassins would kill to possess it. But I suspect you already know that."

"Would you?" I ask, since we're being honest with each other. "Kill me for it, I mean?"

He surprises me by laughing. "I don't want it. I prefer to kill with my hands. Or, if I'm in a hurry, with a gun."

He gestures to the bedside table where he left his weapon. I guess he did that to make me feel more secure since I can reach it before he can.

"Well, the plant won't do anyone any good," I say. "It's protected by a spell that makes it completely untouchable." I slide out of bed, my legs wobbling, an exasperated grumble on my lips. "I don't care about the poison, but I do want the sap. But there's no way through that protective shield so... um... *Oh...*"

My cheeks flare as I realize that the buttons on my pajama shirt are mismatched. By lifting my hand to point at the verdan, a ginormous section of material just gaped open. Right at my bust level.

I drop my arm as fast as I can, but it only serves to unbalance me and I end up clutching the bedside table with one hand, supporting my pounding head with the other.

Vlad's sole response to my display is a slightly raised eyebrow. "It looks like you had some difficulty dressing last night."

Wow. He's totally unmoved by the fact that I just flashed him a solid look at my breasts. I'm impressed. He's blunt and focused, and not easily distracted.

I sigh. "I need a shower."

He grunts a response. "You need to wash off the tear tracks. They don't suit you." He stiffens a little as if he just replayed what he said in his mind. "That was intended as a compliment."

"I'll take it as one." I eye the feather he's still holding. I don't want to turn my back on him until I know the feather's safely back in my possession. I square my shoulders. "You're going to put that on the box and leave now."

He ponders the Clave for a moment before raising

himself off the trunk, saying, "I fully intended to leave this morning and never look back, but I think we can help each other."

I narrow my eyes at him, suspicious of his intentions. "How?"

"I can help with the verdan." He quickly lifts his free hand before I can ask more questions. "First, get yourself cleaned up. We can talk over breakfast."

It sounds like a perfectly reasonable proposal. A little too reasonable. This guy is like a hibernating bear, all calm and relaxed, but I have no doubt he will be unforgiving if provoked.

If he was offering information about anything other than the verdan, I'd walk away, but the plant's protective shield is a significant frustration.

He turns the Clave over in his hand and asks, far too casually, "If I walk out of this room with this feather right now, could you stop me?"

It's a forthright question. Despite my determined glare, there's no doubt he already knows the answer. The fact that I'm clutching the doorframe is a dead giveaway.

I respond with the same directness he has shown me. "I couldn't."

"Well, then." He stands, takes the feather to my satchel, places it inside, and brings the whole thing to me, waiting for me to take it.

I stare at my bag in surprise before gathering it into my arms.

"Assassins never trust each other," he says. "Let's make this a first step in that direction."

He gives me a quick nod before relocating to the far side

of the room to where his own belongings are contained in a large satchel.

I close the door and drop my bag in the corner behind it so that if Vlad does anything sneaky, like opening the door, the satchel will end up trapped in the corner behind it. Not that I'm expecting him to do anything underhanded after that gesture. He's had plenty of opportunities to attack me and hasn't.

I pull off my pajamas and stand under the shower.

Cold water doesn't work as well as it used to. There's a painful hole in my heart that can't be numbed and never will be. I have to live with it now, just as I have to live with the gap in my wings where one of my feathers used to be.

The question is how badly the hole in my heart will fester. How much it will change me.

Dressing as quickly as I can in a pair of jeans and a long-sleeved t-shirt, I return to the bedroom to find two plates on the small table, both piled with bacon and eggs, a bowl of fruit perched at the side and... *Oh my...* coffee! I make a beeline for it, inhaling as I draw the cup to my lips.

Vlad leans back in one of the chairs, an intrigued smile playing with his lips. "They don't serve coffee in the Realm, do they?"

I pause while the liquid sloshes against my top lip. "Not a drop."

He seems far too pleased that he hooked me with it. I'm certain he's trying to butter me up for something.

I put the cup down without drinking from it, showing him that I won't be bought. I'll have to make do with coffee fumes instead.

I ignore my rumbling stomach while I remain standing,

maintaining my distance. "Tell me exactly how you think we can help each other."

"You want to get through the protective spell around the verdan. I can tell you how."

I squash my rising optimism before he sees it. I need to maintain a level negotiating field. "In return for what?"

"I'll tell you, but first I have a question."

"What is it?"

He asks, "Is Slade Baines the new Master of the Legion?"

Just hearing Slade's name hurts. I flinch and it doesn't seem to escape Vlad's notice but he doesn't say anything.

I keep the emotion out of my voice. "Slade took Gareth back in chains two nights ago after Gareth tried to kill us. The Guardian and Cain Carter were waiting for one of us to return so, yes, Slade is now the Legion Master."

Vlad purses his lips. "You weren't exaggerating when you said you had a bad night."

"Deception may be my friend," I say, "but I don't often exaggerate."

"Noted."

I consider his thoughtful expression before I ask, "If you help me remove the protective shield from the verdan, what do you want in return?"

He leans forward. "I need an audience with Slade and Cain. I have important information that they both need to hear. Can you get me in to see them?"

My stomach sinks. His request is a difficult one. I can't go back to the Realm. I have to stay away from Slade. When Valkyries bond, we're supposed to remain near our bonded partner until we can separate without pain. I wrenched myself away from Slade after only a day. I don't know what will happen if I see him again.

On top of that, I stole both the verdan and the Clave. It's possible that Slade will tell everyone that the verdan was destroyed but Gareth could accuse me of stealing the Clave and Slade will be honor-bound as Master of the Legion to take action against me.

Despite all that, I need the verdan sap and I'm annoyed to admit I have no idea how to get through the protective shield around the plant.

I counter Vlad's request with a question. "Why can't you go to the Realm yourself?"

He shifts a little on the spot, appearing uncomfortable for the first time. "I may have had a falling out with Master Gareth and now the Realm won't open for me."

I sigh. It's time to take a seat. Folding my arms across my chest, I sink into the chair. "I don't think I can help you. I stole the feather so there's a big risk that I'll be apprehended as soon as I set foot in the Realm."

"What if I told you that I can take care of that problem for you?"

I narrow my eyes at him. "How? You said you can't get into the Realm, but you can somehow protect me from retribution for stealing the feather?"

He is back to his confident self. He rubs his hand over his shaved head, a smug smile on his lips. "I guarantee I can."

I wait for him to elaborate. Frustratingly, he doesn't.

He leans forward again, elbows on the table, and asks, "Unless there's another reason you don't want to go back?"

I exhale slowly. I have a choice to make.

How badly do I want the sap versus... how badly do I need to stay away from Slade? Can I stand in the same space as him and not be torn apart from the inside?

I have to try. I need the sap. The alternative is to run and hide for the rest of my life.

I never hide. And I'm already sick of running.

Or… I could beat the answer out of Vlad. I pretend to study the coffee cup, flicking a casual glance at him to ascertain his position on his chair, his balance, the location of his fists and legs.

I play it out in my mind: I could pull the table out from under him, he would go down, and his head would meet my boot. But he won't be much use to me unconscious, since I need him to talk.

He seems to read my mind. He may be a big, dangerous bear but he's perceptive, I'll give him that. He shifts away from me, slides one hand down to his thigh, pulls the gun out of the holster, and places it on the table.

He positions it with the handle toward me.

Damn him. He's daring me to take it.

He keeps his tone casual. "Trust is a tricky thing, Hunter. Like I said, I know who you are. I know what you're capable of. But you need to know that I'm deadly serious about talking with Slade and Cain. Lives depend on it. More lives than you could possibly know. I won't help you unless you help me."

I wasn't expecting him to talk about lives being at risk, let alone say so much about it. The mere fact that he's strung so many words together tells me how serious he is.

Quietly, I ask, "What's going on, Vlad?"

"I'm afraid I can't say anything more until I speak with Slade and Cain."

I contemplate him for a moment while I decide what to do. What he says about trust is true. It can take years to build but can be torn apart in seconds.

Like when Slade found out I'm Valkyrie...

I need to start building bridges, not tearing them down.

"I will help you," I say. "But I need you to carry out your part of the bargain first—tell me how to remove the verdan's shield and then I'll take you to the Realm."

He presses his lips together. He doesn't look happy about my request.

I persist. "We can't do both things at once. One of us has to trust the other. I won't break my word. I will get you into the Realm."

His lips twist into a wry line. "Says she who lies."

I shrug. "Don't we all?"

"I prefer to keep my words to a minimum. There's less call for deception that way."

Come to think of it, he's been completely open with me so far, which only makes me scowl. So he's an honest, old bear. Actually... maybe not so old.

He grins as I scrutinize him, asking me, "What do you want to know, Hunter?"

The moment he smiles, he looks younger and now I can't place his age at all. "How old are you?"

"Not much older than you."

My forehead creases. He knows I'm twenty years old because I was recently a Novice. If he's a similar age then it means he was a Novice not very long ago, too. It's odd that he would be stationed all the way out here so soon after becoming a Superior, but maybe that's how much Gareth hates him.

I'm perplexed. "It must be your nose."

"What about my nose?"

I wrinkle my own. "Squished. It makes you look five years older."

He raises an eyebrow. "I'll take that as a compliment. Are you going to eat your breakfast or not?"

I try to catch up with his change of subject. "I guess."

"Good." He picks up his knife and fork, leaving his gun where I can grab it.

I carefully angle a finger at it and very slowly prod it toward him. "Put that away."

He grins again, revealing a row of even, white teeth. His laughter is a rumble in his chest, but he leaves the gun right where it is. "Don't think for a second that you can boss me around, woman."

Now I'm really tempted to dive for the gun just to see what he does.

I've already visually ascertained that the safety catch is on so it won't go off by accident.

Deciding not to push our relationship, I leave the gun alone and finish my breakfast, knowing I will feel better with a full stomach.

When we're finished, Vlad stands up, stretches, and says, "We need warm clothes."

Then a slow smile spreads across his face. "And a helicopter."

CHAPTER THREE

I eye the motorcycle stationed at the front of the motel as Vlad settles his big frame onto it.

He raises a challenging eyebrow at me. "We have to get to the airstrip somehow."

I adjust my backpack and check that my katana is secured across my shoulders. Everything important is on my back: the Clave and the Keres ring are tucked away in the bottom of my backpack. I've wrapped them in cloth this time and secured them inside internal pockets.

The verdan plant is also inside my bag, along with several changes of clothes and my assassin's ledger. It makes for a heavy bag but I'm not leaving any of it behind. I'm uncomfortable enough about leaving Mom's ledger. Before I exited the room, I locked everything in the trunk and threatened Harry with annihilation if he let anyone in again.

I continue to consider the motorcycle warily. "This is yours?"

I don't know much about motorcycles, but this one is a

sleek, black beast that looks like it cost more than Vlad could afford.

He answers me by turning the ignition, at which the engine purrs like a jungle cat. "Hop on."

I slide in behind him, find the footrests, and can't help but appreciate how comfortable the motorcycle is despite the fact that I'm totally exposed to the weather.

Vlad hands me a helmet, waiting for me to clip it in place before he drives the motorcycle out onto the deserted road.

I settle in where I am, eventually giving up on keeping my hands at my sides and slide them around his waist instead. He gives me no indication of what he thinks about this as we speed along the road.

Two hours later, I'm concerned about our location and lean in to shout over the wind. "This is Dominion territory."

He answers me with a nod. "We have to cross the Faction border to get to the nearest airstrip."

"Are you sure that's a good idea?"

I catch the grin in his voice. "You have your katana. I have my gun. We'll be fine."

I'm not so sure. I keep my eyes peeled, my nerves stretching thin with every town we pass through.

Finally, we speed toward a large fenced-off area and through the open gate. At the end of the road, we reach an expansive hanger. Three helicopters rest on the tarmac.

I narrow my eyes at it all. This is a private hanger. The signs on the building tell me as much. But the helicopters aren't made for sightseeing. Their make and build make it clear they're military.

When Vlad stops the motorcycle, I slide to the ground, stretching out my cramped legs. Three men emerge from the hanger, all heavily armed, and I instinctively check for assassin's rings, frustrated that I can't tell at this distance.

The men stop in their tracks as soon as they catch sight of Vlad.

He leans down to me with a murmur. "Wait here. I know these people. Let me handle this."

He strides across the asphalt to meet the guys. All three step toward him in unison. Vlad raises his hand in their direction and they stop where they are.

One of them says something I can't hear. Vlad inclines his head in my direction.

I'm just about to harness my ability to overhear their conversation when Vlad turns swiftly in my direction. He strides back to me while the three men scatter.

Well, that was fast.

"They'll have the helicopter ready in a few minutes. In the meantime, you must be hungry."

"And curious," I say, following him along the path to the hanger. True to his word, the men busy themselves preparing one of the helicopters, fueling it, and loading it with what looks like hiking gear. "How do you know these people?"

"Keeping the peace at the border requires making friends. They trust me. I trust them. It comes in handy."

One of the men brings me a sandwich and points me to a nearby seat. It's easy now to identify his assassin's ring up close. Another one offers me a warm coat. All without speaking, removing their weapons, or altering their carefully blank expressions. They may as well be machines.

"Thank you," I say, watching to see if my response has any impact on them.

The guy handing me the coat twitches and casts a quick

glance in Vlad's direction, but still says nothing. It seems the Dominion assassins are neither my friends nor my enemies.

I turn back to Vlad. "When are you going to tell me where we're going?"

Vlad stuffs a sandwich into his mouth instead of replying.

Hmm. I guess I'll have to make do with a shrug.

When the first man gives him a nod, Vlad strides over to the helicopter and climbs into the pilot's seat.

I follow him and make myself comfortable in the co-pilot's chair. "You're flying the helicopter?"

Vlad grins at me, seeming pleased about my surprise before he gives the men a wave and wastes no time taking off.

He handles the helicopter like he's flown a thousand times before. Comfortable that he knows what he's doing, I close my eyes and inhale the crisp air as we soar up and into the sky.

We travel for at least an hour before I catch sight of mountains dusted in snow. I lean forward, trying to identify them. Taking into account how far we rode on the motorcycle and how long we've traveled by air, we could be in South Dakota now. I would be more stressed about my location if I didn't have my own wings to get me out of here if I need to escape.

I finally ask Vlad, "When did you learn to fly?"

He replies, "My old man taught me."

"You're close to him?"

"I was until he died a year ago." Vlad doesn't take his eyes off the mountain peaks. "That's when a lot of things changed for me."

"I'm sorry."

He glances at me, his expression more piercing than I expected. "At least I had the chance to know him."

I look away. Everyone in the assassin's world thinks that the former Legion Master, Soren, was my father. He died soon after I was born so it's a common perception that I never knew him.

Only three people know that Ridley, my combat teacher, is actually my dad: me, Ridley, and Slade.

I pretend to study the mountain peaks below us and the way the early afternoon sunlight casts brilliant reflections off them. "Well, I had my mother, and she taught me everything she knew."

"You're going to need every skill you've got when we land."

I wait for him to tell me why but he remains infuriatingly tight-lipped. I don't blame him for keeping things to himself. As he says, trust is tricky. But at some point, he's going to have to tell me what's going on.

"We're flying into the heart of this next mountain," he says. "However, it's heavily guarded by an occupant who won't like our intrusion."

I raise an eyebrow. "A non-human occupant?"

His answer is grim. "A draugr."

My eyes widen. "That's an undead warrior." My Valkyrie power is no use against a draugr. They exist in the place where they died, usually for the purpose of protecting the treasure that led them to die there in the first place. They are incredibly strong and can increase in size and weight at will.

"As soon as we step into its territory, the draugr will retaliate," Vlad says.

I pull my sword from my pack. A draugr can only be

killed by decapitation. Ideally, its body should also be burned to prevent it from rising again. "I'll be ready."

Vlad surprises me when he says, "I would prefer not to kill it unless we have no other choice."

"Why is that?"

"We have no fight with it. We are trespassers, after all."

I chew my lip. "It would help if you tell me why we have to go into the heart of the mountain in the first place."

"You'll see as soon as we get there," he says.

I sigh into the crisp air. I'm not going to get anything out of him until he's ready to share. Valkyrie run hot but even so, I'm feeling the cold. I'm glad now for the thick coat and gloves the guys gave me at the hanger.

Vlad points. "We'll land over there."

The snow cover swirls as we set the helicopter down. When I grab my pack, Vlad shakes his head at me.

"Take only the plant and your sword," he says. "But keep your gloves on. You don't want to touch the sap by mistake."

I follow his instructions, but I shove one more thing into my pocket: a small glass vial that I took from the kitchen at the motel before I left. I can use it to collect the sap. I'm not sure what will happen when the shield comes off the plant. The verdan may even self-destruct. I might need to move fast.

Vlad pulls several daggers from his pack and slides them into various holsters around his body. The only other thing he takes is a flashlight. I consider asking for one too, but both my hands are needed to carry the plant and use my sword if I need to.

Vlad strides ahead of me, remarkably light on his feet, especially as the snow cover deepens.

An opening in the mountain yawns in front of us,

revealing a deep cave, which we enter and follow for another ten minutes before Vlad slows down in front of me, finally drawing to a halt. The tunnel walls close in ahead of us, becoming an even tighter walkway, leading to a dark, narrow opening.

He lowers his voice to a rumble. "We need to go single-file."

I wrinkle my nose. The air here is very stale. But I suspect it's more than a lack of air flow. The draugr will reek of decay. The scent in the air tells me that the creature is close by.

"The draugr's lair is through that opening," Vlad says. "Unfortunately, our destination is right on top of his treasure. I need to turn off the flashlight now."

Is he suggesting that we walk in the dark?

I grimace. "I don't think that's a good idea."

He replies, "Trust me, Hunter. You'll understand as soon as I turn off the light."

CHAPTER FOUR

lad doesn't wait for me to agree. There's a soft *click*.

As the golden light fades, another bursts into life.

I gasp as the verdan casts crimson light around the tunnel.

Each petal of the orchard-like plant glows bright red and dark as blood, the gaps in its light throwing strange shadows across Vlad's massive body. It makes me realize how much he has to hunch over in the low tunnel. The color of his eyes turns red in the reflected verdan light. The image he presents is gruesome, fearsome, and strangely gorgeous all at the same time.

I understand now why we're here.

I breathe out my surprise. "The verdan's shield disappears in the dark."

"But only in true dark," he says. "You have to bring the verdan to a place where no light reaches. You probably thought that the shield was put on the plant by someone trying to stop others from using it. It wasn't. It's a self-generated shield that is triggered by light hitting the leaves."

He inclines his head toward the plant with a warning. "Walk carefully, Hunter. The shield will completely disappear as soon as we enter the lair. The poison rests on the surface of the flowers. You don't want to stumble and touch them by accident."

"I understand."

Vlad says, "The draugr won't come out here, but it will fight us as soon as we step into its territory. Are you ready to go in?"

I shoot back a challenge. "Are you?"

He grins at me, his teeth appearing blood-red. His answer is to present me with his back as he leads the way forward.

He has to angle his body to slip through the narrow opening and I quickly follow, holding the plant away from all parts of my body, holding my breath until I make it through.

Inside, a cavern rises high above us, around fifty paces wide and deep. The floor sparkles with gold, silver, jewels, and coins all piled up in the middle. All of it is cursed because the draugr died here. I won't touch any of it and I certainly won't try to take any of it with me. There's not a lot that can physically harm me but I don't need more bad luck in my life.

As soon as we enter the space, a humanoid shape rises up from the pile of treasure, displacing coins and jewels as it unfurls, scattering gold across the clearing. A single coin rolls across the rocky floor and hits Vlad's foot. He is tense and ready to fight. I hang back, knowing that there's only so much I can do while I'm holding the plant.

The draugr's skin is dark blue, a color that blends with the crimson verdan light to create a weird purple. Its stench makes my eyes water, creating a physical sensation like acid inside my nose. Its face is misshapen, barely human.

It was once a man but it's possible that it has lain here for hundreds of years without being disturbed. It growls at us, attempting to form sounds, but it has long ago forgotten how to speak.

Vlad quickly positions himself between me and the creature. At the same time, I slide my hand through the space next to the plant to check whether the shield is still operational.

It's gone.

Vlad points me toward a spot at the side of the cave that is furthest from the draugr. "I'll keep him busy. Do what you need to do. But do it fast."

His feet thud the ground as he runs at the draugr and barrels straight into it, wrestling the beast to the ground. Coins scatter and clink as the two collide. The only way to restrain the draugr is through sheer strength alone. I don't have time to admire the fact that Vlad approaches the task with impressive efficiency.

I race to the spot where Vlad pointed, balance the plant on the rocky ground, unsheathe my sword, and prepare to pierce the curved stem with the blade. I need to make a large enough cut to release the sap and I don't have time to be delicate.

I slide the tip through the part of the stem that curves horizontal so the drips will fall straight down, placing the glass vial beneath it to catch the oozing liquid without allowing it to touch my skin.

The sap is thick and the first droplet forms more slowly than I need it to.

Too slowly.

Shifting air behind me is my only warning when the draugr breaks free from Vlad's hold and rushes toward me, drawn by the plant's light, its eyes filled with an eerie glow.

I jump to my feet, prepared to use my sword. But before the creature reaches me, it suddenly slips forward, barely missing me as it crashes face first into the dirt, its legs pulled out from under it.

Vlad takes hold of one of its feet and drags it backward as it flails and claws at the ground. He shouts, "Hurry up, Hunter!"

The beast roars, curls its body around, and hits back with a fist, launching itself at Vlad. Vlad ducks the swing like a professional boxer and retaliates with a crunching blow to the draugr's torso, followed by two quick hits to its face.

The draugr stumbles backward and Vlad follows it, wrestling it to the ground again. I can't see the strain on Vlad's arms and legs because he is covered in furs, but the bulging cords in his neck tell me how much effort it's taking to restrain the draugr right now.

I spin back to the verdan just in time to catch the first drop of sap in the glass vial.

Three drops follow it before the liquid stops flowing.

I don't have time to pierce it again. What I've collected will have to be enough. I cork the bottle and shove it into my pocket. My heart is pounding, but not because of the draugr.

The sap is said to be poisonous to all creatures. I can't assume I'm safe just because I'm Valkyrie. None of it dripped on me but my sword's tip is now smeared with crimson liquid. It's well and truly poisonous.

"Vlad! I'm done!"

Vlad lands a final blow on the draugr's nose, shoving it

backward. The creature falls with a roar, never taking its eyes off Vlad. It's not giving up.

Vlad shouts, "Run, Hunter!"

I take off at a quick pace without sheathing my sword, not wanting to spread the poison inside the scabbard. I squeeze through the gap at the entrance to the cave and race along the corridor, gripping the plant by its pot. I'm incredibly grateful now that the self-forming shield is returning to the plant.

The verdan is a deadly object that puts up a barrier between itself and the world to protect others.

I swallow hard as I realize… this plant is a lot like me.

I'm twenty paces along the path before I notice the absence of running feet behind me. I skid to a stop, kicking up dust and pebbles, spinning back to the cave's entrance.

Vlad isn't there.

I wait another second.

He put away his flashlight to fight the creature. I'm carrying the only light source he had. It's unlikely he'll be able to reach for his flashlight, let alone fight with it in his hand.

I race back to the entrance, my feet and heart pounding. Sliding through, I come upon the draugr holding Vlad off the ground, one of Vlad's arms in each of its enormous hands.

The breath catches in my throat. The creature is now twice the size it was before, its head bumping the ceiling. Vlad struggles to break free, but the more he fights, the more the draugr pulls.

It's preparing to rip his arms off.

Vlad gives a roar, changing tactics, pulling his arms inward instead of struggling, straining against the draugr's opposing force, dragging the creature's hands closer together through strength of will alone.

There is no good end to this fight.

Vlad's back is to me. The light source—the verdan—is also behind him. I can't see Vlad's expression, but he won't be able to hold on for long. I may feel uneasy about our alliance, but I won't let him die here.

I place the verdan on the ground and harness my inner power without releasing my wings, using it to speed up my movements as I run straight for the creature, curve out to the left, flip my katana into my left hand, and leap from the ground.

The draugr's neck is bare to me.

I fly through the air, swinging my sword arm. The weapon slices in the direction away from Vlad's position.

The draugr's eerie eyes widen.

My sword sizzles as the verdan meets the draugr's blood.

I land on the other side, knees bent, the whispering thud of my landing filling the silence in the suddenly quiet cave.

Behind me, the draugr's body topples to the ground.

Now free, Vlad drops to his feet and rolls out of the way of the falling body. Luckily, the draugr's power fades as it falls, shrinking back to its normal, human size, easily missing Vlad's location. He steadies himself, his chest heaving from exertion as he considers the draugr and then me.

I take a moment to check my sword, glad to see it is completely clean now. The draugr's cursed blood has consumed the verdan. It wasn't why I killed it, but it's a lucky consequence.

I replace the sword in its scabbard before turning to Vlad with an apology on my lips. "I'm sorry."

He slowly regains his breath. "For saving my life?"

I shrug. "You didn't want to kill it."

He contemplates me for so long that I shift on the spot, uncomfortable now under his scrutiny.

Finally, he says, "You could have run and not looked back. You had the sap. You could have left me here to die. But you didn't."

I shrug, unhappily. "Do you really think I'm that merciless?"

He pauses. Then, "I'm starting to believe you're not."

I turn away before he can say anything else. "Let's get out of here. The stench is giving me a headache."

His response washes over me as he follows close behind. "I'll fly us as close to Boston as I can. We'll need to refuel a few times, but we should be able to land at one of the airstrips near the city."

I miss a step.

Damn. Boston.

I shudder so hard I almost topple over. My fearlessness abandons me. Now I have to hold up my part of the bargain.

CHAPTER FIVE

I never expected to return to Boston so soon. It's only been three days since Slade and I went to Mount Greylock.

Vlad and I flew most of the afternoon after defeating the draugr and then found a place to land and huddle in the helicopter overnight. It took us another five hours this morning to reach Boston.

When the helicopter sets down, everything inside me fights to turn around and leave. The closer I get to Slade's location, the more my insides twist and turn.

I try to focus on the other challenges ahead. Vlad wants to see both Slade and Cain at the same time, and I'm not sure how to make that happen.

Cain is the Heir Apparent of the Horde. He was given permission to stay in Boston to reconnect with his family. He remains here strictly as a civilian, not as a future Master Assassin so his presence doesn't challenge the Legion's control of its territory. But he only visited the Realm when he was invited. I have no idea how I'll make sure he's there today.

More important to me is the safety of the Clave. I went through so much to get it out of the Realm and away from Gareth. I won't walk back in there with it in my backpack.

My steps are heavy as I climb out of the helicopter and wait for Vlad. I plant my feet on the tarmac before he can progress toward the hanger.

He takes one look at my face and pulls up sharp, slowly tugging his backpack over his shoulders. "What is it, Hunter?"

"When I left the Realm..." I swallow hard, curling my fingertips into my palms. I stare up at the mid-morning sky and take a deep breath. "Coming back here is dangerous for me. I really hope this is important."

His expression softens. "It's dangerous for me, too. Gareth has allies in unexpected places. We both need to watch our backs."

I shudder. Watching each other's backs was what pulled Slade and me together. "I can't take the feather into the Realm. I promise I'm not trying to stall or back out on our deal, but I can't walk in there with everything I fought so hard to get out in the first place."

He gives me a cautious look. It will take a lot for him to trust me right now. From his point of view, I might be trying to trick him. I hope my actions saving him from the draugr will help alleviate that concern.

He asks, "What do you propose?"

"I want to leave my things in a safe place. Then, I can take you to the Realm."

His big hands close around the straps of his backpack,

adjusting it as he considers my request. "Where is this 'safe' place?"

"I'll tell you, but I need to warn you that the occupants are not all human."

The last thing I need is for him to go all assassin on Tansy or Dean. Tansy is a witch and Dean is an empath. What's more, Tansy distrusts assassins—especially me.

Then there's William who is human, but owns a bookshop called 'The Tomb' that contains rare and precious books about magical creatures that most people would see as oddities. I haven't met the other occupants of Saber Lane but I'm sure there are more magical people among them.

Vlad doesn't flinch. "Magical beings don't worry me. Where is it located, Hunter?"

For someone who kept our destination from me for an entire day, he's pushing me hard for a location.

"It's called Saber Lane," I say. "It's a twenty-minute walk from the Realm so it's not out of our way."

I don't have to hold my breath for long.

Vlad gives me a quick nod of agreement and says, "Then let's go."

I step onto Saber Lane, my boots thudding on the pavement, the sight of the familiar shops making my heart warm in unexpected ways.

When I first came here, I was sent to kill William. Luckily, I figured out that Gareth was trying to trick me into breaking the Assassin's Code—a crime that would have resulted in me being kicked out of the Legion.

Gareth's real target was the Keres Coda, an ancient book

about my sworn enemy. I ended up getting to know William and discovered that I had spent the first four years of my life living in the home above the bookshop—Mom went there after she left the Legion. William was the closest thing to a father that I had before I met Ridley.

Vlad sticks close beside me. His gun is concealed at the back of his jeans, but my katana is difficult to hide. Short of acquiring a violin case, there's not much I can do about it, so I choose to carry it in plain sight slung across my back.

The street is quiet for a Saturday when the tourists are usually out in force. In fact, the silence is oppressive. I pass by the bakery, worried about the 'Closed' sign in the door. The next shop is closed, too.

"This isn't normal," I whisper to Vlad. "Keep your eyes peeled."

"Always."

A lone woman hurrying in the opposite direction squeaks in alarm as I stride past. She side-steps me, staring at my sword.

"Oh, it's an antique," I say, forcing a laugh and gesturing toward the apothecary's shop, which is the most ancient-looking of them all, as if I'm taking it there to be valued.

She darts a glance at Vlad and hurries away.

I let her go, turning back to find only one other person walking along the street.

"Briar!"

The old lady stops in her tracks. "Milady!" Her shocked expression clears and she races toward me, her coat flapping around her bony legs. "Thank goodness, you're alive!"

Briar was my first client. She came to the Realm to seek the assassination of a known criminal who was harming women. She has no money to her name, so she offered me her loyalty as payment instead. She had pointed to my tattoo and told me I was my mother's daughter.

I didn't know at the time, but she was trying to tell me I needed to take my mother's place. Since then, she became my eyes and ears on the streets of Boston.

She shocks me by throwing her arms around me in a giant hug. I stiffen before allowing myself to relax into it. She's bony but somehow her embrace is one of the most calming I've experienced.

"Briar, it's good to see you—"

"No time for that. You need to get to the Tomb right now —" She stops abruptly, gasping when she sees Vlad. Her mouth snaps shut. She glances at me. And back at him. "He is with you?"

"This is Vlad." I hesitate to call him my friend. "Our interests are aligned at the present time."

She speaks carefully and I guess it's his monstrous size and boxer's face that cause her to take a step back. "Very well. I have to go, but please hurry to the bookshop."

"Thank you, Briar." I have another thought and catch her before she rushes away. "Wait… there's something I need your help with."

"Yes, Milady?"

"I need Cain Carter to be at the Realm today. Is there any way you can get a message to him?" I'm frustrated to realize that I don't know where he lives.

Briar says, "That won't be difficult. Former Master Gareth is being tried today. Cain Carter will be at the Realm for the hearing. Along with the Guardian."

"Thank you, Briar." I consider the way she keeps darting glances at Vlad.

Does she know him? I guess it's not impossible—he's a

Legion assassin so she could have run into him at some point.

I ask her, "Are you sure you're okay?"

She casts another furtive look at Vlad. "Yes, Milady. I'm relieved you're back."

I pick up my pace along the street. Vlad remains quiet beside me, light on his feet as always. I take the steps at the front of the shop two at a time, knocking despite the 'Closed' sign. Vlad remains a step behind me, still taller than me despite standing a step down.

Tansy's face appears in the glass pane.

I brace, not expecting a warm welcome. She wasn't exactly happy to see me the first time I showed up here. Then, when I brought Slade to her, begging her to heal him, she refused, her fear of assassins too great for her to overcome.

She pulls the door open, her features ashen, and shocks me when she says, "Hunter! We thought you were dead."

CHAPTER SIX

They thought I was dead?

I can only stare at Tansy. "What? Why?"

She shocks me again when she grabs my arm and pulls me into the shop.

I nearly freeze at the contact. She never willingly touched me before.

She speaks rapidly. "Come out of the street. Quickly. And bring your… friend."

Tansy's speech slows. Her eyes grow wide as she takes in Vlad's assassin's ring, shaved head, been-in-too-many-fights nose, and incredible height.

Her power glows in her eyes, her fear of assassins rising fast and furious in a palpable force around her.

Vlad sucks in a breath at my side, quickly turns both hands palms out at his sides, and drops his gaze to the ground. "Blessings on your power and your home," he says.

The force fades from Tansy's eyes, replaced with curiosity. "How do you know the witch's greeting?"

Vlad raises his eyes. A smile plays around his mouth. "I'm Vlad."

A perplexed expression crosses her face. "You didn't answer my question."

"You're right. I didn't."

She blinks at him. Then she shakes herself. She checks the street again before she says, "Come inside. Both of you."

She hurries inside, calling out to William as her heels clack on the floor and her golden hair bounces against her back.

I follow her, turning the lock in the door as soon as Vlad is safely inside. I inhale the familiar scent of the paper and ink as we stride past the rows of books and climb the stairs. I want to stop and absorb the calming atmosphere, the comforting sight and smell of this place, but Tansy is already racing up the stairs.

As soon as we appear at the top, William shoots to his feet, rising from his seat at the kitchen table.

"Hunter! My dear child!" He hurries around the table and pulls me into a hug. "We thought you were dead."

I'm astounded by how many hugs I've received today. More than I've had in… well… a long time. But he's the third person to tell me they thought I was dead and I need answers. Sure, I disappeared after I left for Mount Greylock —without sending word about my plans actually, a fact about which I suddenly feel very guilty given how worried they were.

I force myself to pull back. "William, why would you think that?"

"After you left that morning, we heard a rumor… Briar told us it was spreading like wildfire through the underground..." His voice trails off. Just like Briar and Tansy, it took William a minute to notice Vlad's presence.

For such a massive guy, Vlad definitely has the knack of disappearing into the background. It's an assassin's skill. One that Cain Carter has also mastered. I still remember with some embarrassment the time I tripped right over him at a high-end charity ball on the night of my first mission. As it turned out, Cain himself was hosting the ball.

Unlike Briar and Tansy, William doesn't wait for introductions. I guess he is faster to accept that I wouldn't bring someone to his home unless I trusted them.

William returns his attention to me. But what he says next shocks me. "We heard that Slade Baines had killed you."

I'm so shocked that I can barely form sound, forcing a whisper, "Slade would never do that."

Tansy takes up position on the other side of the table. "The underground went wild, Hunter. It wasn't this bad when your Mom died. You were still here then. Your presence kept them all in check. Now that they think you're dead too... and that Slade killed you no less... Suddenly..."

She shudders so hard that she has to grip the table to keep her balance.

I ask, "What happened?"

She presses her lips together for a moment, the blood leaving them. "People have started disappearing. Humans and non-humans. It's only been a few days but nobody is safe."

That would explain why all the shops are closed. Anyone who is aware of the underground, or has opposed it, is in fear for their life right now.

I slip off my backpack and katana and sink into the

nearest chair while Vlad chooses to remain standing behind me, staying quiet for now.

I shake my head in disbelief. "I knew Mom had a reputation. She destroyed all of Patrick Ryan's rivals and kept everyone in line, but I didn't think that I…"

"That you had such an impact?" William takes a seat beside me, leaning forward to take my hands in his, a warm grip. "Your friend may as well know that there are whispers in the underground that you are—or *were* according to the rumors—superhuman. That you could kill anything and not be killed. That belief kept everything in balance."

William is speaking carefully now. He and Tansy know that I'm Valkyrie, but Vlad doesn't.

William says, "When the rumor spread that Slade killed you, it was like a green light to every criminal and mobster out there."

I argue, "But Slade is ferocious. Surely, they're afraid of *him*."

William shakes his head. "He killed you, Hunter. To their eyes, he gave them his blessing."

"Then the good people—the people who would have supported him—will turn away from him." I press my lips together. It's a cruel strategy on the part of the person who started the rumor. By claiming that Slade killed me, the good people will fear Slade instead of supporting him, which in turn will hamstring Slade and enable the underground to rise up and take control.

I ask, "Who started the rumor?"

William says, "The new leader of the underground."

I'm surprised. "Not Gareth?"

"He's imprisoned in the Realm. He's facing trial today in fact."

Vlad speaks up for the first time. "The leader of the underground is a woman, yes?"

William and Tansy give him surprised looks. It's a stereotype, but until now, the underground's leaders have been male.

"That's correct," Tansy says to him. "How did you know?"

He shrugs. "News travels."

Tansy pauses as if she wants to push for more information, but he already played word games with her once on the front steps.

She speaks to me instead, "You were right to be concerned about the Tirelli Family, Hunter. The woman at their head has stepped out of the shadows. They call her Lady Tirelli."

My first target was associated with the Tirelli Family. I was careful to kill him in a way that looked like an accident so I didn't bring the entire family's wrath down upon myself. Now it looks like Lady Tirelli is a lot more powerful than I feared.

I chew my lip. "I overheard Gareth talking in his office before I left. He said that Lady Tirelli wanted her prize. I don't know what that means, but he also said she wanted to control Slade. This must be how she's trying to manipulate him."

William nods. "By making everyone believe Slade killed you."

"Except he didn't," I say.

Tansy runs her hand across her eyes. She looks tired, her expression dull, sapped of strength. "We were worried because of what happened between you and Slade... We knew your death at his hand was possible so when people asked us, and when you didn't come back, we couldn't stop the rumor."

My shoulders slump. "You thought he did it."

Tansy's pretty mouth presses into an apologetic line. "We knew he was strong enough."

When I used my feather to heal Slade, I made it impossible for myself to ever kill him. William had begged me not to take that risk, but Slade's life was at stake. It means that Slade has more power over me than bonding would normally give him.

I sigh into the sudden silence.

There's so much I need to tell William and Tansy about the Clave and the verdan, but I can't speak freely in front of Vlad. I need to tell them that I have everything to reveal the weapon that Mom was protecting. I thought I needed to do it alone but now... knowing how worried they were for my safety—even Tansy—makes me realize I don't want to.

My relationship with Tansy is still fragile but I know she won't do anything to jeopardize anyone's safety.

And William... he was the first man to step into the role of father to me. I might not remember it because I was so young, but photos in Mom's old room tell me she trusted him more than anyone else.

I'm tired of being on my own, of only trusting myself.

I have to take a leap of faith. I have to trust them.

But first I have to honor my promise to Vlad by taking him to the Realm. Then I'll be free to come back here and release the Clave.

"Everyone thinks I'm dead." A grin grows on my face as I remove my jacket, exposing my tattoo. "I think it's time for me to take a walk through the streets of Boston."

efore I leave the bookshop, I relocate my backpack and sword to the room where Mom and I stayed when I was little.

William calls it my room now. I hug him and decide not to argue.

Inside my room, I run my hand across Mom's picture where it rests on top of the chest of drawers, sensing the weight of everything she did.

I still don't understand why she chose to help the former mob boss, Patrick Ryan, to rise to power and remain king of the underground for so many years, but I'm beginning to understand the weight of responsibility she must have felt about it.

I wish I'd brought Mom's ledger back with me. It belongs here. I'll have to retrieve it as soon as I can.

When I return to the kitchen, I find Tansy reciting a spell at the same time as she holds a mug of water. I'm surprised she isn't reading from a piece of paper. Tansy was injured as a child when her aunt tried to steal her powers. Mom killed her aunt but not in time to prevent the damage that was done to Tansy's brain. She can't hold spells in her head like other witches. Instead, she has to read spells aloud.

Vlad leans against the table opposite her, nodding as she sounds out each word. The water in the mug begins to boil and Tansy lets out a laugh. "I didn't think that would work."

Vlad grins, his focus entirely on Tansy, his gray eyes warm. "It should help if you think in pictures, not in words."

Tansy's face lights up. "It does! Thank you."

I study them both as William draws me aside. He whispers, "Who is Vlad? Really?"

I smile. "Why do you ask?"

"Because somehow he got Tansy to tell him about the problem with her power *and* he gave her tips about how to overcome it. Is he really human?"

Despite the humor in William's eyes, it's a serious question. As a human, William can't sense a magical being's aura like assassins and other magical beings can.

"Vlad has no aura." As a Valkyrie, I'm the only non-human that doesn't have an aura. The Keres would be the same if they weren't extinct. It's one of the reasons Valkyrie are so dangerous. Nobody can detect my power, except another Valkyrie.

William smiles. "Then I guess Vlad must be human."

Vlad finally casts me an arrogant grin, the glow around his chunky black ring telling me that he's using his assassin's magic to listen to everything William and I are saying.

He gives Tansy a polite bow when she thanks him again. For a second, I think she's going to hug him but she appears to reconsider after a quick assessment of his giant arms and general ferociousness.

"It was a pleasure, Solnyshka," Vlad says to her.

She tilts her head, a curious crease growing across her delicate forehead. "What does that mean?"

He smiles again. "Thank you for your hospitality."

She purses her lips in a way that says she doesn't believe him. "I don't think that's what it means."

"You're right. It isn't."

He seems very happy to infuriate her. The furrow in her brow deepens to a scowl as he lumbers down the stairs without waiting for me. I note that he has left his backpack on the floor against the kitchen wall. It means a lot to me that Vlad trusts my friends.

William says, "We'll keep everything safe until you return."

I take a deep breath. "I'll be back soon."

I hope.

I hold my head high as we stride along Shawmut Avenue. It's freezing in Boston now that winter has set in. Vlad keeps his coat on but I prefer to ensure that my tattoo is visible so I'm easily recognizable. Vlad looks at me as if I'm nuts but he doesn't voice his thoughts as we pass cafes and shops inside which patrons huddle over warm drinks.

We've picked up a number of followers, only one of them from the Legion. The others, I don't recognize.

The non-Legion pursuers back off as we approach the Boston Common where the Realm is hidden. The fact that they are leaving at this point confirms that they're Lady Tirelli's people.

That's right. Run back to your Mistress and tell her that the games stop now.

Only the Legion observer follows us all the way, keeping at a safe distance from us.

I glare right at him so he can be in no doubt that I've spotted him. It's too soon for any new Novices to be admitted to the Legion so I can only assume the guy tailing us is a Superior. Not all assassins are as good as Vlad, Cain, and Slade at concealing their presence.

A knot grows in my stomach the closer we get to the Realm. My heart rate speeds up and my breathing increases.

I convince myself it's because of our quick pace.

But with every step, I'm forced to acknowledge that my emotions are going haywire about seeing Slade again.

I try to shut down everything that I feel right now... fear... anticipation... awful, horrible hope... but mostly fear. The mask across Slade's emotions when he last looked at me is eating at me like acid.

Vlad called me a machine. That's what I have to become if I'm going to get through seeing Slade again.

I lead Vlad to the tall memorial plaque that I need to place my palm on to give me access to the Realm. Vlad has to take my arm if he wants to follow me inside.

My open palm hovers over the memorial. "You know there's a chance my permission to access the Realm has been revoked."

He contemplates me for a long moment as if he sees through my lame excuse for trying to back out.

Then he carefully takes my hand in his. His palm is rough, calloused, but strong and comforting. "You didn't tell me what happened between you and Slade before the night you disturbed my sleep."

"You mean the night you trespassed in my room."

He holds my gaze. "Don't avoid the question, Hunter."

"You didn't ask one."

He laughs suddenly, the low, rumbling vibration extending all the way to our clasped hands. It's contagious, lifting my heart just enough that I can breathe again.

"I get it," he says. "There are some things you can't talk about. But I made a promise to you that everything will be okay. I will make good on that promise today, Hunter. I need you to trust me on that."

"I'm still not sure how you're going to do that. But... okay."

I lift the hand that he holds, twist it so that my palm is clear but his remains a comforting pressure against the back of it.

I press against the memorial.

The Realm materializes, the door and wall becoming visible to me. I can tell it's also visible to Vlad as soon as his focus shifts from the distant trees to the wide mahogany door in front of us.

He won't be able to follow me through if I break the contact between our bodies, so I grip his hand firmly as I push open the door and we step inside.

The moment we pass through the entrance, an alarm blares above our heads, breaking the calm as soon as our feet hit the pebbled pathway.

My eyes widen. We've definitely triggered something.

Assassins run from all directions but only a few of them are fully armed. The rest look like they grabbed whatever they had on hand, including my favorite weapon—a steak knife.

Vlad and I stand very still and raise our hands at our sides while the assassins form a defensive ring around us, their guns and daggers ready.

We aren't armed but we're both wearing our assassin's rings. Everyone in this place knows I don't need a weapon to do a lot of damage.

Their expressions range from shock to fear. They can't seem to stop looking between me and Vlad.

Vlad meets my eyes briefly, flicking me an apologetic glance followed by a slight shrug. I'm not completely sure why he's trying to silently apologize right now.

One of the Legion assassins shouts, "Step away from him, Hunter!"

The man who shouted is one of the older assassins, not somebody I ever talked with much, if at all. I'm concerned about the way he and the others point their weapons… not at me… but at Vlad.

Just then, someone pushes through the protective ring.

Rowan Robertson barrels his way through but pulls up sharp, his face draining. He was a Novice with me. He tried to kill me after Gareth attempted to trick him. By stopping him, I saved his life and after that, we became wary allies.

His expression is far from the arrogant guy I met on my first day in the Realm.

He exhales into the sudden tension, shock and relief at war in his expression. "Slade was telling the truth."

I remain very calm. "You thought I was dead."

Slade would have insisted that he left me alive. But, as I feared, it looks like many of the assassins didn't believe him.

Rowan assesses me from head to toe in the same way he used to check that I was okay, taking in my bare arms, my tattoo, my hair cast across one shoulder, finally lingering on my assassin's ring.

Then his focus lands on Vlad.

Rowan's eyes widen. His tone takes on a deep warning,

his shoulders angling toward me in a protective gesture, his fist clenching around the dagger he's clutching.

He speaks very carefully, a dangerously low tone. "Hunter? What are you doing with him?"

I cast a quick glance at Vlad who remains silent, but grim beside me. Vlad promised me that he would make my problems go away. I sincerely hope his plan isn't to overshadow my sins with his own.

My stomach sinks rapidly. I murmur to the side, "Vlad? What is going on?"

Vlad takes a step toward the assassins.

That single movement has an effect like breaking glass. Each of the men, including Rowan, jumps backward, defensive, muscles bunched. Weapons extend and triggers are ready. The tension rises. All it will take is a spark and this situation will explode.

What the hell did Vlad do?

He murmurs to me, "I'm sorry, Hunter. I may not have been completely truthful about who I am."

I lick my suddenly dry lips, hoping I won't have to step between him and a bullet. "Vlad?"

He turns his attention to the assassins and raises his voice in an authoritative command. "I am Alexei Vladimir Mason, newly appointed Master of the Dominion. You will take me to the Legion Master."

CHAPTER EIGHT

My stomach falls beyond my feet.

I should have seen it. The way Vlad navigated through Dominion territory.

The way the men at the airstrip practically bowed to him (because now that I think about it, that's what they were about to do before Vlad stopped them).

The way he used a respectful tone when he talked about the Dominion and his comment about the Heir Apparent wanting to form an alliance with me.

He wanted to form an alliance with me.

Not to mention... he offered me a favor and indicated that it was a big deal.

A Master offering a favor to an assassin in a different Faction?

Yep. That is a pretty big deal.

I file away the knowledge that I haven't asked him for that favor yet. Although I'm not sure I ever will. Favors tend to backfire even with the best intentions.

The barrier of assassins parts and Rowan gestures us forward with a stern expression.

I stride alongside Vlad as we follow quietly where Rowan leads. I try to ignore the assassins who reform a guard on either side of us and the weapons they hold ready to use if Vlad so much as twitches in the wrong direction.

He walks tall and strong beside me, a big, brute of a man with a nose that I now know has been in too many fights. I didn't learn much about Alexei Mason during my training in the Legion, but I did hear that he trained as a boxer. Also that he kills with his hands just like he told me.

The way he subdued the draugr confirmed how strong he is.

But what the whispers didn't say is that he's quiet. Calm. Resolute. And very, very blunt. He also likes a good night's sleep, without which he becomes a grumpy bear.

I'm surprised to realize that I won't have any hesitation protecting him if someone flies off the handle.

Vlad had every opportunity to harm me and didn't. He told me it was a matter of life and death that he speaks with Slade and Cain together. I know a lie when I hear one and Vlad wasn't lying about that.

Technically, he didn't lie about his name either.

I actually have to admire the way he managed to tell me the truth at nearly every turn. He just left some really important parts out.

He casts me a guarded glance as we arrive at the Cathedral. I wasn't sure if Rowan would take us to the administration building but it seems that Slade is currently located here. If Briar is right, then Cain and the Guardian are located in this building, too.

I allow a small smile to cross my lips in response to the

question in Vlad's eyes. I'm not going to judge him for having secrets. "Master, huh?"

He inclines his shaved head. He sighs but it sounds relieved. "It was difficult keeping that from you."

I grin but I feel no humor. "I let you in here, which makes me a traitor. You'd better have a plan, because I'm in deep trouble right now."

He gives me a serious nod. "Unfortunately, we all are. That's why I'm here."

Two figures peel themselves off the Cathedral wall as we arrive at the door. Lutz Logan casts an arrogant glance in my direction and Brandon Baker assesses me with his steely-eyes. It's difficult to read their expressions but there's an edge of tension in the set of their shoulders.

They have a quick, silent exchange with Rowan that I can't interpret.

Rowan says, "Wait here while Slade decides whether to remove the protective barriers that are in place against the Dominion Master."

Now that I'm a Superior, I have the right to enter and leave the Cathedral as I please. But the same does not apply to Vlad. The protective spells around the Cathedral will annihilate him if he tries to enter without permission.

We wait, holding our breath for Slade to decide whether he will see Vlad. I'm not sure if he will. The protective spells are designed to thwart an assassination attempt on the Master's life. The Cathedral is the only place where Slade can sleep safely. He once told me he didn't want to be the Master and end up a sad, old man, living alone for the rest of his life.

I told him he wouldn't.

So much of what we said to each other was wiped out the moment I revealed my wings to him. The moment I told him

I gave him my feather and made him... not so human anymore.

As soon as a guard appears from within the Cathedral and gives Rowan the go-ahead, he spins to us. "It's safe to pass through the barrier, but I don't know how safe you'll be once Slade sees you. He's different now, Hunter."

The warning in his voice is compounded by the tension in his posture. He's worried. Despite their stern expressions, so are Lutz and Brandon. They were never friends with Slade but they weren't his enemy like Gareth was. Brandon even told me he would follow Slade if Slade became the Master.

But now... they look like they're itching to get me the hell out of here.

A shiver runs down my spine, but I step forward into the entrance room with Vlad.

All of the other assassins remain outside while Lutz and Brandon fall in behind Vlad and Rowan directs us toward the dining hall.

Rowan keeps his voice low. "When Slade came back without you, he said you decided not to return to the Realm. We didn't believe him. You fought hard to be here. You wouldn't just walk away."

I had walked away, but not without a lot of pain.

I ask, "What happened?"

"The Guardian named him Master and they put Gareth in a cell under the Cathedral. But Slade was more brutal than normal."

I'm startled to hear Slade described as 'brutal.' When we were training, he always kept his strength hidden. He blended in, never revealing his true skill or the extent of his ability to use assassin's magic.

Rowan says, "Then we heard that he killed you. All hell broke loose."

I dart a surprised look at him while Vlad remains silent beside me.

Every now and then Vlad flicks me a quick assessing glance. He's already taken in every aspect of our surroundings from the high ceilings to the ornate paintings to the absence of any exit other than the door we entered through.

Carefully, I ask, "What sort of hell?"

It's cold inside the Cathedral. Somehow even colder than outside.

I sense the violence seeping through the air around me. It's icy but awfully familiar... Slade's power. I recognize it without thinking.

What happened here?

My steps slow but I force myself to keep moving. The door to the dining hall is a few paces away and I sense that Slade is inside.

You are a machine, Hunter. You have no emotions. Just put one foot in front of the other.

Lutz speaks up behind me, "Ridley lost it."

I miss a step. "What?"

"When he heard that Slade killed you, Ridley went after Slade. In a bad way. We had to put Ridley in a cell to stop him breaking the Assassin's Code and killing his own Master. He's underneath the Cathedral in a cell beside Gareth's."

I jolt to a stop and grab Lutz's arm while the others stand clear of me. I haven't told Vlad anything about Ridley being my father so he doesn't know what this is about, but I appreciate that he knows it's important enough to give me space.

Before I left, nobody knew that Ridley was my dad. I'm guessing that's changed. Ridley told Slade before we went on the Fury mission that if anything happened to me, he'd kill Slade despite the code.

Lutz stares at the contact between my hand and his muscled forearm as if it's startling that I would willingly touch him. His surprised eyes meet mine.

"Let Ridley out," I say. "Now."

"Only Slade can do that."

I growl at him. "Ridley doesn't belong in a cell. Definitely not right beside Gareth. I'm certain he won't cause any trouble when he knows I'm okay."

There was a time that Ridley didn't want to know if I was his daughter because it meant he would have to watch out for me. I guess that must have changed. Dramatically.

Lutz plucks my hand from his arm, making an annoyed sound deep in his throat, but he says, "I'll see what I can do."

He and Rowan push open the doors to the dining hall, but they don't follow us inside. As I pass him, Lutz darts a look at the figures standing at the far end of the room and back at me. The tension around his eyes and mouth hits me hard. Lutz Logan isn't the type to worry. Certainly not about me.

This room is the place where I first saw the Clave; where I first heard Gareth talk about it. The gruesome tapestries still hang from the walls, depicting Valkyrie and Keres killing each other over the souls of dying humans.

I had hoped Slade would take the tapestries down. Even the Guardian expressed a dislike of them.

Three figures stand at the opposite end of the room, in

front of the dais. Two of them wait at the side, separated from the third.

The Guardian is as regal as always, her head held high, her intelligent gaze taking in everything from my appearance to the fact that I don't carry any weapons, gliding over Vlad from his boots to his shaved head. She would have been present when he was declared Master.

Despite her calm façade, tension is revealed in the tightness around her eyes, the stillness of her lips, and the way her hands clasp in front of her, turning white because she's pressing them together so hard.

Cain, on the other hand, isn't trying to hide the fact that he's on edge right now.

It surprises me to see that he's wearing his assassin's ring today. He wouldn't be able to do that without Slade's permission. The thick gold band glints as he runs his hand through his almost-black hair.

His focus flicks between me, Vlad, and… Slade.

Slade paces like a caged lion in front of the dais. His gaze is piercing, his focus never straying from me despite his constant prowling back and forth.

He is tall and powerful, muscles bunching beneath a short-sleeved shirt and supple black pants. Like me, he is not wearing a coat. Like me, he will run warmer than most humans now.

My heart skips a beat when his blue eyes level with mine and pierce me like a blade.

Within moments, he scrutinizes every inch of me from my eyes, to my lips, all the way down to my waist, and back up to my mouth. My entire body comes alive under his gaze as if he reached out and stroked a hand down my bare skin, as if his fingers curled around my hips, drawing me closer…

A shiver runs the length of my spine as his power reaches out to me, sparking across the distance.

Silver lights dance in the depths of his eyes, the same lights that shone when I bonded with him.

The nature of his power is unmistakable.

It is Valkyrie. And very, *very* dangerous.

Everyone else will think it's coming from Slade's assassin's ring. After all, the Guardian gave him one of the most powerful rings in existence. But this power is part of him.

I'm part of him.

He is harnessing raw Valkyrie power. He was lethal before. But now he is deadly to everyone.

No wonder Cain and the Guardian are keeping their distance.

Fear rockets through me. My heart pounds harder in my chest; so hard I have to press my fist against it.

Rowan warned us that we wouldn't be safe once Slade sees us. I need to warn Vlad but we're too close to Slade for even a whisper now.

As we draw to a stop several paces from Slade's position, I try to control my breathing, try to calm my pounding heart, but my power scatters across my torso like shivers, responding to the force pulsing off Slade in waves.

Despite the danger, the pull toward him is like a magnet, dragging at me while I fight it as hard as I can.

His lips part. "Hunter."

The way he says my name is like… *holy damn…* It's like tearing me apart and putting me back together at the same time.

My heart splits and burns, shivers and breaks, kicking hard inside my chest.

I never should have come back.

CHAPTER NINE

I should have stayed away from Slade.

I should have found another way to release the verdan, something, anything other than standing in front of Slade while he's angry and ferocious and… wants me to go to him, pulling me with his every breath.

Then his gaze shifts upward to a spot above my shoulders, to the place where my wings would be if I let them out, and it's like a bucket of ice poured over me.

He's remembering my wings.

He holds my gaze for another moment, his intense scrutiny as hot as burning coals. I can't begin to read his thoughts as his focus finally shifts away from me.

He strides rapidly toward Vlad. "Alexei Mason, you have trespassed into my Legion without permission. That is a crime for which I am entitled to take your life."

I inhale sharply. Slade has been brushing up on all of the rules in the Assassin's Code. It's the seventh rule: a Master Assassin must not trespass on another Master's territory.

The consequence is death. Slade has the right to kill Vlad for what is effectively an invasion of the Legion by the Dominion.

Vlad has taken a major risk coming here today. A risk I would have cautioned him against if I'd known that he wasn't a member of the Legion. More so because of the change in Slade that I'm now witnessing.

Slade demands, "Why are you here?"

Vlad draws himself up to his full height, taller than Slade. Vlad is incredibly strong, and a ferocious fighter, but he has no idea what he's facing if he tries to fight Slade.

I prepare myself to get between them if I have to.

Vlad remains poised, responding to Slade's threat with an equally powerful stance. "I'm here to warn you."

Slade is like a fully primed weapon about to go off. "Warn me?"

"Your life is in danger. Along with Cain Carter's."

At the side of the room, Cain and the Guardian both startle, casting alarmed and questioning glances at me but I have no answers, no reassurance I can give them. Vlad didn't tell me why he needed to speak with them.

Slade's eyes narrow to dangerous slits. He has no problem invading Vlad's space. "The only danger I see right now is you."

"I am not a threat to you, Legion Master."

"Prove it." Slade pauses. "Leave right now. I'll give you one chance."

Vlad stands his ground. "You need to hear—"

Slade's open hand shoots out and closes around Vlad's throat like a vice. Vlad doesn't have time to draw breath before Slade wrenches him off the ground. Vlad gives a strangled shout as Slade elevates him above the ground with a single upstretched arm.

At the side of the room, Cain lurches forward and the Guardian follows, a cry on her lips. But neither of them has authority here.

I'm already moving. "Slade, stop!"

Before I can get between them, mere seconds after Slade grabbed him, Vlad's instincts kick in and he retaliates.

It's the worst thing he could do.

I shout, but it's too late. "Vlad, don't!"

Vlad's giant fist meets Slade's chest, a solid hit that would have forced anyone else to let go. It's a defensive move, the same approach he used on the draugr. He follows it up with two more hits—another to Slade's torso and one cracking blow to Slade's temple.

Slade absorbs the hits and barely flinches. He forces Vlad higher, thrusting him into the air and letting go. He follows Vlad's descent to the ground with so many rapid blows that I can't count them.

Slade's fists, both left and right, crack across Vlad's torso, shoulder, neck, and finally smash into his face, the force and momentum spinning Vlad backward mid-air. I know what it feels like to experience the full force of Slade's fist and mine was only one blow.

Vlad took five.

It's fast, brutal, and over in seconds. Vlad lands with a crunch several feet away, bouncing before coming to rest on the floor.

I'm amazed when he pushes up on his hands, still conscious. But the way his limbs shake tells me he's partially concussed.

Vlad told me he would make everything okay for me but it's time for me to protect him.

"No!" I race forward, harnessing my strength to reach Slade faster than the Guardian and Cain can, wrenching Slade's arm back before he can land another blow.

I gasp as soon as my hand connects with his arm.

In that awful moment, I realize I've made a terrible mistake.

Instant agony shoots through me, fiery pain burning up my arm and into my chest. The shock forces my hand to clamp around Slade's wrist like I'm being electrified.

The power flowing through him…

I know it because it's my own.

It is Valkyrie killing power. Not just strength. Not just speed. But death.

I can't let go. No matter how hard I try to force my fingers apart. My hand won't open. But it's my heart that is in the most pain.

I knew he carried some of my power, that it would make him stronger and allow him to heal faster but I didn't anticipate that he would become like me.

There has never been a male Valkyrie. I didn't think it was possible. Mom told me that Valkyrie sometimes gave their birth feathers to their mortal partner to extend their mortal life.

But I gave Slade one of my permanent feathers.

What have I done?

"Hunter!" Slade shouts and jolts. Shock flashes across his face and his body instantly tenses.

His focus shoots to my fist clenched around his arm.

I sense his inhale like it's my own, his skin like it's part of me, his power as it sears my blood, awareness of his body rushing straight into my heart.

He was about to unleash death on Vlad, to take Vlad's life. He harnessed the Valkyrie power when I grabbed him and now I'm absorbing it instead.

There's a moment of calm as I take the darkness into my body, inhale into the sudden silence…

Then I scream as intense pain rips me apart.

CHAPTER TEN

Agony scorches my insides, tearing and clawing at me.

It feels like every part of me is being shredded and gouged.

Slade pulls away from me, trying to break the connection, but it's no use.

He grabs my hand with his free one, muscles straining as he tries to pry my fingers apart. "Hunter, let go!"

There's nothing he can do. My fingers won't unclench until the surge of power fades—until I've absorbed every bit of the death that he intended for Vlad.

Tears stream down my cheeks. I sob in a breath and scream it out again.

Valkyrie power can't kill me. Only Keres power can. But it's hurting me. Badly.

Slade roars, *"Let go, Hunter!"*

Sob-screams tear out of me. *"I... can't..."*

The Guardian screams, racing toward us. "Hunter! Stop touching him."

Vlad struggles to get up, wobbling and falling, crawling on his hands and knees to get to me.

Cain reaches me first, green eyes blazing with assassin's power, the angle of his body and his line of sight telling me he's going to pull me away from Slade.

Just in time, my free hand shoots up into the space between us. "Don't touch me or you'll die!"

Cain skids to a halt, muscles bunched, fists clenching. He backs away with a frustrated shout, taking glances between me and Slade. He can't help me and the look on his face tells me he hates it.

Slade takes hold of my wrist but stops before he tries to pull my hand away again. His voice lowers to a whisper. "Hunter, please…"

I can barely hear him over the sound of my screams ripping through my throat, echoing around the room.

The far door bursts open and Rowan, Lutz, and Brandon appear on the other side of it, but Slade lifts a hand and that's all it takes for the door to slam shut again. This time he's using his assassin's ring, the same way he closed the training room one time so he could kiss me.

My knees buckle, and Slade catches me with his free arm, sliding it around my back and drawing me closer, enclosing our connected hands between his chest and mine, his big hand soothing down my back.

He closes his eyes, an expression of concentration falls over his harsh features, and the power shrieking through me reduces marginally. It's enough that I don't have to scream out the pain anymore.

Whimpers and sobs pour out of me instead.

Every sound makes Slade wince.

I have no choice but to curl over the tangle of our hands

between us and drop my forehead to his shoulder, crying softly as the pain finally begins to recede.

Slade whispers into my hair. "I never wanted to hurt you again, Hunter. I wanted you to stay as far away from me as possible. Nothing good happens to you when you're near me."

My mouth is dry. I can't speak and my thoughts are jumbled.

I want to tell him that's not true. Lots of good things happened when we were together. I slept soundly. I had an ally. I felt liked and not feared.

The killing force reduces again and finally… it disappears. But my insides burn. I won't walk away from this unscathed. It will take time to heal.

Time I don't have right now because Slade continues to speak softly. "I can't let Alexei walk out of here alive. It will send the wrong message to anyone who wants to attack us. It will make the Legion more vulnerable than it already is."

I grip his shoulder with my free hand, my clenched hand finally uncurling from his arm, the blood returning to my fingers in painful increments.

My voice grates against my throat like I swallowed barbed steel. "I won't let you do that, Slade."

I push away from him, my legs unstable and trembling.

He reaches out to steady me but I push my hands into the space between us to stop him. I back up and around, wobbly steps, placing myself resolutely between him and Vlad.

I had better heal fast because I'm not sure if I have the power to fight Slade right now.

In fact, I don't think I do.

Slade shakes his head at me, an edge of ferocity entering his voice again. "Don't do this. I don't want to fight you."

I grit my teeth. "I won't let you kill him."

Slade sucks in a deep breath, pausing, a muscle at the edge of his jaw ticking. He changes tactic so rapidly it shocks me. "As your Master, I'm ordering you to step aside."

My eyes widen. He's playing the Master role. I'm still a member of the Legion. Slade is the Legion Master. That means I have to do whatever he says and if I don't... well... I don't know what he'll do, but it's his choice to impose whatever punishment he wants.

I could end up in a cell next to Ridley.

I tilt my chin up, stubbornly refusing. "I will not."

His eyes narrow. He steps right up to me. The air between us is charged, the light in his eyes as bright as before, but my own power is dull now. There's nothing left of it. I am empty except for my human emotions and that damn bond that won't go away, that makes me want to close the final gap, kiss him, and tell him he's being stubborn and needs to change his mind...

I shake myself but Slade's focus has shifted to my lips as if he followed my thoughts.

He quietly asks, "Are you refusing to obey a direct order from your Master?"

As he gazes at me, the friction between us worsens, intensifying like a physical force. I can withstand a lot but I'm barely upright and the extra pressure on my nerves is beyond my endurance.

I won't win. The only way I can stop him killing Vlad is to spread my wings and let my deepest power loose.

My true nature already cost me everything I wanted. If I show Cain, Vlad, and the Guardian what I am, I will lose everything else.

Emotions race across Slade's expression so fast I can't

catch them. There's a war going on in his mind. He never once chose to fight me. In fact, he always refused. I was the one who stepped into the punch that knocked me out. I was the one who grabbed his hand just now to stop him killing Vlad.

The way his lips press together in a line of concern tells me he knows I have no strength left. *Damn him.* I thought I could bluff my way through this.

I clench my teeth, shut my eyes, and harness what little is left of my power.

I can do this. Somehow. Even if I'm simply a human shield.

Even if it means a cell next to Gareth.

Vlad's voice rumbles behind me, a soft groan. I tilt toward him, but not enough to make Slade think he has an opening.

Vlad has recovered enough to draw up to his knees, a trickle of blood running from his left temple. He leaves it to run to his chin.

He appears to still be dazed, but says, "There's an easy solution, Hunter."

"Really?" I definitely don't see one. "What is that, Vlad?"

Vlad doesn't try to get up. He's smart enough to know he has to stay where he is if he doesn't want to fall flat on his face and bust up his nose again. "You don't have to obey the Legion Master if you're not a member of the Legion."

I stare at him in confusion. *Is Vlad asking me to defect? To join the Dominion? Is that his idea of helping me?*

He grins, his warm gray eyes like a storm over the sea. "Declare yourself Rogue."

I suck in a breath. My mother was Rogue.

She broke all ties with the Legion and became her own

Master. But if I do that, I won't be able to step foot inside the Realm again without an invitation.

I will break any official connection I have with Slade once and for all.

Slade's eyes shoot wide, one hand rising into the space between us. He shakes his head, the smallest shake, as if that's the last thing he wants… before he carefully relaxes his arm and waits for my decision.

The idea of cutting my final ties with him tears at my heart. Seceding from the Legion is like declaring that I'm an enemy of the Legion and everyone in it. It's not true. They might not be my allies, but many of the assassins here have my respect: Rowan, Brandon, Superior Lincoln, Slade's cousin Thomas. Even Lutz. And especially Ridley.

But I have to be free to return to Saber Lane and find out what weapon the Clave is hiding and then destroy it.

In fact, I need to be free to follow my own path separate from the Legion in all things.

If I declare myself Rogue right now, Slade can't fight me. One glance at Cain tells me he's considering moving to stand beside me. The determination I've shown appears to be swaying him.

Two of us facing Slade will stop him from killing Vlad.

Just as Cain steps forward, Slade steps back from me, his shoulders squared, visibly prepared for my decision.

I swallow the pain of cutting ties with him.

Taking a determined breath, I say, "I'm going Rogue."

CHAPTER ELEVEN

*V*lad rises to his feet, hands flat on his knees as he leans forward while he gets his balance.

Upright once more, he says, "I will support Hunter's bid for freedom. The same way my Master gave his support for the Glass Fox to become her own Master."

Before an assassin goes Rogue, they need the support of at least one Master. That's what makes it so rare—what Master would willingly support the creation of a rival?

I consider Vlad with surprise. I never guessed it was the Dominion Master who supported my mother.

The Guardian doesn't miss a beat. "Your support is sufficient." Her dress swishes around her long legs as she turns to me, her previous alarm and fear quickly disappearing, tucked away behind a regal veneer again. "Hunter Cassidy, where is your chosen territory?"

"Saber Lane," I say, without hesitation. It's a small chunk of land to take away from the Legion so it shouldn't be too much for the Guardian to approve.

She replies, firmly, "Sanctioned. All Masters will

respect the boundary." A smile curves her lips. "You are now your own Master, Hunter. But remember, a Rogue Master has no Faction." Her smile fades, sadness creeping into her voice. "You are, from this day on, alone."

It's done so quickly that I'm left with a sense of shock, as if the world shifted and I'm only now registering the earthquake beneath my feet.

Cain unfolds his arms from across his broad chest. "The Horde will respect the boundary." The weapons he is carrying about his massive body glint as he gives me a formal, acknowledging nod. I recognize the daggers marked with his initials. One of them looks like the very dagger I returned to him.

Vlad says, "The Dominion will also respect the boundary."

As Vlad speaks, Cain contemplates him with wary respect. It will take a lot for them to move past their existing distrust, but for now, they seem to have reached a silent truce.

Slade is the last to respond. He moves further away from me, his boots thudding one after the other, increasing the space between us.

His eyes are dull, the flickers of his power concealed. I sense it lurking beneath the surface, the pull toward him just as strong as it was before. Except that now it's like I've built a wall made of explosives between us.

If either of us breaches it, we won't survive.

A perfectly blank expression conceals whatever Slade is feeling. "The Legion will respect the boundary."

The Guardian's countenance remains formal as she addresses the previous problem. "Slade Baines, do you wish to carry out the sentence on Alexei Mason or will you hear him out?"

Slade's expression is neutral. "If Hunter thinks it's worth risking death to save him, then I will listen."

Vlad dabs a thumb to the cut on his forehead as I move to stand beside him. He told me that coming here was important enough to risk our safety. I have to believe that he didn't lie to me. But... *dammit...* he'd better have a spectacular reason after everything I just did for him.

Vlad gives me a short, formal nod, but beneath the cool gesture, gratitude warms the depths of his eyes and lifts my heart just a little.

"First," he says, "I need to verify that Hunter did *not* know who I was when she brought me here."

The Guardian clasps her slender hands in front of herself. "Duly noted."

Vlad addresses both Slade and Cain. "I came to warn you about a powerful and dangerous woman."

Slade's eyes narrow to glinting, blue slits, taking on a little of his former ferocity. "There are many dangerous women in this world. One of the most dangerous is standing right beside you."

Vlad appears to assess the continuing friction between Slade and me. He's probably wishing that he'd pushed me harder to tell him what really happened between us.

He focusses back on Slade. "This woman has the power to interfere with our ledgers."

"What?" The Guardian and Cain Carter both speak at once, their shock reflecting my own.

Tension renews in the angle of Cain's shoulders and the set of his jaw. He and I aren't exactly friends. In fact, he told me once that there's no such thing as a friend in the assassin's world, but he certainly isn't my enemy or my rival."

He demands, "How is that possible?"

Vlad replies to Cain, but watches Slade carefully, knowing that it's Slade he has to convince. "Somehow, she has hijacked the Guardian's power and uses it to sanction assassinations for her own purposes."

The Guardian gasps. "Who is this woman?"

"You know her as Lady Tirelli."

The Guardian hisses, "Lady Tirelli! I know her violence very well. She is responsible for multiple murders in the last three days alone."

Vlad continues, "She gets someone who works for her to pose as a client and write in the ledger. Then she sanctions the killing herself. The assassin has no idea that the assassination isn't really sanctioned. As for the magic behind it, we haven't figured out exactly how she does it, but we have ascertained that she can only affect the entry being made by the person she sent. She can't read or change any of the other existing or future entries."

The Guardian is aghast. "For her to do this, she has to conceal from me the fact that the entry is being made at all. I should be able to see every entry in every ledger! How... I can't... how did you find out about this?"

Vlad sighs. "Lady Tirelli is playing a long game. It began twenty years ago, when the Dominion Master—the Master I just replaced—fell prey to her scheme. He was given his first assassination. Determined to prove himself, he tracked his target across the country. He carried out the mission only to discover that the woman was innocent. It was a tragedy he could never atone for."

The Guardian clenches her fists, advancing on Vlad. It's the angriest I've ever seen her. "Why didn't he notify me?"

Vlad meets her accusation with an even gaze. "He couldn't come forward. He carried out an unsanctioned assassination. That means exile, which ultimately leads to death. And… unfortunately… there were other unsanctioned killings before he discovered what was going on. Other assassins were implicated. *Good* assassins. I'm here now because Lady Tirelli has moved her base of operations from the Dominion's territory to the Legion's."

It's easy to see that the Guardian has a thousand questions bubbling on her lips, but Slade gets in first. He demands, "Why haven't you killed her?"

Vlad exhales. Slowly. He swallows. It's his first sign of defeat. Even when Slade knocked him across the room, he didn't appear this beaten. His shoulders take on the same slump that they did when he apologized for offending me.

He exchanges a glance with the Guardian as he says, "Two months ago, my Master wrote her name in my ledger and the Guardian sanctioned the kill."

The Guardian sucks in a breath. "So that's why your Master wrote her name! I sanctioned it because of the other atrocities she committed."

Vlad nods. "I waited for Lady Tirelli to enter Dominion territory. I took a shot at her. I was sure I hit her but… she got away."

A muscle in Slade's jaw ticks. "A failed assassination can't be attempted again."

Vlad lifts his chin. "Not by the Dominion."

It's the fourth rule in the Assassin's Code, which means Vlad can't try again.

Cain paces at the edge of our group. His distrust of Vlad

has returned to his features. "Why haven't you tried to warn us before now?"

Vlad shoots back with his first sign of irritation, "Would you have believed me?"

He levels his gaze with Cain. "I know you don't trust me, Cain Carter, because you heard rumors of unsanctioned killings. Well, it's true. But it's not our doing. We have been tricked in the same way that you will be tricked unless we work together to deal with this problem."

Slade shakes his head. "You expect us to believe any of this after you gain access to my Legion by subterfuge?"

Vlad shakes his head. "I couldn't make this an official visit and let others know I was traveling here—not even my own people. Lady Tirelli has infiltrated all Factions. You know who your traitors are: Master Gareth and Superior Fallon. But even after all these years, we have not discovered ours."

His focus is suddenly on me and I'm not sure why as he continues. "Lady Tirelli is waiting for the chance to take us all out. Then she will be able to get to her ultimate target."

He pauses before he exhales a heavy breath and says, "She will be able to get to Hunter."

CHAPTER TWELVE

I'm wary and unsettled as I return Vlad's steady gaze. "I'm her ultimate target?"

Vlad nods. "Twenty years ago, my former Master tracked his target all the way here." His hand shoots up as Slade growls. "Yes, I know, he trespassed into Legion territory which he shouldn't have done."

Vlad returns his attention to me. "Your mother intervened but not soon enough. You see, the target was a woman with a baby. My Master found out, years later, that it was the child that Lady Tirelli wanted."

I touch Vlad's arm, needing to anchor myself. There's too much I don't know about my mother's past. "What did Mom do?"

"She fought my Master," he says. "She sent him packing. But not before she made him promise to support her to go Rogue. The last he saw of her, she was walking away with the child in her arms."

A chill speeds down my spine. "What happened to that baby?"

Vlad shakes his head. "My Master searched for the little girl for years. He wanted to make amends, to look after her, but she disappeared completely. Whatever your mother did to protect that child from Lady Tirelli, she did it well. My Master couldn't find her. But neither did Lady Tirelli."

I pause to consider everything Vlad has told us. "Why would all of that make me her target now?"

Vlad replies, simply, "She thinks you know where the child is."

"Not a child anymore," I say. "That girl would be the same age as us now. A woman. I have no idea where she is. This is the first I've heard of her. At least it's obvious what Lady Tirelli can gain from tampering with our ledgers."

Cain nods. "She can annihilate her competition without us knowing we are pawns in her game. She can even turn us against each other." He gives Vlad a solemn nod and once more they are back to a quiet truce.

Vlad turns to Slade. He spreads his arms wide in an open gesture. "Do you still want to kill me, Legion Master?"

Slade exhales. "No." He turns to the Guardian. "From now on, we will communicate directly with you instead of relying on our ledgers."

The Guardian nods. "Perhaps I should stay in Boston for a while. It will make communication easier. With your permission of course, Slade?"

"Granted."

Cain also indicates his agreement with this plan. He doesn't take up the role of Horde Master for another four months but he says, "I will warn my Master, although it sounds like this is mostly a Legion problem for now. I have no doubt it could become a Horde problem too, so I will help in any way that I can."

Despite the general agreement, Slade is no more relaxed than he was when we first arrived. "That takes care of the problem with our ledgers, but it doesn't deal with Lady Tirelli herself."

Vlad says, "She lives in the shadows. Only a handful of people have seen her or even know what she looks like. You need to draw her out."

"How do you propose we do that?"

"We need to be seen together, all four of us, in a public place. She won't be able to resist the temptation to strike."

Cain says, "I can help with that. I'll put on a charity event and leak the guest list so she knows we're all going." He considers the tension between Slade, Vlad, and me with a wry smile. "We can pretend to be friends."

A muscle in Slade's jaw continues to tick. "How long do you need to set that up?"

"Three weeks. Is that soon enough?"

Slade nods. "It will have to be."

Vlad says, "Thank you. In the meantime, I request permission to stay in Boston. I can't fight Lady Tirelli, but I can pass on my knowledge of her organization."

Slade takes a deep breath. "Permission granted. But from now on, you will respect the boundaries between Factions. The rules exist for a reason. Do not trespass in the Realm without an invitation."

Vlad relaxes for the first time. "You have my word."

Slade isn't finished. He is quiet and doesn't look at me as he says, "Likewise, Hunter, as your own Master, you will not step foot inside this Realm unless I ask you to. Just as… I will not come to Saber Lane without an invitation."

I flinch. Whatever words he's speaking, it's his emotions I'm sensing now. He is pushing back against my presence, pushing back as hard as he can. He knows he can't breach the wall I've constructed between us. What I don't know… is whether I can either.

I focus on a spot beside his face, trying to quell the emptiness creeping into my heart. I've done what I had to do. I will make it through this.

I nod. "Understood."

Cain speaks from the side. "I'll make the preparations to draw Lady Tirelli into the open and let you all know the details."

We're almost done but there's one more thing I need to know before I can leave. "What about Gareth?"

Slade's expression hardens. "He will be imprisoned here for the next year. After that, he will be exiled."

"Exiled? Not executed? But… he tried to kill you."

Slade folds his arms across his chest, muscles bulging as he presses tight. "He tried but didn't succeed. If he had succeeded, the Guardian could execute him, but as it is, he hasn't broken the code. All I can do is banish him from the Realm."

I exclaim, "So attempted murder isn't a crime?"

Slade's ferocity returns. "If it was, then your father would have to die, too."

I jolt. "No… that's…"

"Different?" Slade exhales and deep frustration fills his expression. Gareth was determined to kill both of us. He will continue to be a lethal threat. He won't stop until he has the feather and the verdan.

But Slade is right. Ridley attacked him. Slade can't apply one set of standards to Gareth and another to Ridley. If he executes Gareth, he has to kill Ridley, too.

My heart sinks. If Ridley hadn't gone after Slade, Gareth's

punishment could be more severe.

Slade meets my eyes. "You've already lost your mother. I won't take away your father."

Silence fills the space around us. Slade could have chosen to make a very different decision, but he won't kill my father.

I sense Cain's eyes on me. One of the first times he saw me, I was completely vulnerable after I found out that Ridley could be my dad and that there were things about Mom—important things—that she'd kept from me.

Slade, too, knows how much Mom's death affected me.

I ask, quietly, "What about Fallon?"

"Exiled already. He is no longer part of the Legion."

I bite my lip. Fallon will go to Lady Tirelli. He was already in her pocket. No doubt she will protect him for as long as he is useful to her. That means he's out there somewhere. The Realm is safe from him but nowhere else is.

Especially not Saber Lane.

I have to get back there.

I return my attention to Slade, finding his focus still on me. I bow to him, a formal goodbye. Traditionally, Masters maintain eye contact while bowing to each other. It's an accepted acknowledgment of the distrust between Factions.

I choose instead to lower my eyes to the floor, exposing myself to attack. It's the smallest gesture I can make to ease the tension between us.

He could have chosen to execute my father, but he didn't. I want him to know how much that means to me.

I murmur, "Thank you, Legion Master."

He swallows. "Thank you... Glass Arrow."

Vlad offers Slade a warrior's bow, but the two men never take their eyes off each other. Cain and the Guardian bow quickly after that.

I hold Slade's gaze for another moment before I force myself to walk away.

My reason for being here is at an end. As tough as I'm pretending to be right now, I'm hurting inside, physically and emotionally. Absorbing all that power took its toll and being around Slade is like a battle that never ends, fighting what I want.

My hands have started to shake, tiny tremors, but increasing. I hate that I can't control it. I need to rest and I don't want to collapse here.

The tension eases around me. Cain gives me a small smile before he offers his arm to the Guardian next to him. For a moment, he morphs into the public persona he wears in the outside world. He really does carry off the whole millionaire identity very well. "Guardian, can I have my car take you to your hotel?"

"Thank you, Cain, I would appreciate that."

As Vlad takes up position walking beside me, I manage to catch Cain's eye. "I don't suppose you have two cars? I could use a lift to Saber Lane."

Cain's mouth tugs up at the corner. "I have several. All you have to do is ask."

I sigh, unable to disguise the pain any longer.

Cain's smile slips as concern washes over his features. "Hunter?"

"I'm asking."

He nods and quickly pulls out a phone, speaking rapidly into it. Within moments, he tells me the car will be waiting outside the Realm as soon as I get there.

When we reach the door, a male voice bellows in the distant corridor, "Where's my daughter?"

The door crashes open in front of me. Ridley stands

there, mad as hell. He storms into the room. "Hunter!"

Then he drags me into his arms.

"You're alive." He exhales as he presses me to his chest, his bristles dragging my hair across the top of my head. It looks like he hasn't shaved in days, but I guess you can't trust an angry assassin with a razor blade.

His voice hitches as he says, "I thought I lost you."

It's the most emotional I've ever seen him. He's actually… hugging me. Like a dad would hug his daughter.

I melt into the feeling of having a father. Of having family that cares about me. "I should die more often."

He doesn't pull back for a full minute. Then he takes a good look at me, a crease forming in his forehead. "You're pale. What's wrong?"

I lean into him and whisper, "Do me a favor, please, Dad? Help me to the car outside the Realm? Without it looking like I'm leaning on you."

I'm grateful when he doesn't ask me why. Instead, he shifts, positions one big hand on my shoulder while his other relocates to support my back. He holds me up while making it look like he's hugging me.

He murmurs into my ear, "I'm not against carrying you."

I manage a smile. "I know, but if this is the last time I walk out of the Realm, I'd rather do it on my own two feet."

Ridley keeps his voice low, even though there's no doubt Vlad and Cain can hear us if they want to use their power to do so. "What happened?"

"I'll be fine. I just need a good rest."

"Okay… but what do you mean 'the last time you walk out of here?'"

"I'm my own Master now, Dad." I'm surprised at how

easily calling him 'dad' keeps rolling off my tongue. "I'm Rogue like Mom."

A grin breaks across his face. He drops a kiss to my forehead. "Finally. You're a Master Assassin like you should be." He pulls back a little. "But I claim my right as your father to visit your territory whenever the hell I like. I'm not waiting for an invitation."

It has taken Ridley a very long time to acknowledge me as his daughter and there's no way I'm going to push him away. The pain of leaving Slade a second time is beating me into a bad enough pulp. "Always."

Ridley supports me through the door, but I can't help glancing back.

Slade stands exactly where we left him, a powerful force watching us go.

A *lonely*, powerful force.

I told him he wouldn't be alone when he was Master, but now he is.

CHAPTER THIRTEEN

With Ridley's help, I make it to Cain's car with my feet on the ground where I say goodbye to them both for now.

I even manage to sit upright next to Vlad for the short ride back to Saber Lane.

When the car drops us off at the entrance to the street, I walk on my own while Vlad makes noises about picking me up.

I give him death stares every time he looks like he's about to scoop me into his arms. "No."

I'm relieved to see that Saber Lane looks quiet. I'm worried about Fallon and Lady Tirelli but so far things appear calm here.

Now that I've held up my part of the deal with Vlad, I'm anxious to get back to the bookshop and retrieve the Clave. I've waited long enough to find out the secret it's hiding.

The trouble is, it's time for me to swallow my pride and admit that I won't make it that far.

I stumble to the Diner door, which is located closer than the bookshop. Luckily, William and Tansy are there with Dean, eating an early dinner at one of the tables, which gives me an excuse to make a detour.

William waves to me from the table, appearing a lot more relaxed than earlier today. I hope that means my stroll through Boston has had the desired impact: letting the underground know I won't tolerate their violence.

Whatever game Lady Tirelli was playing by spreading the rumor that Slade killed me, it's at an end.

I hesitate before inviting Vlad inside. Dean is an empath and, depending on Vlad's past, Vlad's emotions could cause Dean extreme pain. The first time I set foot on Saber Lane, Dean nearly collapsed. I still feel bad about it.

Dean calls out to me before I hesitate further. "Come on in, Hunter."

I've barely taken another step when Vlad's big hands dart toward me.

I slip to the side. In a big way. The floor rears up toward me and I make a grab for the nearest table but my legs won't hold me up.

Oh... This isn't good.

Vlad catches me just as I'm about to hit the floor and running footsteps sound before Dean wraps his arms around me, pulling me safely inside the shop.

Dean's face appears above me but he speaks to Vlad, the urgency in his voice a sharp thrum in my ears. "Hunter's hurt. Badly!"

I mumble, confused about why they look so worried, "Vlad is hurt, too. He took multiple hits."

Dean shakes his head. "Your friend is fine. A cut to his

forehead, some bruising. He has a head like stone. Trust me, I sense his wounds and he's okay. But you, Hunter… you're death warmed up. Boiling, in fact."

William and Tansy hover close behind him.

Dean says, "Help me get her upstairs. She's running hot. She needs an ice bath."

"I can carry her," Vlad says.

Dean shrugs him off. "You can bring the ice. See the ice chest outside? I'll need two bags of it."

Vlad doesn't argue, hurrying outside while Dean swings me into his arms, holding me close to his body.

As soon as Dean's chest contacts mine, it's like I'm cushioned in a cloud. My head suddenly feels like it's floating.

Wow. I don't feel pain any more.

I peer up at Dean as he carries me upstairs. I'm not surprised to see that he lives above the shop like William does. But the effect that his empathic nearness has on my body is a little too intense, a little too much like…

Oh. Wow.

Something I would never do with Dean.

A sigh escapes my throat. I clear it, pointedly. *Ahem.*

I may be close to losing consciousness but I'm still in control, thank you very much. I growl at him, "Dean, what are you doing to me?"

"Soothing your pain."

"Well, it's making me feel… *hmm…*" I press my lips together. Not exactly what I should feel around him.

"Your mind needed lifting from the dark place it was descending into. I promise I won't take advantage." He switches to a mischievous grin. "Unless you want me to."

I pat his arm as he angles me through the bathroom door. "My heart has been broken already, Dean. Besides, aren't you and Tansy…?"

Dean smiles. "I appreciate your thoughtfulness, but empaths can't form romantic relationships, only friendship. A closer attachment is too painful when someone lies to you or is angry with you. We're better off alone."

"That's not very fair."

"Life isn't. But I'm okay with it." He gives me an unexpectedly sly smile, his voice oozing honey at me, dragging my attention to his lips. "That doesn't mean we don't indulge when we want to."

He has nice lips, full and soft-looking…

I shake myself with a laugh. "Well, don't develop any hopes about indulging with me, *baby*."

He winks at me. "Shucks. And here I was hoping I could soothe your frazzled nerves."

He slides me into the bath fully clothed, my feet pointed toward the faucet end. When he turns on the cold water, the liquid sizzles, steaming off my skin.

I give a start. "You weren't joking when you said I was running hot."

He becomes grim. "You don't have to tell me what happened, but I think you should tell William. He knows more about Valk—"

I place my fingers against his lips, stopping him from speaking as I shake my head and point toward the sound of Vlad's footsteps coming up the stairs.

Dean gives me a nod of understanding.

"I will, thank you, Dean," I say. "And for helping me."

He shifts to the side when Vlad enters carrying two

enormous bags of ice, opening them without any fuss and pouring them into the bath. The water was warming much too fast because of my body heat, but the second bag of ice does the trick and everything finally cools down.

When he's done, Vlad hunches down beside the bath, gripping the edge with his big hands. "You took a death blow for me today, Hunter. I'm not sure how you did that and survived."

He levels his gaze at me. "But what is clear to me is that Slade Baines was in more pain than you were."

I stare at him, wide eyed, before I run my hand across my face, icy water dripping down my cheeks. I wasn't expecting this conversation so soon. I should have remembered that Vlad always gets right to the point.

My voice turns to a strangled whisper, "I know."

As blunt as always, Vlad asks, "Why?"

Dean scowls from the side. "Hunter doesn't have to explain anything to you."

Vlad nods. "Okay. You're right. She doesn't. But when she's ready to explain, I'll be ready to listen. In the meantime, there's something you need to know, Hunter."

I draw my hand away from my eyes, allowing the water to drip rivers down my cheeks. "Yes?"

"If our roles were reversed and Slade infiltrated the Dominion, I would kill him. Just like he tried to kill me."

I inhale sharply. "Without listening to him?"

"Absolutely. He gave me a lot more air than I would have given him."

I splutter. "But… then… why did you take that chance today?"

He grins but it carries no humor. "Because I was sure I could beat Slade in a fight."

I groan. "There's no beating Slade."

He nods, a grim smile remaining on his lips as he taps the edge of the bath with a thick finger. "I heard rumors that Slade had assimilated with assassin's magic in a way that nobody has ever seen before. I thought it was only stories. I couldn't have been more wrong. What he did today was beyond my worst nightmare."

He holds up his fist, showing me his assassin's ring. "Do you know what these are made of Hunter?"

I whisper. "Do you?"

He nods. "It's a secret passed from one Master to the next. Since you're now a Master and I supported you, I'm allowed to tell you."

I glance at Dean, but Vlad doesn't seem to mind that he's still watching over me—and listening to us.

I hold up my hand to stop Vlad from saying the words, my fingers splashing water across the space between us. "I already know. They're made from stolen feathers."

"Ah, so Gareth told you." Vlad turns his ring, the chunky rubies catching the light. "This ring is made from a Valkyrie feather. So is Slade's. So was my Master's. There are a few rare rings that are made from Keres feathers, but sadly, it was the Valkyrie who were imprisoned and ripped apart to make most of the rings."

My eyes widen at the way he describes the way my ancestors were treated. From everything William told me about Mom, she didn't know about this either.

She kept a lot from me, but William told me she was genuinely confused about why she couldn't wear an assassin's ring without feeling ill. That's why she had her glass ring made in secret and tricked the former Guardian into giving it to her.

Vlad shakes his head with disgust. "Those peaceful women were treated like animals and we wonder why they became our worst enemies?"

I still remember the pain I felt when I ripped out my feather, how it feels like a part of me is missing, and the only time I feel whole again is…

When I'm near Slade.

Vlad continues, "Slade's ring is made from the feather that was stolen from the Valkyrie Queen herself. He has harnessed the true killing power of the Valkyrie. No Master has ever done that before. They've tried. But never succeeded."

I look away. I can't tell Vlad it's because I gave Slade the key to unlocking that power, that it's not only coming from the ring, but from inside his heart and soul.

Vlad gives a resolute sigh. "I will never beat Slade in a fight. Nobody will. He's too powerful now. Which is why I am eternally grateful, but also astonished, that you took a death blow and survived today."

I'm not about to tell him why.

I need to know what he's thinking, even if it's dangerous to ask. "Your theory is?"

"That he loves the hell out of you."

I suck in a breath.

Vlad plows on, "He didn't want to hurt you. He put a stranglehold on his own power. He probably would have cut off his own arm if he thought it would make your pain stop. Any idiot can see what he feels for you." Vlad points at himself. "Even a concussed one."

I run my hand over my eyes again. Hot tears leak from beneath my eyelids but thankfully the ice water disguises them. Vlad has seen enough tear tracks from me. "I don't know what to do, Vlad. I'm stuck in a place with no exits."

"I can't tell you, Hunter. But you need to sort it out because a love like that either becomes something amazing or it turns into something really bad. You need to decide which you want."

CHAPTER FOURTEEN

ith that, Vlad draws to his feet, eases out his shoulders from hunching beside the bath for so long, and swings to Dean. "If you disclose any of our conversation to anyone, I will rip your arms off."

Dean observes Vlad with a curious expression. I remember now that I was worried about Dean reacting badly to Vlad's presence. It wasn't threats I was worried about so much as Vlad's emotions.

But Dean tilts his head to the side, studying Vlad with a curious expression.

Dean says, "You have no emotions."

Vlad gives him a grin like a wolf about to eat dinner. "I see the world with clarity, not clouded with feeling."

Hmm. I take note of that. It's certainly something I've already observed about Vlad, the way he reacts with logic rather than sentiment, almost to the point of being *un-feeling.*

Brandon once described me as a stone cold assassin but

Vlad is like an ice serpent—emotionless but capable of sudden movement. I'm not totally sure that it's possible to clamp down on all emotions to the point of not feeling anything though.

After Vlad leaves the room, Dean leans across to me. "Do you want me to stay?"

I shake my head. "I'm fine, Dean. I'm cooling off now, thank you."

"Okay. Call me if you need anything."

As soon as the door clicks closed, my mask falls away.

This is the second time Slade's actions have put me in an ice bath. Neither time was because he wanted to. In fact, Vlad is right. Slade has tried at every opportunity not to hurt me. Vlad's assessment of Slade's reaction today is painfully accurate. I just don't want to acknowledge it. I can't. Slade pushed me away. He wanted me gone. It's too much of a risk for me to hope there's any future for us.

Half an hour later, I'm about to get out of the bath when there's a tentative knock on the door. Tansy pushes it open a crack. "May I come in?"

"Uh, sure." I lean back against the bath, not sure what to expect as she twists her hands in front of herself, taking only a few small steps inside the room.

"Vlad told us what you did for him," she says. "I wanted to thank you."

My eyes shoot wide with surprise. I never expected Tansy to thank me for anything. She continues in a rush before I can think too much about what she said, "Can I get you some dry clothes?"

"Yes, please."

She disappears and I take a moment to drag myself, dripping like a wet cat, out of the bath. I feel much stronger.

Not entirely healed, that will take longer, but my body has dealt with the worst of the death it absorbed.

When Tansy returns, she offers me one of Dean's long shirts. From the look of it, it will cover my backside and extend halfway down my thighs. It's decent enough.

She grimaces. "Sorry, I don't think any of his jeans will fit you."

I swallow a laugh. "I'll pretend I've taken a swim then. Wet underwear and a shirt-dress. In the middle of winter. Lucky the cold is what I need right now."

"There's food downstairs if you want it. I'll wait outside."

She disappears again and I take off my wet outerwear and dry myself off as much as I can before I slip on the shirt and roll my wet clothing into a ball.

Downstairs, William rises to give me another warm, welcoming hug. I have definitely had more hugs today than I ever expected.

I try not to make the seat wet while I shovel down warm vegetable stew. I need to get back to the bookshop and the Clave.

I'm grateful to discover that Vlad has filled the others in on all the important information while I was in the bath—that I'm my own Master now, Saber Lane is my territory, that Vlad himself is the Dominion Master, and Gareth is being held for a year before being released.

I wasn't sure how Tansy would take the news that I claimed Saber Lane as my own but she's remarkably calm about it.

When I finish my meal, Vlad swings his backpack over his shoulder. He must have retrieved it from the bookshop while I was in the bath.

Tansy's answering smile to Vlad's polite bow lights up the

room. She doesn't seem to notice that her response has triggered her instinctive magic. The space around us brightens as she asks, "How long will you stay in Boston?"

Vlad replies, "For the next three weeks before I return to the Dominion's Realm in Portland."

Her smile fades as she contemplates his backpack. "You'll stay here on Saber Lane, won't you?"

Vlad seems thrown. "I thought I would find a hotel..."

I glance at William. I hadn't thought that far ahead, but it's better if Vlad stays close. However, there is only one spare bedroom above the bookshop and that's mine.

"We could find a fold-up cot for my room." I look to William for an answer. "Maybe?"

Tansy scowls at me, interrupting William before he can reply. "There are plenty of spare rooms at my place. A proper bed is better than a fold up one." She clears her throat and glances at Vlad. "If that's okay with you?"

"Thank you, Solnyshka. It is appreciated."

I hide a smile. Tansy is so prickly and protective, but for some reason, Vlad has gotten under her skin in a good way. If she can open herself up to trusting him, then maybe there's hope for me.

After Tansy and Vlad leave for Tansy's brownstone at the corner of Saber Lane, William and I say goodnight to Dean at the Diner door.

Dean peers after Vlad as he and Tansy disappear up the street. As tall as she is, Tansy looks like a slender wraith walking beside the giant assassin.

Dean speaks quietly. "Vlad is not a total machine like he claims to be. I might not be able to get a read on him but there are some emotions he doesn't hide as well as others."

"Really? Like what?"

Dean inclines his head at Tansy. She and Vlad are halfway back to her place now. "My dearest friend has captivated the cynical warrior."

I'm glad to know that Dean doesn't have any romantic feelings toward Tansy, even if there is a hint of sadness in what he said.

I drop a kiss on his cheek. "Good night, Dean."

"Good night, Hun—" He freezes. "Wait."

My heart skips a beat.

I sense it, too. A presence that can't be seen.

Someone is blurring nearby…

My arm shoots out to stop William from stepping forward. I drop my balled up clothing on the doorstep and meet his alarmed gaze, speaking quickly to both of them. "Go inside the shop and lock the door."

I trust them to follow my instructions as I step onto the street, scanning the Lane, seeking the location of the magic I sense. I'm grateful to hear a click that tells me Dean has locked the door behind me.

The trail of magic is a mere wisp but grows thicker and stronger as I hurry up the street after Vlad and Tansy.

It's definitely coming from their direction. I can see through any assassin's blur but I need to be closer to see who it is.

I try to identify the magic from this distance. The invader is not Slade. And it's not Gareth. Even if I thought Gareth had escaped, I know what both their blurs feel like. This person's aura is slimy, shadowy, and makes my skin crawl.

It has to be Fallon.

I finally locate his position at the entrance to the street. He is creeping toward Tansy, his blur making him invisible.

But… Vlad should have seen him.

Confusion washes through me. *Why hasn't Vlad sensed Fallon?*

In fact, they're walking straight toward him but Vlad hasn't made a move at all.

Fallon's magic flairs, coating his body in icy blue flames. He projects ropes of light that curl around Tansy's hips, forming chains of fire around her thighs, waist, and chest.

He tugs on the ropes, making her walk away from Vlad, as pliant as a doll.

She doesn't scream and, to my horror, Vlad doesn't react. He keeps walking and that's when I realize…

It's what Fallon does best.

He has created a magical illusion to lure his prey into believing that nothing is wrong. He did it to me while I was training.

Right now, Vlad will think that Tansy is still walking beside him. He's caught in a deadly mind trap. He has never been exposed to Fallon's magic before so even if he realizes he's caught in an illusion, he might not know how to fight it.

He'll keep walking even if Tansy is dying…

Fallon drags Tansy up against his chest, his dagger flashing to her throat.

I'm running before I know it, my legs pounding, harnessing the last shreds of my power. The force inside me is far too slow to respond. I'm too drained. I can barely feel my strength, flickering and sputtering inside me.

I prepare to release my wings, desperate to harness their power. I sense my back shift and then stop… My wings are heavy and sluggish, refusing to open.

Frustration shrieks through me.

Tansy and I have never been friends, but she doesn't deserve to die like this.

Dark liquid drips down her neck as he takes his time pressing the blade into her skin as if she is a plaything.

Please, wings! Please!

They don't respond. I run harder, pushing myself faster, drawing on everything inside myself.

Tansy is quiet and pliant in Fallon's arms, completely vulnerable. Her head tips back against his shoulder as he wraps one arm around her waist in a sickening caress while his other hand tugs on the blade.

I'm too far away to stop him.

CHAPTER FIFTEEN

Awash of silver light flashes across the entrance to the street.

A blurred figure races into view, running straight toward Fallon, much closer to him than I am.

Slade!

He sprints at full pace but skids to a halt before he enters Saber Lane, flinging out one arm, his power spearing through the air.

Fallon's blade arm flies wide, forced away from Tansy's throat by the powerful force Slade directs at him.

The blade clatters onto the cobbled pavement.

Fallon shouts, a muffled sound within his blur, and attempts to throw a line of blue flame at Slade, trying to strike him without letting Tansy go.

Slade evades the blow and flicks his other hand to the side, using his power to force Fallon's other arm away from Tansy's waist.

Fallon now stands with both arms spread wide. But Slade

is also stuck in that position, straining to keep Fallon from grabbing Tansy again.

She slips forward and I catch her before she hits the pavement. I pull her into my arms and away from Fallon. She is limp and heavy in my arms, her face completely blank.

Her neck oozes a little but the cut is superficial.

It was lucky Fallon decided to play with his prey instead of going for a quick kill.

While Slade uses his power to keep Fallon immobilized, Slade remains outside the street. He hasn't stepped foot onto Saber Lane, respecting the boundary like he promised.

Fallon ignores me, struggling and cursing, spitting at Slade, trying to harness his power to fight back. When that doesn't work, Fallon's features settle into a mask of concentration.

Slade winces, flinching.

My eyes widen. Fallon must be trying to get inside Slade's mind. Just like he got inside Vlad's and Tansy's.

If he succeeds, Slade will become like them: completely vulnerable.

I need to get Tansy to safety and then help Slade. I gather her into my arms and carry her to the side of the street, propping her against the steps at the front of her house.

I don't have keys to place her safely inside her home and Slade's pained groan tells me he won't hold out against Fallon much longer.

I have no choice but to leave her here. I make sure she is stable and won't fall against anything that might hurt her. At least she's out of the line of fire now.

She stares blankly at the sky, slumped, not registering anything around her. She's still trapped inside whatever illusion Fallon created to make her pliant.

Vlad too has stopped walking and stares at nothing, becoming a statue in the middle of the street.

I race back to Slade and Fallon, taking note of the sweat beading on Slade's forehead. He is physically stronger and more powerful than Fallon, but nobody knows mind games better than our former teacher.

Slade's expression twists and another groan escapes his lips. His widespread arms falter, his power loosening on Fallon's arms.

I don't know what Fallon is making Slade see but it's causing him too much pain.

Fallon struggles against Slade's power, hissing between his teeth, pushing harder to get free, a cruel smile lighting up his face.

I'm not strong enough to fight Fallon physically right now, not in my depleted state. But I'm immune to his mind games and he can't control me when I'm inside his illusions.

I need to keep Slade strong, help him overcome whatever illusion Fallon has immersed him in.

I approach Slade cautiously, wary of what he might do if Fallon makes him see something that isn't there. Slade could strike me without meaning to.

Fallon's foul gaze rakes across me. "You're tired, Valkyrie. Useless. *Weak.* Your friend would be dead right now if her safety was left up to you."

I push away the cruel truth in what Fallon said. Slade saved Tansy, not me.

I fix my gaze on Slade, on his pale blue eyes, the way his face resembles unyielding stone, all hard lines and determination. "Slade… focus on me."

Slade twitches but doesn't look at me. His gaze remains far away. His chest rises and falls rapidly. Too rapidly.

Then… tears leak from his eyes.

I freeze in shock.

Slade never cries.

I spin to Fallon. "What are you doing to him?"

Fallon laughs. "Playing with his soul."

Slade's fists clench slowly in the air. He shakes his head, as if he's trying to stop something from happening, but he can't.

He whispers, "No… Hunter…"

He's not talking to me, not in the present. He's talking inside the illusion. That means it's about me. The fact that it's causing him this much pain wrenches my heart inside my chest.

I'm close enough to touch him.

I take a deep breath as I reach across the distance, preparing myself for what making contact will do to me.

My heart pounds as I wrap my fingers around his outstretched arm. His body is warm beneath my hand, strong, and so intensely connected to my own. I don't try to fight the way my heart thumps or the way my hand tingles.

I keep my voice soft, whispering to him, "Slade… you don't have to stay outside the street."

His focus shifts to me with an intensity that takes my breath away. His arm shudders beneath my palm in a way that tells me shock struck straight through him.

"Hunter?"

I sigh with relief. His eyes are focused. He sees me again.

I give him a small smile. "I'm here. You don't have to stay at the entrance. You can come into my territory."

His gaze travels to my hand on his arm and then back to my face, tracing the outline of my cheeks and my lips. He doesn't try to shake me off, closing his eyes briefly and taking a deep breath before he steps forward, allowing my hand to remain on his arm. One foot after the other, he steps onto the Lane.

Fallon growls unhappily as Slade's focus remains on me. He won't like that I've interrupted his spell.

The darkness around Fallon increases, a force that crawls up my spine, making me shudder. He's trying to drag Slade under again, his magic like oil sliding over my back and arms, trying to get past the mental barrier I've given Slade.

As long as I'm touching Slade, as long as he is focused on me, Fallon can't invade his mind.

Right now, that's all that matters.

I know Fallon can hear everything I say, and telling Slade that I can't fight right now is dangerous, but Fallon has already sensed that I'm weak and Slade needs to know my limitations.

"I don't have my strength back," I say.

Slade's fierce eyes rest on mine, an undeniable force. "I can fight him. But we need to release Alexei and Tansy from the mind trap first. Otherwise, he will damage their minds."

"How can we release them?"

Slade says, "We have to fight Fallon inside the illusion. Like we did that time in class. It's the only way to break his hold over them."

I wasn't prepared for that. Whatever Fallon made Slade see caused him too much pain.

I consider the tear tracks down his cheeks. I'm not sure that I want to willingly immerse myself in an illusion that does that to him.

I can't go in there without knowing what I'm about to face. My demand is harsh as I ask, "What did he make you see?"

Slade's response is soft. "Something that will never happen." He swallows and hurries on, "You're keeping the mind trap at bay for both of us, but it will suck us down as soon as you choose to let it. Are you ready?"

Am I? I glance along the deserted street. We're lucky nobody has walked past at this time of night. They won't see Fallon because he's blurred. My best course of action is to blur Slade and me. That way only Vlad and Tansy will be visible to an outsider.

I just hope Dean and William stay away until it's safe again.

I draw Slade into a blur with me, concealing us both completely, even from Fallon, and say, "Yes."

I stop pushing away Fallon's power, allowing the oily sensation to creep under my skin, through my ribs, into my chest, up into my mind, allowing it to pass to Slade.

There is a pause as the illusion sucks us under and the world around us turns into mottled gray and vague shapes.

Slade's eyes meet mine for a quiet moment. Fear burns deep inside his gaze for the first time. "Hunter, please don't believe—"

The illusion takes hold.

Trees form around us, along with a clearing and a cabin. Vibrant colors and a carpet of red leaves settle into place beneath our feet.

I know this place. It's the Fury cabin where Slade found out what I was.

Our hands are connected. We stand a single step apart. I'm still wearing Dean's shirt. I am the same as I was on the street. Except that I'm holding an object out to Slade.

It glints, a copper force contained within a leaf.

It's the Keres ring. The one that can kill me.

I offered it to Slade in the real world but he refused to take it. But now... it already rests in his palm, the leaf protecting his body from the contact that would sear his skin; such a small object disappearing inside his upturned hand.

He raises his head as his fist closes around it, the dry leaf crunching between his fingers. His voice doesn't sound like his own. "Did you kill my brother, Hunter?"

"No."

Fury washes through his harsh features. The danger and threat surrounding him builds. "Don't lie to me!"

My eyes widen. "You know I can't."

The gray rims around his irises darken and shadows cast across his face as if a cloud passed over him even though the sky is clear above us.

"If it wasn't you, then who?"

I whisper, "I don't know."

I inhale sharply. Did I speak the truth or lie?

I don't know for sure that my mother killed his brother. I only know what Slade told me: that it was a woman with wings. A woman like me.

Guilt and sadness wash through me before I can hide them.

His expression twists. He shakes his head at me. He could always read me too well.

He roars, "Now I know you're lying!"

He takes a step forward, his closed fist lighting up with copper flame. Keres power, sharp and biting, licks along his arm and leaps out at me. Another inch closer and it will strike me.

"Slade... no..." I shudder, my breathing speeding up, my back shifting in response to the threat. I jolt as my wings strike out into the air on either side of me, silver light surrounding them.

I'm ready to fly but Slade is faster. His free hand clamps around my shoulder, biting into me, holding me tight. His face is barely recognizable to me; it is full of so much hatred. "You deserve to die, Hunter. Just like your mother."

He slams the Keres fire against my heart.

A scream wrenches out of me, agony rips through me, and my knees buckle. He forces me down, driving his fist harder against my chest, surrounding me in Keres fire.

This isn't real! Slade would never do this. This is... my worst fear... my own fear striking back at me...

My body won't listen. My heart cracks inside my chest and my Valkyrie power fades, consumed by the Keres flames that light up my body within seconds. I fall to the ground, my wings crumpling beneath me. My whole world bursts into pain and light as my wings catch fire.

Then... suddenly... shockingly... the flames disappear.

The pain stops.

Slade falls to his knees beside me, wraps his arms around me, and pulls me close. One hand supports my head and his voice reaches me from very far away. "Hunter! No..."

His face wafts across my vision, blurred, unfocused. He draws me up against his hard chest, dragging his hands through my hair, trying to wake me. "Hunter, please."

He lifts his head and roars across me, shouting into the trees. "Stop making me do this!"

His attention returns to me, raw and unyielding.

He whispers, "I will never do this to you."

CHAPTER SIXTEEN

y vision clears. I'm finally able to focus on him again.

My hand shakes as I reach up to brush away the tear dragging down his cheek. I shudder as remnant pain courses through me. "Slade…"

Cruel laughter at the edge of the clearing tells me Fallon has finally materialized.

Fear darkens Slade's expression. "As soon as we stand up, Fallon will make it happen again. He's caught me in a cycle of killing you and trying to save you."

My palm rests against his cheek for another second. "I won't let him."

For a brief moment, Slade allows me to touch him and the friction between us disappears. His hand rests against my lower back, having found its way under my shirt. He strokes my skin, soft and slow, responding to the gentle press of my fingertips to his jaw.

I'm caught up in his arms, my head tilted back, pressed close to his chest. A different kind of tension builds between us. Having him so close to me is like being offered a drink of water in the desert.

Slade's gaze deepens… then he shakes himself.

His arms loosen around me and I have no choice but to remove my hand, focusing on a spot on his shoulder instead.

I grit my teeth. "Fallon shouldn't have given me wings in this illusion."

I roll free, deliberately propelling myself away from Slade, catapulting to my feet, and launching into the air in one fluid movement, spreading my wings at the same time.

Slade jumps to his feet, observing my flight across the clearing.

Fallon's laughter stops as I drop neatly to the ground in front of him. He sneers at me, begins to speak, but I don't allow him to say a word.

My fist darts out and wraps around his throat, halting his gloating in its tracks. He is creating this illusion using his assassin's magic, which is derived from a Valkyrie feather. He never taught us how to create illusions in class. Our training was cut a whole month short. But any skill that Fallon has must be something that I can do.

I draw on the power deep inside my chest, my killing power, sensing how alike it is to the power that fills every part of the illusion around me, every detail in the trees, the earth, even the cabin. This whole place lives in Slade and my memories.

I gasp as I recognize the power Fallon is using. I've used it too.

When Slade was knocked unconscious on our first day in the Realm, I used this aspect of my power to draw out his consciousness. I sought out his memories and brought them to the surface. That's what this is.

Movement from the side of the clearing draws my attention.

In the distance, the clearing morphs into an illusion of Saber Lane. A quick glance shows me that Vlad and Tansy are walking along it, talking to each other.

No matter how many steps they take, they don't move along the street. Their minds are trapped in this illusion.

I refocus on Fallon as he strikes back, icy flames hitting me square in the stomach, but because my wings are spread, I am at my strongest and the attack rolls off me. Icy light flickers around us as Fallon unleashes everything he's got, trying to make me let go.

He roars at me, snarling and striking out, every flash of his power hitting me and dying. He strikes again and again, but it fades into the background as I splay my fingers across his temple and close my eyes, diving deep into his subconscious.

Loneliness hits me hard. I search for memories of his family and friends.

Finding none, I dive further into his past until I finally find… shouting… dirty feet… a burst of pain across his cheek… a lock clicking… a confined space…

Fallon screams, a fearful shriek, terror passing across his features as I surface to focus on his face.

I can't withhold my sympathy when I say, "You have a lot of pain."

He gasps for breath. "Get out of my head."

My anger returns. "As soon as you get out of Slade's. And Vlad's. And Tansy's."

Fallon's lips twist. "I'm only here to bring you a message."

"Then spit it out."

"Lady Tirelli wants you to bring her the feather and the

verdan. If you bring them personally, she will let your friends live."

I narrow my eyes at him. It's a very specific request.

She doesn't only want the Clave and the verdan, she wants me to take them to her. Vlad was right. She must believe I know what happened to that mystery baby. She wants to question me.

I scoff, "She has no idea what she's dealing with if she wants to take me on."

"She knows what you are. That's why she plans to kill your friends if you don't do what she wants. All of them. One by one. She will tear your life apart. Piece by piece."

A shiver runs down my spine. I can't deny that his threats shake me.

I can't protect everyone all the time. I can't protect Briar when she's out and about. Tansy lives right on the corner of Saber Lane, furthest from the bookshop, in the most vulnerable location…

Fallon oozes menace as he voices my fears, "Lady Tirelli can get to anyone."

I draw on his memories again, dragging him back to the darkness of his childhood. "I'm done with your threats. Release my friends or I'll leave you in your own darkness."

He is quick to give in. "No! I delivered the message. I'll… let them go."

The trees immediately peel back around us. The sky and the leaf-covered ground thin and give way to the buildings and shops of Saber Lane. Slade and I are in exactly the same position—my hand on his arm, my wings gone, standing several paces away from Fallon. Vlad is frozen in the middle of the street and Tansy slumps against her front steps.

The mind trap breaks with a *pop*.

Tansy wakes up screaming, her instinctive power igniting around her, burning the air. She jumps to her feet but Vlad leaps in front of her, restraining her as she stretches toward Fallon.

She screams, "I'll kill him!"

"No, Solnyshka." Vlad steadies her, both hands on her shoulders, demanding her attention. "I will."

At the same time, Fallon strikes out at Slade, taking advantage of the time it takes us to orientate ourselves. Fallon delivered his message to me. He made it clear how vulnerable my friends are. Now he will try to escape.

Fallon throws two daggers at us as he attempts to dart away.

I grit my teeth, dodge the weapons, run at him, and knock him down. We crash against the pavement, grazing our elbows and knees. I jump back to my feet, ready to use my fists, but Fallon is suddenly wrenched backward.

Vlad's thick arm snaps around Fallon's throat at lightning speed, lifting the smaller man right off his feet.

For such a big guy, Vlad's movements are rapid and brutal. Fallon barely has time to draw breath before Vlad lands a quick fist to Fallon's lower back.

Fallon's eyes widen with pain as Vlad forces him to his knees, a boot to the back of his calf, wrenching his head back at the same time.

Vlad doesn't carry any weapons. Only a fist like an iron clamp around Fallon's slender jaw.

Vlad told me he preferred to kill with his hands, but the first rule of the Assassin's Code will prevent any bloodshed today.

He growls into Fallon's ear, "You have trespassed onto the

Glass Arrow's territory. I may not be allowed to kill you, but I can make your life painful."

Maintaining his hold on Fallon's jaw with one hand, he pulls his arm back at an angle it doesn't want to go. Fallon screams but I step forward.

"Vlad." I place a warning into my voice. "We need to let him go. But not before we give him a message to take back to his Lady."

Vlad lowers his voice to a dangerous whisper to Fallon. "It's only because I'm in another Master's territory that I have to honor her wishes. Otherwise, I would break both your legs and watch you drag yourself out of here using your hands."

It isn't an idle threat. Violence is second nature to Vlad. Just like rage is second nature to Slade. Oddly enough, I've never seen Cain exhibit either of those traits. I should probably be wary of the characteristic that caused Cain to be picked as the next Master of the Horde. Possibly, it's his effortless ability to inspire loyalty.

I force Fallon to meet my eyes, aware that Slade stands clear behind me. He was prepared to fight Fallon as soon as the mind trap broke, but now he is respecting Vlad's right to fight back against the trap he was placed in.

"Tell Lady Tirelli that I won't do a damn thing she wants," I say. "If she harms my friends, I will hunt her down and end her. She knows I can."

I give Vlad a nod. He hefts Fallon upward and throws him across the pavement. "Don't come back."

I wish I could believe he won't.

After Fallon disappears into the night, and only after waiting another few moments to make sure he's gone, I turn to face the silence behind me. Slade is already edging toward the pavement outside the street. Every step tells me he plans to leave now.

I'm not ready for him to go. I want to talk to him about what happened in the illusion.

Before he can say 'goodbye,' Tansy runs to us, her face ashen in the dim light. Her power has dimmed but her features are pulled taut with anger. "How long was that monster watching us?"

"Not long," I assure her. "He must have arrived just as we came out of the Diner."

Tansy shudders. "We were walking along the street. I thought it was real…"

Vlad says, "It's okay now. You're safe. I'll sense him the moment he tries to come near us again." His lip curls. "I know what he smells like now."

"I hate assassins." Tansy stops, realizing what she said.

Vlad doesn't flinch. I admire his ability to take the same bluntness he dishes out.

She chews her lip, saying to Vlad, "Other than you."

I notice that she doesn't make an exception for me, but I shrug it off. It's baby steps with Tansy. The trauma she suffered as a child will remain with her for life.

William and Dean hurry toward us from the distance. For some reason, Dean slows and stops further away. He looks as pale as Tansy and I'm not sure why. I don't think he's hurt…

William demands my attention. "Are you okay?"

I'm glad to see that he includes Slade in his quick visual assessment.

"We are," I say. "But only because of Slade."

Slade was inching further away but stops, pinned in my sights.

I ask, "How did you know Fallon was here?"

He shrugs, a deliberate movement, as if he's trying to ease out the tension in his shoulders. Moments ago, inside the illusion, he held me in his arms and begged me to be okay. But now... I guess we're back in the real world.

"I was following him," he says. "I thought he might lead me to Lady Tirelli, but he came here instead."

"You saved Tansy's life. Thank you."

Tansy startles. She was inside the illusion the whole time and doesn't know what really happened around her.

She seeks Vlad's confirmation. "What did Slade do?"

He shakes his head. "I was under the whole time."

I decide to be as blunt as Vlad. "Slade stopped Fallon from slitting your throat."

Tansy's hand flies to her neck, finding blood there.

Her comment about hating assassins must have hit me harder than I thought because I have to hold my tongue before I remind her that she chose not to save Slade's life once.

I sigh inwardly, letting go of my momentary anger, exhaling it. My relationship with Tansy is perpetually fraught. It won't get better overnight.

She scrubs at her neck, wiping away the blood. I already ascertained that the cut was superficial, which is why I'm not rushing her to a hospital right now. But the way she's rubbing at her neck... it's like it doesn't hurt at all.

I peer closer, my forehead creasing. "The cut is gone."

She stares at the blood on her fingertips. "I've healed already. I don't know how... I can't heal myself without a spell..."

I purse my lips in thought. The flash of power she gave off when she woke up was intense.

She seems more frightened by the fact that she healed

herself, than the fact that she almost died. A faint gleam enters her eyes, a glimmer of power and for a second, I do a double-take. Her aura brightens and a force glows behind her eyes, but it's tightly controlled and deeply hidden.

My eyes widen as I realize that Tansy wears her own mask; one so permanently fixed that maybe she doesn't know about it.

She takes a deep breath and says, "I need to go home."

But she pauses mid-turn, giving Slade her full attention. "Thank you, Slade. You did more for me than I did for you. I'm humbled by your actions."

He gives her a respectful nod.

Vlad glances between us. He doesn't know the history and I can't tell him because that would require revealing my true nature—as well as Slade's non-human attributes.

"I'll see you in the morning, Hunter," Vlad says.

"Please watch over Tansy."

He hesitates as if he's about to say something else. Then he gives me a nod and follows Tansy quietly to her front door and inside.

I turn to Dean. He hasn't moved any closer to us.

I say to him, "Make sure you lock all your doors and windows. Blurring makes Fallon invisible, but it doesn't give him the ability to move through solid objects. Keep everything locked and you'll be safe."

He backs away with faltering steps. Fallon didn't hurt Dean—he was in the Diner the whole time—but he looks ill.

"Dean, are you okay?"

He nods rapidly, continuing to shuffle backward. "I will be. I'll talk to you tomorrow, Hunter."

I want to go after him because despite what he said, he doesn't look okay, but Slade is also making moves to leave.

He bows to me, eyes down the same way I bowed to him earlier.

It's a small peace offering that I wasn't expecting.

"I should go," he says.

"No." My response is so sharp that I have to inhale a calming breath. "I need you to stay. Will you please... stay?"

What are you doing, Hunter? I'm about to take a massive risk, but my instincts scream at me that it's a risk I need to take.

I need him to stay for what I'm about to do next.

CHAPTER SEVENTEEN

Slade glances at the open street beyond the Lane and then to me and William.

Only now, I have the chance to assess Slade's appearance. He is wearing full protective gear, which means he would have blurred the whole way here.

Assassins only wear protective gear when they're going into battle and can be assured they won't be seen. He looks like he wants to blur and leave. Right now.

He clears his throat, obviously working hard to keep his tone even. "Why, Hunter?"

It doesn't hurt me to tell him the truth. "Because I need to show you something. You and William both. Back at the shop. Will you please come with me?"

I hold my breath as he hesitates. His eyes drill into mine. The tension between us intensifies for a long moment, filling with a thousand stolen breaths and a hundred nights sleeping back to back, never touching each other.

The friction eases as he exhales. "Yes."

"Thank you."

I meet William's questioning gaze as I turn toward the shop. He casts a quick glance at Slade before following me without asking what's going on.

Slade quickly draws level with me, remaining at the edge of my sight, keeping his distance.

By the time we reach the bookshop stairs, I'm questioning myself. My instincts tell me I need Slade here, but my heart tells me I can't take any more punishment. I have no idea how Slade will react to the revelations I'm about to give him.

William unlocks the door and we pass through the downstairs area but Slade stops at the bottom of the internal stairs.

This place has as many memories for him as it does for me. It doesn't help that I'm scantily clad in a shirt that doesn't reach past my upper thighs.

I try to remain unemotional, to put on my own mask, as I stop halfway up the stairs and say, "Please come upstairs. It's important."

He pulls away from me and for a moment, I think he's going to walk right out of here. I'm too far up the staircase to stop him and I won't make him stay if he doesn't want to.

"You need to know why I came to the Legion," I say. "You need to know why Gareth wants me dead, and why Fallon came here tonight. There are some things I don't know yet, but I need you to be here when I find the answers."

William has also paused further up the stairs. He catches on fast. "You have the Clave and the verdan."

When I left the shop the last time, I had neither of those things. I had only just found out that the verdan would reveal the weapon that the feather was hiding.

"I do," I say.

"Then… you're ready to reveal it."

"I am."

William runs his hand across his forehead and eyes, clearly coming to grips with this new information.

Below me on the stairs, Slade folds his arms. He still hasn't budged. "What is a Clave?"

"It's a very small, fragile feather that changed the course of my life. Please. I will tell you everything upstairs."

He glances at the door. Now I know how William felt that day when he had so much to tell me about my childhood and I nearly bolted instead of listening to him.

Slade says, "I can't stay away from the Realm for long."

"I understand."

He remains stiff and guarded as he inclines his head toward the upstairs. "Okay."

When we reach the kitchen, I don't take a seat, knowing that Slade will want to stand, and I want him to be as comfortable as possible.

He's come this far but I can't assume he won't leave at the first opportunity.

He takes up position as close to the top of the stairs as possible. I hate that he feels like he needs a quick exit from this situation.

I get right to the point. "Twenty years ago, my mother came into possession of a very dangerous object. It was a feather that belonged to the last Keres."

Slade's forehead creases. "Your mortal enemy."

"That's right. We… that is William and I… don't know where she got it. She came home with it one day when I was still a baby. It was while she and I were living here."

William gives me a confirmatory nod. He already told me

everything he knows: that Mom went out on a mission and didn't come back for days. When she returned, she had the feather. After that she was relentless in her protection of Patrick Ryan, the underground king.

I continue, "She told me that the feather was the key to locating a very dangerous weapon but she wouldn't tell me what the weapon is. This feather was so important that..."

My voice catches. I swallow hard. "Protecting the feather was so important that my mother gave her life's blood to coat the feather so the weapon could never be revealed. It's why she chose to die."

Slade's gaze deepens, but I hurry on. "I believe that Lady Tirelli asked Gareth to keep the feather safe in the Realm until they could figure out how to get the resin off. I don't think they realized how important the feather was until recently. A week ago, William discovered that the resin could be removed with the sap from the verdan plant. Unfortunately, Gareth found out, too. He sent us to destroy the Furies for him. He planned to steal the verdan and take both the plant and the feather to Lady Tirelli."

Slade asks, "Is that why you wanted to destroy the plant?"

"Yes." I lift my shoulders in a slow shrug. "But everything changed after that night. And now... I have both the feather and the verdan. I need to find the weapon so I can destroy it once and for all."

Slade's voice lowers. "Why am I here, Hunter?"

"Because I need..." I stumble over the truth. "I need you to help me destroy it. My mother couldn't do it, so it must be something very powerful. I can't do it alone."

"But why me? Why not Vlad? Or even Cain?"

I shake my head. "They don't know the truth about me. I can't show them this."

He asks, "Who does know the truth, Hunter?"

"William, Tansy, Dean, Gareth, and Fallon. Apparently Lady Tirelli knows too."

Slade looks surprised but not for the reason I thought. "Ridley doesn't know?"

I shake my head. "Mom never revealed her wings to him. He doesn't know what I am."

"Are you going to tell him?"

"No." The truth is awful. I squeeze my eyes shut for a moment. "I've lost too much because of what I am. I won't lose anything else."

Slade is quiet. Pensive and withdrawn now. He lifts himself off the wall.

I'm wary of where his line of questioning could go. I need to pull the conversation back to the feather before he asks me things I don't want to answer... like whether Mom bonded with Ridley and when do our wings reveal themselves?

I stare at the floor, my heart pounding, speaking before he does. "Knowing what the weapon is comes with risks. If I destroy the feather, then knowledge of the weapon will exist only in your mind. You will have information that Lady Tirelli wants. She has threatened to kill everyone I care about. She will come after you, Slade. And you too, William."

Slade pauses at the edge of the table opposite me as William takes my hands in his.

William says, "I've been part of this ever since your Mom walked through my door, ever since the moment I witnessed your birth."

I'm surprised. "You were there for my birth?"

A gentle smile touches his lips. "I want to be clear that I never felt anything toward your mother other than friendship, but the moment of your birth made me wish you were mine, Hunter."

He squeezes my hands as my eyes burn with sudden tears. Knowing he was there when I was born means more to me than I expected.

"I know the danger," he says. "If I was worried, I wouldn't have decoded the Keres Coda. I'll be with you every step of the way. I'll give you as much help as this old, human body can give."

I don't let go of his hands, appreciating the strength and comfort in them, turning to Slade, a question on my lips: *is he in?*

He nods. "If Lady Tirelli wants this weapon, then I'll do everything in my power to destroy it."

I give William's hands a final squeeze before I leave the room to retrieve my backpack. I pull the feather and the vial of verdan sap out of it. The feather fits into the palm of my hand, smaller than it should be for the impact it had on my life.

I carry it back to the kitchen. "I cut the verdan with steel so I know the sap won't burn through metal. William, do you have some sort of baking tray I can rest the feather on? I don't know if the sap will damage your table."

As soon as he places a tray in front of me, I rest the feather on it.

Slade remains quiet. His focus is on me, rather than the feather. "That casing around the feather is…?"

I swallow. "My mother's life blood. This is the reason I came to the Legion. Gareth stole the feather from my mother when she died. I needed to get it back."

I don't tell him that Valkyrie blood triggers the feather to reveal the weapon—that Mom's blood both triggered and concealed it at the same time.

I whisper, "Mom died for this."

William places a hand on my shoulder, a steadying gesture. "You can do this, Hunter."

I sense William holding his breath beside me as I unplug the glass bottle and tip it directly over the top of the feather. The sap drips onto the resin, changing from clear to crimson as soon as it hits the surface.

The transformation is slow at first, the resin turning into thick liquid and then… it collapses, pouring off the copper edges.

The feather rises above the surface of the tray, completely clean, glowing brightly as it floats above the surface.

At the same time, it projects colors and shapes upward, forming images in the air at eye level with us. It's going to show us the weapon…

I can't breathe. My heart is pounding.

I grip the table as the colors form shapes… or… *one* shape…

The object has smooth edges and delicate curves. It is soft and fragile. It is…

Not an object.

I jolt, shock slamming through me.

Slade's eyes are wide. He whispers, "We can't destroy this."

My mouth turns dry.

The weapon is a baby.

A gorgeous baby girl with eyes the color of violets, purple flecks that shine brightly in her perfect, innocent face. She gurgles within the image, her tiny fists shifting across a bed of golden—

I stumble backward. "No!"

A bed of *copper* feathers.

She has copper feathers.

My hand flies across my mouth to smother the scream rising in my throat.

The weapon is a Keres baby.

CHAPTER EIGHTEEN

Slade stares at the image.

He will recognize the baby's wings from the tapestries that hang in the meeting hall. "The Keres are extinct."

William also stares, transfixed by the image of the baby girl. His eyes are wider than I've ever seen them.

I shake my head from side to side, trying to make sense of the image. "If this baby is the weapon, then that means it's alive today. It must have been a baby when my mother got this feather... It's why my mother... *Oh... no...*"

I sink into the nearest chair.

Slade is quick to catch on. I'm grateful because right now I'm finding it difficult to be coherent.

"That's the baby that Vlad was talking about," he says.

A groan wrenches out of me. "From twenty years ago. It's the baby that Mom saved, the one that Lady Tirelli wanted... The baby and the weapon are the same thing."

William wasn't at the Cathedral and Vlad would not have

revealed this secret to him at dinner. He casts me a worried look. "Hunter? Explain, please."

I quickly fill him in on the story—that my mother intervened in an assassination that left a baby without a mother. She saved the child and then hid it from the world.

"It has to be this Keres baby. And this is its birth feather." I drop my head into my hands. "What else could a birth feather lead to but the child to which it belongs? I've been so blind…"

William is ashen, shaken. "You mother wouldn't let you out of her arms when she came back that night, Hunter. She was exhausted, devastated. She wouldn't talk about what happened but she cried herself to sleep. If she witnessed a murder and had to save that baby—after becoming a new mother herself—it's no wonder she was upset."

My stomach twists. I feel sick. "But she saved a *Keres* baby. It's the only magical being that can kill me. She saved a creature that can kill her own daughter. Why would she do that?"

William whispers, "Just because you're born into darkness…"

It was Mom's mantra. The words she lived by. Her final words to me.

I finish for him. "Doesn't mean you can't overcome it."

Tears drip down my cheeks. I don't care that I'm crying in front of Slade. "She said that to me when she died."

William takes my hands. "You aren't enemies with someone just because you're told to be. Just because someone is born a Keres doesn't mean they can't be good and beautiful. Just like you control your Valkyrie power. That Keres woman came all the way from the Dominion to ask your mother for help. What if she was never your mother's enemy? This Lady Tirelli must have been hunting her. Well… your mother hunted the hunters. It must have taken enormous faith and trust for that Keres woman to ask for your mother's help."

Tansy once said that the Keres were misjudged and that the Valkyrie were the real killing machines. But Vlad had described the Valkyrie as gentle too—that we became vengeful after our ancestors were ripped apart for their feathers.

"Mom got there too late." Just like Mom was too late to save Tansy's mother. It must have eaten her up inside to fail two children. "A Keres can only be killed by a Valkyrie. The Dominion Master who killed the mother of this baby had a Valkyrie ring. Vlad told me that tonight. That must have been how he killed her. The same way the Keres ring can kill me."

Slade remains standing, his expression unreadable, but he flinches at the mention of the Keres ring. "We need to find that child before Lady Tirelli does."

"That child is a grown woman now," I say. "She could be anywhere. I will be able to sense her, but only if I am very close. If I had come across anyone like that in Boston, I would have known about it already."

Slade is grim. "At least we have the clue that Lady Tirelli wants."

I raise my eyebrows at him. "Clue?"

He points. "The violet flecks in her eyes. That's very unusual. Anyone who saw her will remember her."

A laugh wrenches out of me, but there's no humor in it. "I'm about to go looking for the only woman who can kill me. And then what? Convince her not to be the weapon she's destined to be? Also, that she shouldn't kill me. Or fear me, since I'm the only creature that can kill her. Oh, along with a hundred assassins who have Valkyrie rings." I spin to William. "You're right. She has more to fear than I do."

William reaches out to rub my back in the same way he calms Tansy. "She lost her mother like you did. She's the last Keres, just like you're the last Valkyrie. You may have been born enemies, but that doesn't mean you have to choose that path."

I can't help glancing at Slade. We started off as rivals, then we became something very different, and now…

Well, I don't know what we are now.

William says, "We have to be careful with this knowledge. What will you do with the feather now?"

I ask, "Do you have a match?"

He retrieves a box of matches and brings it to me.

"Mom burned my birth feather when I was born," I say. "To ensure it couldn't be misused."

I strike a match and drop it onto the feather. It lights up and burns very quickly. As it curls and turns to ash, it sinks back to the tray and the baby's image fades and disappears.

A pile of dust is all that remains.

"Now only the three of us know what the feather was hiding." I sink to my chair, my hands shaking. I clasp them in front of myself on the table. "Mom could have burned this feather years ago. She could have saved herself…"

My voice chokes. "She needed me to see this. She needed me… to change the course of our future. The Keres and the Valkyrie. I don't know how, but I have to find this woman. Somehow."

Slade leans across the table toward me. His hand almost touches mine before he stops himself. "We'll find her."

He clears his throat, his expression closing over again, withdrawing from the solidarity he almost showed me.

Before I can say anything, he steps away again, his boots thudding in the heavy silence. "I have to return to the Realm now. I won't come back again unless there's an emergency. I'll communicate through Briar. It's better if we aren't seen together until the charity event."

I jump up. He's pushing me away again and I'm not letting him do it so easily this time. "Better for who?"

"For all of us."

"Slade…" I lean against the table, my bare legs pressing into it. There are so many immovable obstacles between us. The feather is a small pile of ash in front of me. If only my heart could be as lifeless.

I want to ask him to stay, but he gives me a quick shake of his head. There's nothing I can do to stop him leaving.

I exhale. Slowly. "Goodnight, Slade."

"Goodnight, Hunter. William."

I wait for his steps to fade. Then for the bookshop door to click closed again, telling me he has left the building. The spot where he stood opposite me is suddenly a yawning chasm.

I sink back into the chair. "How am I going to do this, William? How will I find her? I know she has distinctive eyes, but Mom is bound to have done something to help her hide that feature."

"Your mother was smart, Hunter. She kept that feather so you would know the truth. She *wants* you to find this woman. Take some time to think. Your mother must have planted clues in your memory."

I shake my head. "I don't remember anything… I didn't even remember we lived here…"

"Don't try now, Hunter. You're exhausted. Your strength took a massive hit today and you need to rest."

Tears burn at the back of my eyes. Is this how William was with Mom? So caring and supportive. "I wish Mom had stayed here instead of leaving."

"Me, too." He pats my arm. "But she and I... had a disagreement... about something you don't need to worry about right now. Get some rest. Tomorrow is a new day."

Before I go to bed, I put away the Keres ring and the verdan, hiding them both at the back of my closet. The Clave is gone now and it feels like I've closed the door on a part of my life that caused me too much heartache.

What's left is confusion and frustration.

Despite William's insistence that I shouldn't try to search my memories, I toss and turn in bed, wishing I could remember every detail of everything she told me, something that might give me a clue about the Keres woman's whereabouts.

The more I seek the answer, the more it eludes me, until I fall asleep out of sheer exhaustion.

Born into darkness, born into darkness, born into...

Mom's voice echoes in my mind. I wrench out of bed, my body heavy and sluggish as I try to escape the remnant nightmares... the memory of Mom's death... the dirty brick wall she leaned against... her lank hair... her hands resting across her stomach, palms upward...

I double over, trying to banish the images from my mind.

The sound of knocking at my door forces me to find my feet and wobble over to it, opening it a crack. A quick backward squint at the clock on my bedside table tells me it's only five a.m..

"William?"

He appears disheveled and caught unawares—a bit like me. His hair sticks out at all angles as if he didn't have time to brush it. "Hunter, you need to come downstairs."

I'm immediately alert. "What is it?"

"Get dressed. And bring your ledger."

My ledger? I'm suddenly fully awake.

I race to the bathroom to wash my face, brush my hair, and change as quickly as I can.

I only slow my steps when I descend the stairs. The hum of voices reaches me, hushing when I appear.

Briar stands at the entrance to the shop right next to the door. She's wearing the coat I gave her while her old green beanie is pulled low over her ears to keep out the cold.

In front of her, two women and a man wait. William pats the corner of the counter in the same place that Mom kept her ledger. His warm gaze tells me he wants me to place mine there, too.

I put it in the exact spot he indicates and, as if they already decided who is going to approach me first, one of the women steps forward and holds out her hand for the pen.

They're here for me. But not for Hunter Cassidy. They're here for the assassin.

I open my ledger and hand her the pen.

She startles me by writing the name of the target first. Most people write the target last so they have the chance to back out if they change their mind at the last minute.

Geno Tirelli.

I recognize that name immediately. He is the oldest son in the Tirelli family.

I have yet to figure out the relationship between Lady Tirelli and the Tirelli men. I'm not convinced she is their actual mother, especially since the Tirelli Family have lived in Boston for years but Vlad said Lady Tirelli moved here recently.

I suspect it's more likely that she ingratiated herself with them, needing a pack to run with and a base of operations. Somehow, she must have convinced them to hand over control of their business to her.

In the offered payment section, the client writes a dollar amount with more zeros than I was expecting and in the 'why' section she writes:

For my son.

Tears sparkle in her eyes when she looks up at me without speaking.

I sign my name without hesitation and wait for the Guardian's response. I will have to verify the response with her in person, but I'm sure that this client is genuine. It would be very strange for Lady Tirelli to send someone to request the death of her right hand man.

Not impossible though, which is why I'll be careful.

The Guardian's curvy script glows golden across the page within seconds.

Sanctioned.

I consider for a moment what I've just taken on.

Geno Tirelli will be a difficult target. As the male head of the Tirelli Family, he is a businessman and surrounded by bodyguards at all times.

I won't be able to employ subterfuge like I did with my first assassination, making it look like an accident.

Geno Tirelli's death will be an obvious assassination. I'll

have to watch out for retribution from his two brothers, Vincent and Enric.

I give the woman a nod, and the next takes her place.

I hide my surprise when she writes:

Vincent Tirelli.

He's the second Tirelli son, known for getting his hands dirty. He never bothers with bodyguards because he's more brutal than they ever will be.

I consider the man still waiting to write in my ledger, wondering… Is he here for the third son?

Sure enough, when the man steps up, he writes the third son's name:

Enric Tirelli.

Enric is the expert marksman in the family. He never misses a shot unless he intends to.

The assassinations of all three Tirelli men are sanctioned. The heart and soul of the Tirelli family. Each client has offered me a large sum of money and each has lost a family member to the Tirelli's brutality.

If I can pull this off, it will be a strike that could break down Lady Tirelli's foundations. It will make her vulnerable in a way she hasn't been before.

Then she will seek me out, and I will end her.

Briar ushers the clients out of the shop, but she remains behind for a moment, racing across the distance to me and surprising me with a hug.

When she pulls back, her eyes are lit with a new fire. "Welcome home, Hunter."

Before I can do more than gasp at the warmth in what she said, she hurries out of the shop to see the clients on their way. For such a reserved lady, she gives the most amazing hugs. My heart fills with the trust she places in me.

I turn to William, determination flowing through me, triggering my inner power. My back burns with it. "I'm taking down the Tirelli Family."

He grins. "Just like your mother tore down Patrick Ryan's rivals."

Mom's purpose was to help Patrick Ryan rise to the top of the underground.

Mine is to tear it apart once and for all.

CHAPTER NINETEEN

After an early breakfast that morning, William pushes his chair back and says, "There's time before the shop opens."

I give his cryptic statement the puzzled response it deserves. "To do what?"

He smiles. "For you to meet everyone who lives on Saber Lane. They're looking forward to meeting you."

I slip a coat around my shoulders before we leave the shop. Our breath frosts in the air as we step outside. William takes me to the bakery first, telling me we should start there.

He introduces me to the middle-aged couple who run the shop. They offer us coffee and freshly baked cupcakes that are smothered in bright pink and green icing. The entire atmosphere could be pulled from a 1950s movie. They both have the aura of fairies but when I ask them about it, they emphasize that their magic only manifests in their creativity, after which they show me the latest wedding cake they've made.

By the time I leave the store I feel like I should be wearing a puffy dress and a big, yellow bow in my hair.

Next, we visit the grocery store with the orange and cream checkered linoleum floor. The owner is a younger man who introduces himself as Christopher James. He has the aura of a dryad—a tree spirit—and he appears youthful, despite telling me he's lived in Boston for fifty years.

He manages to speak coherently around a wad of bubblegum, gesturing at the fluorescent green graffiti on the window as he asks, "Do you like it?"

William grins broadly while I peer at the painting until I recognize that it's a replica of my tattoo: a design that resembles an 'A.'

Christopher says, "This is your street now."

"You don't mind that I've claimed it?" I ask.

"Hell, no. We're protected now. The same way we were when your Mom was alive."

The Apothecary's store is next, run by an elderly woman with starry eyes I could get lost in, as if her youth is somehow trapped inside her. Her aura is strong, a white glow all around her, but I can't identify it.

She shows me the rows of herbal medications that she says are good for treating all sorts of ailments from headaches to cuts and bruises.

Then she glides to a cabinet at the side of the room and pushes it aside to reveal a set of hidden shelves.

My jaw drops when I recognize all the poisons I learned about while I was training in the Realm.

She winks. "You can come here for all your medicinal needs, dearest. We have everything you could possibly want. And if we don't have it, we can get it."

I grin at her. "Thank you. I will." I can't leave the shop without asking, "Forgive me, but I can't identify your aura."

She winks at me, her long lashes resting against her cheek for a moment. "I'm a will-o'-the-wisp. You can call me 'Willow.'"

William nudges me when we continue to the end of the street. "You'll like the next one just as much."

I've never ventured this far along Saber Lane. There are only a few shops back here, but right at the back is a building painted black on the outside.

As we approach, a large man pushes open the wide doors of the building situated furthest back, sliding them open to reveal…

A dojo.

The glint of steel winks at me from the back wall where multiple weapons are housed.

I break into another grin. This morning is full of pleasant surprises.

The man folds his arms across his broad chest. He reminds me of Ridley: straight-backed, stern features, forbidding. Definitely no-nonsense. He wears black training gear, pulled tight across powerful arms and thighs. His eyebrows draw down into a scowl as we approach.

"This is Drake," William whispers. "He's all human. Don't be deceived by his unwelcoming act. He's a big softy. He teaches kids self-respect and women self-defense."

I bow low when I reach Drake's position, deciding to be up front about what I want. "May I train with you?"

Drake breaks into a smile and spreads his arms wide, angling to indicate the side of the dojo. A katana sword rests proudly on a display stand.

Drake says, "It would be an honor. I open these doors

every morning at six. Classes don't start until seven. The space is yours until then."

My heart lightens and I promise to be back tomorrow.

When Drake heads back inside the dojo, a nasty scar is visible across the back of his neck, stretching beneath the neckline of his shirt. It's broad enough that I'm surprised he survived it.

William murmurs to me as we walk, "Many of the inhabitants of Saber Lane were once running from danger. They found safety here, the same way your mother did, among those who are willing to protect each other."

"Is that why Tansy struggles to accept me?"

William gives me a sad nod. "It's one reason. She sees you as a threat—someone who could tear down the protective environment we've worked hard to create here."

"I promise you, I won't," I say.

"I know, Hunter. Give Tansy time. She'll see it, too."

We end up outside the Diner where Dean waits, shivering in the cold. "Come on in," he says. "I'll make you a cup of cocoa."

I'm not sure I can eat anything more after the coffee and cake I consumed at the bakery, which was on top of the hearty breakfast I had at William's, but Dean appears to have something on his mind.

"William, may I have a few minutes alone with Hunter?" he asks.

"Of course, I'll go to Tansy's to see how she is this morning." William smiles before he takes his leave.

As I follow Dean to the counter, I'm glad he looks better than he did last night. He busies himself behind the worktop, quietly pouring out a single cup of hot chocolate, sprinkling it with chocolate powder.

I nurse the warm drink in my hands, unable to stand his silence any longer. "It's about last night, isn't it? Something was wrong."

He pauses in the middle of wiping the table top, his eyes filled with deep concern. "There's no easy way to say it, Hunter, but I sense a dangerous shift in Slade."

I stiffen. Rowan described Slade as different now and when I first encountered him yesterday he was far more ruthless toward Vlad than I expected.

I'm afraid to know the answer but I ask, "What kind of shift?"

Dean says, "The Valkyrie and human forces inside him are at war. His internal battle is like a gale force wind. One minute it pulls; the next it pushes. He is becoming very powerful, but if he steps down the wrong path, he could become your worst nightmare."

I shiver so hard my drink sloshes. Fallon's illusion yesterday revealed two opposing sides of Slade: the murderous one and the one that tried to protect me.

Dean quickly wipes up the spill and levels his gaze with mine. "You have the power to determine which path Slade chooses."

I ask, "What can I do?"

"He may not want you around, but he needs you, Hunter. You have to teach him how the Valkyrie power can coexist with his humanity."

Frustration rises inside me. "I can't get close to him. He won't let me."

Dean grabs my hand, compelling me to listen. "You can't give him a choice. For everyone's sake. Otherwise, Lady Tirelli and all her thugs will seem like butterflies compared to the sledgehammer that Slade will become."

The chocolate dust on my cocoa disappears beneath the surface, sinking like my heart. "I'll try."

Dean strokes my hand. "I feel everything you feel, Hunter. Your heart is broken, you're afraid of your emotions, and Slade is like a wall, thousands of feet high and thousands of feet wide that you can't get through. He stands behind a mask now. You have to break through it."

"How, Dean? Please tell me how?"

His thumb grazes my wrist, a gentle stroke before he breaks the contact. "You know how."

"I really don't—"

Brisk footsteps interrupt us. Tansy appears in the Diner doorway with Vlad close behind her. They look fresh and well-rested despite their ordeal the night before.

I swiftly paste a smile on my face. "Good morning."

Vlad sees through my facade in two seconds flat, his eyes narrowing, but he remains silent. I slide off the bar stool before either of them can ask any questions. "Sorry to leave right away, but I need to visit the Guardian."

Vlad breaks into a grin. "You have clients?"

I smirk, remembering Briar's hug. It was one of the good things that happened this morning. "A few."

"And the targets?"

"Nothing I can't handle."

He side-eyes me. "Let me know if you need help."

I scoff as I pass by. Tansy gives me a nod. She seems more relaxed today and it occurs to me that with both Vlad and me in residence, Saber Lane has never been safer.

I chance a smile in her direction before I head back to the bookshop to change, opting for comfortable clothes—my usual jeans and a sleeveless shirt.

But I also pull my favorite red leather jacket from my

backpack. It was one of the few indulgent items I brought back from the safe house. It's a deep, dark color that brings out the highlights in my mahogany hair and matches my ankle-high boots.

It also has specially cut slits in the back so I can release my wings without any problems. I can run, fight, basically do anything in these boots and this jacket. It's good to wear my own clothes again.

I blur myself completely on the steps to the bookshop before I release my wings, silver feathers spreading and bracing against the cold.

Heat rushes through my body as my power spreads. My recovery from the day before is complete. I sigh with relief to know that my power is back.

I take the quickest route to the Guardian's hotel, landing in the alley behind the hotel, gliding to my feet and tucking away my wings.

My plan is to use the staff entrance and remain blurred until I reach the Guardian's room. That way, nobody will know I came here. I can't assume that Lady Tirelli's people aren't watching the hotel.

I step into the shadows to wait for someone to use the entrance so I can follow them inside.

Ten minutes later, a perky-looking blonde strides up to the door, swipes her access card, and shoves it wide open. I step close to her and glide in behind.

Oomph! Someone pushes in behind me and the speed I need to use to get out of their way nearly catapults me into the young woman's back.

I quickly side-step and press myself flat against the corridor wall, observing the man who followed me in.

He is quiet. Stealthy. He is also packing two guns and a

knife.

The girl senses his presence and squeaks when she sees him.

He snarls at her, "Relax, honey. I'm not here for you. But if you tell anyone you saw me, I'll come for your family. You got me?"

He taps the gun at his waist.

"Y-yes." She hurries away along the corridor, casting fearful glances back at him.

He's none other than Enric Tirelli, the youngest brother. He's blond, wearing black pants and a black shirt.

Before Mom died, the Tirelli Family was a mere blip on the horizon but in the last four years, they've grown far too powerful.

Enric shifts both guns to the back of his pants and swaggers along the corridor. I could take him out right now.

My hands twitch and my power surges, but I restrain myself.

I need to hit all three brothers at the same time. Otherwise, they'll go to ground, fortify their defenses, and my task will become a thousand times harder.

Not to mention, the risk of collateral damage will increase.

Besides, the whole reason I'm here is to ascertain whether the missions are sanctioned. Until I have the Guardian's personal word on it, I can't do anything.

The smart thing is to plan and wait.

I follow Enric through the kitchen area, maintaining my blur as he strides along the corridor and into the service elevator.

I duck in with him moments before the doors close.

My eyes narrow as he hits the button for the same level as

the Guardian. The hairs on the back of my neck prickle. *That can't be a coincidence.*

I stand clear as he leans against the polished mirror adorning the top half of the elevator.

He lights up a cigarette, takes two deep puffs, and when the elevator stops, he steps out and stubs the cigarette into the top of a glossy hall table, burning a circle in its surface.

At the same time, two male staff members pass by dressed in hotel uniforms. They're carrying fresh towels.

But neither of them calls Enric out about damaging hotel property. A closer inspection tells me they're both armed, guns peeking out of the backs of their waistbands.

Not hotel staff after all.

It can't be a coincidence that they're here. Fallon said Lady Tirelli would go after all my friends. I guess she's starting at the top.

Any doubt I had about Enric's intentions disappears.

He's here for the Guardian.

CHAPTER TWENTY

*E*nric stops outside the Guardian's door, knocking briskly and calling out, "Room service."

The men swiftly drop the towels they were carrying to reveal another gun each, complete with silencers. They're ready to fire as soon as the Guardian opens the door.

My blood boils. As a Valkyrie, I could smoke all of these assholes right now. But as an assassin, I'm not allowed to kill them without sanction. Of course… that doesn't mean I can't hurt them.

Movement further down the corridor catches my attention. Two more thugs appear up ahead and three appear behind. They're guarding each end of the corridor in case the Guardian tries to escape.

That makes eight men in total.

Fine by me.

I knock into the nearest one standing outside the Guardian's door and snatch his weapon at the same time, using it to whack him in the face. He jolts backward with a shout, flailing because he can't see what hit him and what's more, he can't see his weapon anymore. I've blurred it with me.

Enric and the other man jump backward, shock flashing across their faces. I snatch the other guy's gun right out of his startled fingers, bending both weapons at once, rendering them useless before I drop them to the ground.

To their eyes, their damaged weapons fall out of thin air and clatter to the floor.

Enric is quick to figure out what's going on, shouting, "It's an assassin!"

He backs up, pressing against the wall. He's smart, I'll give him that. In that position, he's assured that I can't creep up behind him.

He calls out, "Shoot anywhere except at each other!"

Also smart. I may be invisible but bullets can still hurt me. Well, they would if I were completely human.

A snarl grows on my lips.

I dart around the two men I disarmed, snatching the backup weapons tucked in their pants. They're in the middle of trying to move against the wall like Enric did but my movements jolt them around.

I quickly bend those weapons too, hurling them one after the other at the guys' heads. *Smack-smack.*

They don't have time to dodge the weapons that materialize before their eyes. One shouts and grabs his forehead and the other his jaw where I landed direct hits.

Instead of bracing against the wall like they should, they launch themselves at the space where I was, trying to hit me.

I've made them mad.

Keeping them near me means the others won't shoot. For now.

I spin and whirl, moving rapidly, narrowly avoiding their

meaty fists before I land a follow up kick to one guy's chest and two hard fists to the other's. I put all my strength behind the blows, breaking each of their ribs as they fly backward to land, groaning, on the corridor floor.

I keep running. Every time I touch one of them, the others know where I am so I have to move fast. Two quick, quiet bullets hiss past my shoulder, close enough to tell me that Enric may be an asshole, but he's an intuitive shot. His reputation as a marksman is not undeserved.

I won't be able to disarm him as easily as the others.

I need to get rid of the thugs at the end of the corridor or I won't be able to get the Guardian out of here. So far, she hasn't opened her door. No doubt, Enric's shout has warned her to stay in her room. Not to mention, those big guys made a lot of noise when they fell over.

I race down the corridor, landing two quick kicks to the downed men's heads, knocking them out as I pass by.

The corridor is too narrow for me to release my wings properly, so I run at the thugs blocking the fire stairs. Another two bullets whiz past me and I zigzag as fast as I can to dodge them.

I'm not so lucky with the next two. They hit me full in the chest. I duck and roll, drawing on my strength to keep moving, but now my inner power rages inside me.

Pain triggers all sorts of cold intentions. I knocked out the first two guys after soft breaks to their ribs, but I'm done being nice.

I smash into both guys at the end of the corridor, partially releasing my wings at the same time to give me height.

My boot crunches one of them in the face, shattering his jaw.

I use my momentum to backflip and land right in front of

the other one, shoving his gun aside as it goes off, the silenced bullet lodging in the ceiling above us, before I grab his arm, snap the bone, and force him to his knees.

He's screaming but the sound barely registers in my hearing.

I punch a fist into his temple to knock him unconscious. His screaming stops.

The three guys at the other end of the corridor leap into action, running toward their fallen colleagues—they know it's my last location—firing a barrage of bullets. Projectiles stream toward me and there's no way I can avoid them all.

Damn this narrow corridor.

I use my wings to dart upward, bullets biting across my torso, managing to glide several feet above the onslaught, but the width of the corridor defeats me. I can't expand my wings wide enough to stay aloft.

I'm forced to drop to the floor through another shower of bullets and press myself flat against the floor—*under* the stream of projectiles. The corridor walls now bear a multitude of bullet holes. And… so do I.

What's worse, I'm bleeding. My leather jacket will hide the blood so long as nobody stares at me too long, but pressing against the floor has left smears on it. As soon as I stand up, my attackers will see the blood and know exactly where I am.

I count the hits I took: five bullets in addition to the first two. Three of them are lodged inside me.

My blood pumps, my power surges, and I stand up and run.

They're still firing at me when I knock into them right outside the Guardian's door. My fists and feet are a blur. Five rapid hits to one guy's chest and face, four to the next, then I grab the head of the third and ram him into the wall, breaking through the plaster.

Enric creeps up behind me but I kick back at him, knocking him down. A *click* tells me that the Guardian just unlocked her door.

Not now!

Just as I spin to dispatch Enric, the Guardian leaps from her open door, lands a punch to his surprised face, follows it with a roundhouse kick, and lands right on top of him as he falls.

She knocks him out with a fist adorned with a set of golden knuckledusters.

She came prepared.

I stare at her in surprise until I remember that she can't see me.

I take a moment to count my wounds.

Ten.

Ten bullet wounds. Six lodged.

I breathe out the pain, reminding myself that it won't kill me, and materialize so the Guardian knows it's me.

Her eyes widen. "Hunter!"

I take her arm and help her stand. "We need to get you out of here. It isn't safe for you here."

She nods, a rapid up and down motion that makes her caramel hair bob. Despite her efficient method of dealing with Enric, she's shaking. "The Realm. We need to get to the Realm."

"I'll take you there. Do you need to bring anything?"

She taps her head and then her assassin's ring. It's an elaborate design with a large emerald in the middle, smaller emeralds dripping around each side like leaves on a tree interspersed with diamonds. "I have everything I need."

Together, we hurry down the corridor to the fire stairs. I shove the door open, directing the Guardian into the stairwell as fast as I can. But I pull up sharp when a commotion further below reaches us.

The Guardian leans forward, whispering, "What is that?"

A shout echoes upward, followed by a *thud*.

I grimace. "It must be more of Enric's men. Stay behind me."

I can't use my wings now that the Guardian is watching, and I can't blur because I need her to know where I am. That's going to make it harder to fight but by no means impossible.

I brace as two figures race up the stairs. Two more assholes. They just keep coming. I push the Guardian behind me and prepare to unleash my fury on them.

When the first guy reaches me, I duck his fist and thump him in the chest, kicking the second in the face so hard he slams up against the staircase railing and almost falls over it before a third figure speeds up the stairs behind him.

A wash of silver light precedes the newcomer, a luminous form that takes my breath away.

Slade deftly navigates the steps while ramming a needle into the neck of one of the men and another needle into the thigh of the other.

Both men spin and wobble on the stairs, clutching and grabbing at the syringes before collapsing onto the steps as if they've had too much to drink.

Seconds later, they're unconscious.

Slade draws to a halt in front of me, the silver aura around him settling into the space between us, his blue eyes nearly overcome with silver flecks, hardly any blue left.

Unlike me, he's dressed for the occasion, wearing full

combat gear and a protective suit. A row of twenty syringes rests in a harness strapped across his broad chest.

My lips part as I inhale the power around him.

Dean and Vlad were right: Slade's strength is growing.

He asks, "Is the Guardian okay?"

I shift to reveal her, taking a moment to find my voice. "Yes."

"I'm here," the Guardian says. "I'm alive because of Hunter."

Slade gives me a quick nod of appreciation.

I point to the needles he used to subdue the thugs. "What are those?"

"Tranquilizers. Since we're not allowed to kill them."

"That's clever." I hide a sigh and make a mental note to talk to Willow about getting some. It would be so much easier than what I just went through.

Slade's attention shifts to the Guardian, becoming stern and commanding. "Guardian, you need to come to the Realm."

She nods rapidly. "That's where we were going."

Slade freezes. "We?"

"I'm taking her there," I say.

He draws the Guardian to his side, firmly placing her on the step beside him, but his open palm shoots out between us like a giant stop sign. The power flashes in his eyes, a deep burn that calls me closer at the same time as his open palm tells me to stay away.

The moment I step forward, inches away from pressing into his hand, he says, "No, Hunter."

I stare in confusion at the contradictions streaming from his body and voice. The aura around him calls me like a song in the quiet of night, but his outstretched hand and what he said are rejecting me as firmly as possible.

Regardless of what he's saying, he'll need help getting the Guardian to the Realm. I know for certain that I can take bullets without dying but I'm not sure about Slade. "You'll need backup on the way. There are more of those assholes—"

"We'll be fine." He tilts his head. He must be sensing the same thing I am: the men upstairs are reviving.

"Guardian," he says. "We need to go."

She casts worried glances between us, but she has no say about whom Slade allows into the Realm. My heart beats far too fast inside my chest as I finally realize that he meant it last night when he said he wouldn't be seen with me.

He really… actually… meant it.

My mouth is dry and my stomach sinks as I whisper, "You're not going to let me into the Realm again, are you?"

He pauses, half-turned toward me. Half-turned away. One of his fists clenches, his power flashes again, and for the briefest moment, he squeezes his eyes closed before opening them again to look me straight in the eye.

"No," he says.

CHAPTER TWENTY-ONE

he air whooshes out of my lungs because Slade's resolute response hurts.

It hurts more than the bullets.

Dean told me I had to bridge the gap with Slade. I was sure that I'd started to do that last night when I revealed the secret of the Clave to him, but if anything, I've made the gap worse.

Still, Slade promised to help me find the violet-eyed woman. He can't push me away forever if he's going to keep his promise.

Anger rises like a tide inside me. "You promised to help me."

He knows exactly what I'm talking about but he won't reveal it in front of the Guardian. "I will, Hunter. I'll send a message through Briar if I find what you're looking for."

He spins away from me, but I snag his arm, my hand whipping out faster than any human should be able to move. I place all my strength into it, sensing his power rush to the surface in response. He pulls away from me with the same force that I'm using to try to make him listen to me.

The Guardian wisely steps clear of us, navigating around the thugs' prone bodies to find a clear patch of steps to stand on.

I grind out, "Slade, if you keep the Guardian at the Realm, then you can't deny me entrance. I need to see her as much as any other assassin."

He stares at my hand. His expression is as hard as stone. Power bursts alive in his eyes, responding to mine, and his eyes becoming silver pools.

He suddenly stops trying to pull away and pushes instead, moving toward me so rapidly that I end up pressed against the wall, balancing on a single step, his body pressed against mine, chest to chest and thigh to thigh, my hand clamped on his arm but pressed down at our sides.

My senses explode at his nearness. I gasp for air. Heat burns through my chest and legs, unbearable, tingling… overpowering need…

It takes all my self-control not to tilt my head back with a moan.

Damn him. No wonder Mom didn't want me to have this weakness.

His deep growl washes over me. "Yes, I can."

I fight the sensations running the length of my body, grasping at all the logical reasons why he can't keep me out of the Realm forever. "What about when I need a mission sanctioned?"

His mouth is inches from mine, a husky whisper. "Send Briar. The Guardian can direct a message back to you."

"But…"

His hand brushes the side of my thigh, sending a

powerful shiver through me. My breathing is too rapid for him not to notice. So is his for that matter…

His jaw clenches. "You trust Briar, don't you?"

"Yes, but—"

He shifts away from me, lifting his body from mine. I shake my head, trying to clear it. My chest heaves. My voice tears out of my throat. "Stop pushing me away."

For the merest second, the power in his eyes deepens and his gaze intensifies beyond anything I ever imagined. Then his expression becomes a storm of emotions I wasn't expecting: confusion, need, and last of all pain.

Then nothing. A blank slate.

"You pushed first." He steps back with such a sudden burst of power that I have no choice but to open my fingers and release him.

I thought I was the one who built a wall, but Dean was right. Slade's is higher and wider than anything I ever imagined.

Confusion swamps me. I've replayed the final moments on Mount Greylock so many times: revealing my wings, fighting Gareth, telling Slade the truth, and then he told me to leave…

"When?" I whisper. *When did I push him away?*

But Slade isn't looking at me anymore. He's frozen, staring at a spot on the wall behind me. He stands as still as stone, not responding, and it's cracking my heart all over again.

"Damn you, Slade, look at me. When did I push you away? Please… answer me."

He isn't listening to me. His lips part. The tension increases around his eyes, his power fluctuating. An incredulous furrow forms in his brow.

He murmurs, "She said she was alive because of you."

I don't understand what he's talking about. The Guardian maybe?

He finally meets my eyes, fierce alarm hijacking his expression. He looks like he's about to grab me as he demands, "How many bullets did you take?"

I freeze. Then I twist to see what he's looking at.

A large smear of blood stretches across the wall. It's the size of my back. Impossible to miss. I must have left it there when I pressed against the wall just now.

My back is bleeding. Badly. I'm not in good shape, but I'm alive, and… *damn*… he asked me a question so now I have to tell him the truth. If we were alone, that wouldn't be a problem, but the Guardian is listening to every word we say. When I tell him how many bullets I took, she's going to wonder how I'm still alive.

"Ten. Six still inside me."

His eyes widen. "Ten."

Oh, now he's done it.

I glare at Slade, gritting my teeth. He compelled me to say out loud that I've survived an extraordinary number of bullets—too many for a human being. And then he had to go and repeat it just to emphasize the point.

The Guardian races up the steps toward us at a cracking pace. She exclaims, "Ten! But you're not wearing protective gear. How are you still standing?"

Luckily, I'm not compelled to answer *that* question. If I'd known I would encounter bullets today, I would have slipped on my assassin's suit instead of my favorite jeans. I sigh inwardly. I wonder if Willow can make me a crystal ball?

I was prepared to take the Guardian to the Realm as long

as nobody knew I was hurt. I planned to get her there safely and then leave.

But now the Guardian knows I'm injured and she'll insist that one of the Realm's doctors takes a look at me. Surviving cuts and bruises during training is one thing. Explaining to someone how I'm still alive after several bullets hit my major internal organs is another.

The truth is... I don't feel so good. It's nothing like the pain of taking the death-blow yesterday, but my body aches all over. I'm trying to heal but I need to get the bullets out.

I pulled enough bullets out of Mom to know that I've got an hour tops before removing objects gets tricky.

Slade can't seem to tear his eyes off the giant smear on the wall.

The Guardian snaps. "Slade! I have no idea how Hunter is still alive right now but she clearly needs medical help." She points accusingly at the evidence on the wall. "The Realm is closer than Saber Lane. She's coming with us or I will hold you personally responsible."

I groan inside. What the Guardian doesn't know is that I would be better off returning to Saber Lane. William will be able to help me and he won't ask difficult questions because he already knows the answers.

I just wanted to get her to safety... Now I'm trapped...

Slade presses his lips together, leans forward, and plants one hand on the wall beside my head as if he needs to anchor himself somewhere. He once came to me riddled with bullets. My choices after that changed his life.

His voice lowers, softer than before. "Can you walk?"

I respond with a dangerous murmur, "Slade, I can run if you need me to. I'll come to the Realm but as soon as the Guardian is safe, I'm leaving. I never intended to stay."

He lowers his voice even further. "The Guardian is right. You need someone to help you—"

"I can fish out my own damn bullets, do you understand me? If I can't... I'll ask William for help."

A muscle in the side of his jaw ticks. "We'll see. Come on. We need to move."

I glare at his back as he takes the Guardian's arm again and hurries her down the steps. She barely has time to check that I'm following before he whisks her around the corner of the stairwell.

She looks angry that he isn't helping me, but I'm glad he isn't. I don't need his help.

I hurry after them, listening out for our attackers. At minimum, they will send a clean up crew to tend to their wounded. That's if Lady Tirelli doesn't reward failure with a final bullet.

We exit the building through the back and I stay close to Slade as he maneuvers the Guardian along the street. One good thing about my red jacket is that it's hiding the blood pooling down my back. Down my front now, too.

Five steps down the busy street, two guys peel off from the side of a building across the road. Two more are already following us on this side of the street.

I nudge up to Slade. "Two behind us. Two to the right."

"I see them," he says. "Take the Guardian."

We switch places and I walk on the Guardian's right hand side, forming a body shield between her and the thugs.

Behind me, Slade veers into a shadow beneath a shop awning and then disappears completely. He's blurring. I can see it—the silver haze in the air—but nobody else can.

In the next moment, the two guys behind us are suddenly propelled into the nearest alleyway as he barrels into both of them like a bulldozer. They don't come out again.

The ones coming at us from the other side of the street pick up their pace, racing after us now. They don't attempt to hide their weapons—guns with silencers so at least there won't be mass panic.

I grab the Guardian and pull her into a run. It's conspicuous and alarms the people around us, but there's nothing I can do about it.

The Guardian launches into a quick sprint and I bet she's wishing she was dressed in jeans instead of her usual dress as the material flaps around her legs. I stay close, maintaining the shield I've formed with my body. We're only a hundred paces from the Realm now.

Oomph.

I shudder and jolt, stumble, but keep going.

The bullets were quiet. But at least they didn't hit the Guardian.

She gasps, half-turning, still running, eyes widening at the blood now splattering the pavement. "Hunter? Oh my…!"

"Keep going!"

She looks like she's about to scream but she keeps running. The distressed look she gives me tells me she thinks I'm going to die any moment now.

I won't, but I hope I don't pass out.

A second later, the two guys who shot at us suddenly disappear in a silver haze. I don't have time to look back and see what Slade does to them, but our backs are finally safe.

The Guardian reaches the memorial plaque before me. She slaps her hand against it and her point of focus changes. The Realm must have appeared for her, but it won't appear for me and I can't touch the memorial. I've been locked out.

I need her to be safe so I shout, "Go!"

She disappears as she steps inside.

I skid to a halt next to the memorial. I'm not normally winded from running but I guess twelve bullets will do that to me. I lean over, palms on my knees, my vision blurring for the first time. Running has tipped me over the edge and I'm not sure if I'll make it back to Saber Lane.

A hand lands on my shoulder.

I jolt backward, grab the hand and twist it, my fist flying out in a defensive move while I hold tight to stop him grabbing me anywhere else.

Slade side-steps my fist, bumps into the side of the plaque, the Realm appears and...

The momentum propels us both straight through the Realm door.

CHAPTER TWENTY-TWO

*O*h... *shoot.*

I stumble onto the Realm's pathway before I wrench myself away from Slade, my vision swimming.

I stand clear of him, rising up very slowly, waiting for the world to stop spinning around me. Blood trickles down the inside of my jeans from my chest and thighs. One of the bullets is caught in my right hip, another in my right shoulder, left rib, left thigh...

I stop counting.

The Guardian is as pale as snow, her chest heaving. She stands several paces away, already surrounded by assassins. She points toward me. "I'm fine, but Hunter isn't."

I growl at her without forming coherent speech, my responses purely instinctive now. *This woman is going to kill me with kindness.*

The assassins look to Slade, since I'm now a threat in their midst. The only blessing is that I don't see Ridley among them. Hopefully he's out and about somewhere. He'll try to kill Slade all over again if he thinks this is Slade's fault.

I sigh.

Then cough.

Okay, that hurt. Lungs. Hurt lungs. The last bullet must have done that. That would explain why I'm dizzy. I close my eyes. I really need to get the bullets out.

I stumble off the pathway, veering to the left as I mumble, "I'm going to the medical ward." I pause to glare at Slade. "Unless you want to stop me?"

"No."

I pause to make certain I understood him. "*No* you won't stop me? Or *no* I can't go?"

He takes my arm and propels me along the lawn. "You know that your clothes are soaked in blood, right?"

I glance down... then wish I hadn't. No wonder the Guardian looked so shocked. A curse rips out of me that seems to startle Slade more than anything else. I guess I rarely swear.

Despite me being a Rogue Master, every man in our path hurries out of my way instead of challenging me.

It looks like blood-soaked Hunter is a useful spectacle today.

We reach the medical ward within moments and I'm suddenly swarmed by the head doctor and his staff. He's an older assassin, retired, with olive skin, dark eyes, and a kind manner.

He tries to make me lie down on one of the medical beds but I push him away, my protective instincts making me unusually angry. "Get away from me! I don't need your help. I'm not here because I want to be."

He gives me a grim look. "Most people don't choose to be riddled with bullets."

I grit my teeth, trying to suck in a calming breath but it

doesn't work. It turns out that bullets make me cranky. Really cranky.

I shout at nobody in particular, "Hand me the tools. I can do it myself. Now, get out!"

The doctor looks to Slade.

Slade inclines his head at the door, an equally forbidding expression on his face. When the door closes and we're finally alone, Slade approaches me like he would a dangerous animal. "Hunter, you can't do this alone."

"Watch me, asshole."

He doesn't even flinch. Just tips his head in a small acknowledging gesture as if he agrees with me.

I rip off my jacket and shirt, then my jeans, noting the bullet holes in them.

Dressed only in my underwear, I reach for the medical implements. My hands shake as I grip the surgical pliers, trying to angle them toward the bullet in my right shoulder.

I'm right-handed so my left isn't very strong and… *dammit…* I can't get the angle right to pull out the bullet. Not while my hands are shaking.

I swap hands and try for the bullet lodged in my left rib, groaning and almost passing out before I can get hold of it.

Oh, help me. I can't do it.

Now I know why Mom drank a whole bottle of vodka before she asked me to pull out bullets. It's way worse than I expected.

I rest my hand across my forehead and squeeze my eyes shut. Without opening them, I whimper, "I can't do this while you're watching, Slade. Just get the hell out already."

His response is much closer than I expected. "No."

I sigh out my exasperation. "You say that to me a lot."

"Yes."

"That, not so much."

His palm closes over mine, folding around the medical instrument, a soft touch. I refuse to open my eyes because I can't take any more of his hot and cold routine.

I can't stand to see the hard-as-granite I'm-not-going-to-budge look in his eyes or the way his gaze softens when I least expect it.

He murmurs, "You took two more bullets outside the Realm."

I shrug. "What's two more?"

The pliers leave my fingers. One of his arms sweeps behind my back, drawing me close, bracing my lower body against his as he holds my torso tight. His arm is big enough to pass all the way around my back and hold tight to the side of my ribs that he's aiming for.

His muscles tense, gripping me. I almost pass out when he swiftly pulls the bullet from my body.

I squeeze my eyes shut tighter as his hands flex against my back. I allow him to maneuver me over to the medical bed where I feel my way onto it, letting him get to work.

He distracts me while he works over me, somehow managing to place his free hand on a part of my body that doesn't hurt, where his thumb can graze back and forth across my bare skin—on my side, at the top of my shoulder, at my waist, on my thigh, brushing the sensitive skin where my thigh meets my hips...

By the time the final bullet is gone, I float in a strange bubble of pain and pleasure. My voice is croaky and rough as I say, "Thank you."

I try to get up but he places both hands firmly on me—one on my unhurt shoulder and the other on my unhurt hip. "Stay."

My eyes fly open.

He leans over me. His thumb gently passes across my cheek, wiping away the tear that escaped down it. "I haven't finished."

He steps away and I remain where I am until he returns with a sterile cloth and begins wiping down my torso and legs, cleaning up the blood quietly and gently, then setting to work applying patches to the wounds.

Once again, his hands seem to seek out patches of undamaged skin at the same time as he applies the dressings to my wounds, gentle caresses that soothe and fade, stroke and burn, grow and recede, over and over.

Watching him, his forehead creased in concentration, I'm not sure if he realizes he's touching me that way.

I can't bear it. Not when his expression hardens every time his gaze meets mine.

I grab his hand before he finishes the fourth dressing. "I won't have any bare skin left if you patch all my wounds. You really don't need to do that. I'll be fine in an hour. Well… mostly fine."

His eyebrows rise. "You really heal that fast?"

"Usually. It's my first time with bullets so I can't be sure."

He presses his lips together in a disapproving line. "Then you shouldn't take any chances."

I push his hands away. "Slade, stop."

He always respected my right to control what happened to my body. The moment I tell him to stop, he does, stepping away from me and returning the medical supplies to the tray beside the bed.

I reach for my wrecked clothing, dismayed by the holes and blood before I attempt to pull my shirt on. I grimace and yank it off again.

It's too gruesome to wear.

Instead, I pull my jacket directly over my bra and zip it up. But those jeans… *I can't put those back on.* I turn them over in my hands, looking for a patch that isn't shocking so I can focus on it while I pull them on.

Slade suddenly speaks up. "If you promise to wait for five minutes, I can help with your clothing situation."

I make no such promises, but he leaves anyway. He obviously doesn't trust me to wait long because he bursts into a blur as soon as he reaches the doorway.

I slump back to the bed, pushing my ruined jeans as far away from myself as I can. When Slade reappears in the doorway, his presence makes my skin tingle. His chest rises and falls as if he's out of breath. I guess he really hurried in case I left.

He strides forward to offer me clean jeans, a t-shirt, and a new jacket. "All of the clothing in your old room was custom made. I'll have everything sent over to the bookshop."

There's an entire wardrobe in that room, including dresses and slinky underwear that I have no use for. However, I could use some new clothing and there's nothing like custom made.

Before I can thank him, he clears his throat and hands me a book. "This also belongs to you."

I gasp. It's the Valkyrie Vade Mecum. It's the twin for the Keres Coda. I wasn't able to steal it from Gareth before I left the Realm.

Slade didn't have to give me this.

"I… thank you."

I consider him for a moment. I told him that I gave him a piece of me, that he is not completely human anymore.

Which means, this book belongs to him, too.

It suddenly dawns on me that he is the only other creature alive that is like me—even if his Valkyrie nature is a shade compared to mine. Until I have a daughter, he is the closest I have to brethren.

He takes a step back, his gaze never wavering from mine as he murmurs, "I can't give you what you want, Hunter."

I startle. Were my thoughts so obvious just now? Did he see the yearning in my face?

I slam a lid on my feelings. Twice today, I've opened myself up to being hurt—once when I asked him to explain how I pushed him away and again just now. I can't be that vulnerable to him again.

There's nothing I can say to him now, so instead I hurry to dress.

Now that I'm healing and the angry-making pain is fading, my emotional shields are failing and my body is beginning to remember what it was like to fall asleep next to him, wake up next to him, tilt my head back and drink in his kisses, the way everything around me seemed to heat up at his lightest touch...

Once I'm dressed, I find him watching me with an expression I wasn't expecting. Silver power lights his eyes again and flashes of heat fill the space between us.

His lips are slightly parted and softer than usual, all the hard lines gone. His focus lifts from my legs to my eyes.

Goose bumps rise along my skin as he drinks in all of me from my toes to the curve at my waist to the tilt of my neck and my lips.

What did I do to cause this?

All I did was get dressed. He didn't give me that look when I took *off* my clothing.

Despite my promise to myself that I wouldn't make myself vulnerable again, I reach out. "Slade, can we—"

He shakes himself violently and pulls away, powerful backward strides taking him halfway across the room within seconds, the hard lines returning to his face and his suddenly tense body. "No."

I bite my lip. Whisper, "Okay then."

Confused, I roll my damaged jeans and shirt into a ball and leave them on the medical tray. I grip the table for a moment, my knuckles turning white. "You can burn these clothes."

"I will."

I press my lips together before I say, "Make sure Ridley knows that I'm okay."

All I can do now is walk away.

I stride from the room, reaching the corridor outside before my shoulders slump.

So much for building bridges.

When I emerge from the medical wing, the Guardian races across the grass toward me. "Hunter! What are you doing?"

"I'm going home."

Her luminescent brown eyes are aghast. "But you aren't healed. You need to rest—"

"I'm fine."

Her exasperation shows in her deeply furrowed brow and sharp tone. She practically stomps her foot at me. "You're as stubborn as your mother!"

I round on her. She doesn't deserve my anger but I unleash it anyway. "You mean the mother who was killed by the assassin you won't execute?"

She pales. "Do you have proof that Gareth killed Anna?"

I swing away from her. "There's never proof, is there?"

She hurries after me. "Wait, Hunter. You need to know that all three missions are sanctioned."

It was why I went to her hotel room in the first place.

I pause long enough to say, "Consider them done."

Men scatter as I stride along the path, watching me go, the Rogue Assassin who saved the Guardian's life.

CHAPTER TWENTY-THREE

As soon as I arrive at Saber Lane, Vlad descends on me in full fury. "Ten bullets! What were you thinking? You went to the Guardian without protective gear or weapons. Even I wouldn't do something that foolhardy."

I stop in the middle of the street, fury rising fast inside me. "Don't lecture me about personal safety. You're the one who strolled into the Realm knowing that Slade would try to kill you."

He rises up, glowering down at me from his great height, his giant shadow casting me into darkness. "There are people on this street who need you, Hunter. People in this city who can't afford to lose you."

He is as frosty as the winter breeze wafting around us. I can smell snow in the air and it's as crisp and clipped as his tone.

His breath frosts as he says, "*I* don't want to lose you. You can't go around acting like you're invincible."

My eyes widen. He's angry... because he was worried

about me. It takes the wind out my sails. "I'm sorry. I honestly didn't think it would turn into an ambush."

My apology reduces his fury. He exhales quietly. "Next time you leave this street, you need to be prepared."

"I plan to be." My first action will be to ask Willow for tranquilizers.

He says, gently, "Maybe you should let me come with you."

I scowl at him. He might be worried but he's not my bodyguard. "How did you find out about it anyway?"

"The Guardian wrote a message in my ledger. She wanted to let me know she's staying in the Realm. She also let Cain know."

I groan. "I suppose she told him about the bullets?"

I wonder if that means I can expect a visit from Cain today.

Sure enough, Vlad says, "He's on his way here to make sure you're okay."

I growl, "The Guardian really didn't have to do that."

It's Vlad's turn to scowl. "She was worried about you. So were we."

He angles slightly to the side and I'm surprised to see Tansy hovering in her doorway. Despite their concern and my wounds, it's not my body that is causing me the most pain right now.

"Vlad… You told me that I had to find a way to get through to Slade. So did Dean. But every time I go near him, things just get worse."

He gives me a ferocious scowl. "You're Hunter Cassidy. You can accomplish anything. Don't go wobbly on me now, woman."

"Wobbly?" I laugh, pulling the base of my shirt up to

reveal the four patches that Slade put on me before I stopped him applying more. The bullet wounds are still healing and I can't deny that they sting. "Does this look wobbly to you?"

He peers at the patches and I immediately regret my rash decision to show him.

"Actually… that looks bad even for an assassin with your reputation," he says. "How did you survive—?"

Tansy appears behind him, pulling her coat on and blowing on her hands. She exchanges a quick glance with me. For once, she seems to want to help. "Let me see…"

While Tansy maneuvers around him, undertaking a visual inspection of my patched up stomach and hip, Vlad says, "Ten bullets and she's walking around like nothing happened."

Tansy raises her green eyes to mine. She gives me a worried look but clears her expression before she asks, "How many lodged? Do you need them removed?"

"I… um… no. Slade got them out."

"Good. Then everything is fine. You must have been lucky. Vlad, stop hassling her."

He grumbles a response, throwing his hands into the air in defeat. I pick my jaw off the ground when he allows Tansy to tug on his arm and he lumbers away with her.

Dean's quiet whisper behind me makes me jump. "Tansy tamed the bear."

He grins at me, his brown eyes sparkling when I whirl to him.

I ask, "But… how?"

"Witches have ways."

I scowl. "Not with me she doesn't."

"You're unique."

I sigh. Unique and alone. Slade may share my power but he doesn't want to be part of my life.

All my frustration evaporates with the breeze. "I blew it, Dean. Slade is unreachable. He well and truly pushed me away today. I may literally have to die to get him to talk to me."

"Don't do that, Hunter." Dean peers at me, head tilted to the side, his eyes darkening. My senses calm rapidly, telling me he's using his power to assess my emotions. Thankfully, he doesn't try soothing me again. I've had enough of *that* sensation today.

All he says is, "*Hmm.*"

I narrow my eyes. "What?"

He shakes his head at me. "You didn't really try."

What? I splay my hands at my sides as he walks away, leaving me alone in the middle of the street. I exhale my exasperation into the crisp air. *Of course I tried!*

Didn't I?

I drag myself back to the bookshop and slink inside, avoiding the customers as I make my way upstairs. My ledger remains on the corner of the counter. One of the customers innocently opens it and asks William, "What is this book?"

He smiles a response from behind the counter—especially when she blinks rapidly at the entries that appear as nothing more than spider webs across the page. He continues to calmly wrap up her purchases, but the glance he shoots me tells me he's worried about me. Just like Vlad and Tansy.

Guilt isn't something I feel very often but right now I'm drowning in buckets of it. I'm not used to having people in my life who worry about me.

"That book has personal significance," he says. "I'm afraid it's not for sale."

The customer runs her fingertips over the cover, giving William an understanding look. "It's beautiful. If you ever change your mind, please let me know."

I creep up the stairs to the bathroom. I can't remove the patches and take a shower yet—I should be able to do that tonight when the wounds have healed—but I want to make sure that my face is clean. I check my hairline and neck for any signs of the battle but... there are none.

Slade did a very thorough job of cleaning me up.

I lean against the sink, squeezing my eyes closed, trying to forget the way his thumb grazed my side, my hip, my thigh... The way he didn't seem to know he was doing it...

I shove the sensation away, focusing instead on the physical pain. In the last two days, I've taken a death blow and multiple bullets. My body is wrecked.

A growl of frustration rips through me. The bullets hurt less than the mask Slade wears when he looks at me. I never intended to come back to Boston, but now I need to stay. Somehow, I have to find a way to live with him in my life.

I head to my room, pull the Valkyrie Vade from the large pocket inside the jacket that Slade gave me, and curl up on my bed with it. I'm grateful for the jacket and I'm actually looking forward to receiving the clothing he's going to send me. The best thing about assassin's clothing is all the secret pockets.

The Vade is similarly designed to the Coda with a lock on the side that opens at my touch. It's smaller than the Coda, but thicker. The aura around the book is a strong glow, every page infused with magic.

I half hope it isn't written in code but... it is. The pages are filled with illustrations and each is made up of tiny words, none of which make any sense.

I carefully turn the pages until I reach the same illustration that is in the Keres Coda. It depicts a woman holding two babies—one in the crook of each arm—while a single feather floats on each side of her.

I was distracted the first time I saw this image, but now I have time to study it.

The babies' delicate wings are tucked tightly to their sides, but what surprises me is that the one on the woman's left hip is Valkyrie while the one on her right is Keres.

As for the feathers, the one floating in the air beside the Keres baby is silver, while the feather floating in the air beside the Valkyrie baby is copper.

I run my fingertips across the drawing.

Who is this woman to hold both children in her arms as if she loves them?

I jump when William appears in the doorway. That's the second time someone has crept up on me today. My reflexes have definitely taken a beating.

"That drawing confuses me," he says. "I haven't decoded it yet but I'm determined that I will."

The fact that I didn't hear him approach tells me that my strength and senses are significantly dimmed because of the energy I'm using to heal. It's okay for me to let my guard down inside the shop, but I'll need to be on alert if I go outside again today.

I ask, "No more customers?"

"I've closed up for lunch." He props himself on the end of the bed, pointing to the book as he says, "That illustration raises many questions."

I nod, agreeing with him as I say, "Like why she carries a

child of each race, and why the birth feathers are on opposite sides."

William leans forward. "I have a theory that..." His brow suddenly furrows, his fingertips playing around the edge of the book. "Wait a minute... This is not the Keres Coda."

I hand it over to him with a smile. "It's the Valkyrie Vade. Slade gave it to me."

William's eyes widen as he runs his hands over the book in reverence. "He gave this up?"

I nod and shrug. "I didn't ask him to. He probably doesn't know what it's worth."

"Oh, he knows." William sighs, his shoulders sagging where he sits. "When you were gone and the rumor started that he killed you, he came here. He tried to tell me that it wasn't true."

I consider the regret on William's face. "You didn't believe him."

He grimaces. "I may have said some things I regret. I fear... I spoke too harshly."

He falls silent. I sit up a little, propping the pillow behind me and pulling my knees to my chest. "What did you say to him, William?"

He gives a small shake of his head, closing the book and clasping it tight. "That he never deserved you. That you gave up something precious for him—your feather—to save his life. That he would never be worthy of it." William meets my eyes. "Your mother was killed by her bond. I thought you had been, too."

There is so much regret in William's expression and I would do anything to make it go away. He has been nothing but protective and kind toward me. Whatever he said to

Slade was said in fear and pain. Pain that he thought I was dead, betrayed like Mom was betrayed.

I unfurl from my position at the top of the bed. In the last two days, people have hugged me. A lot. But offering a hug is not something that I'm used to doing. It's a form of affection that is completely foreign to me. Mom loved me but her love manifested in the form of training and instruction, in teaching me how to defend myself and how to fight.

Just hugging me for the sake of hugging me... maybe it happened when I was little but not when I was older.

I take a giant leap of faith as I reposition myself beside William, slide my arm around his back, and drop my head to his shoulder. "You thought you lost me."

"I did." He tilts his head to mine, pressing a kiss to my forehead. "I didn't know how I was going to get through that again..."

I curl into his side, giving him the same feeling of warmth and security as he gives me. We are quiet until finally, he pats the book. "I also demanded the Vade from him. I told him he had no right to keep it. He said he would only give it to you."

I inhale and exhale. Slowly. "He kept his word."

"I misjudged him. And I fear I did some damage that I never intended. Words have power, Hunter. If Slade believes everything I said to him..."

William places the book to the side and turns to place both his hands on my cheeks, a sudden urgency in his expression. "Hunter, I need to tell you what your Mom and I argued about. It was a long time ago, but it's affecting your life now—"

A sharp clatter from downstairs interrupts us.

William and I freeze.

I whisper, "I thought you said you closed for lunch? Is Tansy downstairs?"

As soon as he shakes his head, I gesture for him to head across the hall to his room. He will be safe there while I check out what made that noise. Fallon threatened to come after everyone on Saber Lane. After Lady Tirelli's failed attempt on the Guardian's life this morning, I'm not taking any chances.

Once William hurries away from me, I implement a full blur. It's harder than usual, takes me longer to achieve; another sign that I'm depleted. I'm not sure how I can keep fighting today...

I proceed cautiously down the stairs, painfully aware of my limitations. I can't race into an ambush this time. I need to go on the defensive and conserve my energy. I creep down the stairs even though my blur hides any noise I make. I'm almost at the bottom when the scent of roses rises to meet me.

Perfume. Lots of it.

It smells like flowers but it's... off somehow. Like it's masking the scent of something... *rotten.*

I press against the wall as I emerge into the downstairs, not sure what I'll find.

Everything is quiet.

The door is closed.

Nothing moves.

But it's not only the smell now. There's a presence in the shop that is immense, powerful, and yet small and diminished at the same time, overwhelming but also weak, like a tornado and a puff of air, like death and life overlaid on each other. So many contradictions that my senses spin.

I try to get a location on it, to pin it down, to find a shape in the air, but everything is perfectly clear, almost… too sharp.

The oppressive force increases. The scent of roses becomes sickening, making my stomach turn.

It's as if the force is approaching my position. That is *not* possible. My blur is complete and can't be detected.

Whoever it is, they shouldn't be able to see me.

Unless I'm so depleted that I haven't completely blurred after all. The hairs on the back of my neck stand on end.

My defenses rise and my lips part as I spy my ledger, fallen on the floor not two paces away from me as if it was deliberately dropped where I couldn't miss it.

It's splayed open, the pen cupped neatly in the middle fold.

In large letters scrawled across both pages, it says:

You will come to me, Hunter. Or I will kill them all.

CHAPTER TWENTY-FOUR

*R*age spirals through me, but I control it, contain it, and hold it ready.

I have one shot…

I don't know if the presence in the shop is Lady Tirelli herself or a thug she has sent to do her dirty work. Anyone can write in my ledger, but not anyone can blur like me.

I whisper, "Lady Tirelli, you will never have what you want." Not the Clave, not the books, not the Keres girl. None of it.

I close my eyes and stop trying to see with my eyesight, stepping forward into the fumes, the scent growing stronger at double speed as if the owner of the perfume moves toward me at the same pace I'm moving toward them… or *her*.

The gap closes rapidly. One more step…

My fist flies out.

I connect with something solid. It's metallic, some sort of blade. My other fist flies out, grabbing and holding tight to a wad of material encasing some sort of harness.

I unleash my rage. My killing power sizzles through my

hands. I sense a scream in the air, a quiet hiss, before whatever I held is yanked away from me. I'm ready for that, using my boot to land a solid hit, sensing something break before the presence retreats.

The sickening scent of roses recedes in a rush.

The door rips open so fast that the wooden frame cracks and splinters, hitting the wall and shattering the glass panes.

I race through the room after her, my boots crunching on broken glass.

Her presence retreats up the street, taking with it a fading scream.

I want to chase after her but I can't. My strength is draining with every passing second that I maintain the blur. I let it go, materializing, my chest heaving with frustration.

She's going to get away.

Five shops down, a figure stops in the middle of the street, broad shoulders, massive physique, all imposing male.

I've never been so glad to see Cain Carter in my life.

He drops the package he was holding, braces, pauses as if he's sensing... and then charges left. He slams into the presence hard enough that it hits the bakery window, thudding against the window and cracking one of the panes.

At the same time, Vlad storms from Tansy's house, charging down the street. He barrels straight into the spot where gravity dictates that the intruder would land, his arms closing around something that he forces to the ground.

His head snaps back as if she thumped him. He tips to the side, grabbing at air. Cain launches into the space above him, grabs at her... but comes up empty.

As Vlad recovers, Cain casts around. Both of them are tense, paused and searching, before they shake their heads.

She's gone.

Cain offers his hand to Vlad, a warrior's grip to help him to his feet.

As I lean against the broken doorframe, I try to harness my ability to hear their conversation but it's like listening through mud. All I get are muffled snatches.

"… got away…"

"Wh… was it?"

Cain points. "… Hunter… shop…" He retrieves the package he dropped and they both stride in my direction.

I use the last of my strength to turn toward the inside of the shop and call out, "William! It's safe now."

Then I brace against the doorframe and try to make it look like I'm leaning there because I want to.

William clatters down the stairs behind me, appearing so quickly that I suspect he wasn't safe in his room the whole time after all. His hand flies over his nose. Even with the door open, the room stinks.

He asks, "What is that smell? Are you okay?"

I lean in the open doorway, my fists clenched, my blood pounding.

William's eyes widen at the damage to the door. "Hunter?"

Cain and Vlad reach us, both speaking at once. "What was that thing?"

"It was Lady Tirelli," I say. "I'm sure of it."

A dark expression descends over Cain's face. "Then she knows how to blur."

Vlad growls under his breath. "She hijacks our ledgers *and* she blurs. She has to be a trained assassin."

Cain nods. "Which means there will be records of her somewhere. You said she started in your Faction. Could she have been a Dominion assassin?"

"It's possible. I'll see what I can find." Vlad gives me a quick once-over, pausing for the slightest moment, eyes narrowing. He glances at Cain, exchanging some sort of silent communication before he spins on his heel and strides back up the street.

Cain imposes the full force of his stunning green eyes on me. "Vlad thinks you're too proud to accept help, but I'm not afraid to offer. You're hurt. Let me help you."

"I'm fine. I'm *angry*. She came here to threaten me." There's no point showing him my ledger—he can't read it.

Cain reaches out for me. "Anger is understandable, but you're not fine. Let me..."

I evade his hands with a quick backward step. Leaving the support of the doorframe was not a good idea. Pain shoots through my side as soon as I move. But I don't need anyone's help right now. What I need is to end that woman. "No."

He shakes his head at me and keeps advancing. For some reason, William doesn't try to stop him, hurrying out of the way instead.

What are they...?

The pain in my side jabs again. I press it and... *liquid*. My hand comes away coated in blood. One of the bullet wounds must have opened up. Maybe more than one.

Using my power just now must have tipped me over the edge.

Dammit. I'm supposed to be invincible!

I stand still, fixating on the ceiling as Cain veers toward the counter to place the package on it, then drops to a kneeling position in front of me and lifts the bottom of my shirt to examine the patched wounds.

My heart sinks when I give them a quick glance. All of them are bleeding.

"William, do you have a medical kit?" Cain asks.

William rushes away upstairs but I demand answers. "How do you know William?" To my knowledge, he and Cain have never met.

"I've been here before." Cain waves my question away. "Where do you want to do this, Hunter? Here on the floor or upstairs in your room?"

I exhale. "Upstairs. But I can walk."

"I don't believe you, but I'll let you try."

"Oh, you'll let me, huh?" I turn on my heel to prove my point and take each laborious step until I reach the top.

Cain supports my back with one firm hand so I don't topple backward, deftly producing his phone at the same time. "I need repairs at the Tomb Bookshop on Saber Lane immediately. The bakery window was also damaged. Glass and wood. Yep. Good."

When we reach the top of the stairs, he says, "My people will be here in the next few minutes to clean up and repair the damage. You can trust them."

"I… uh…" I scowl at him, disliking my sudden reliance on him. "Thank you."

He arches an eyebrow at me, wrapping an arm around my waist without asking my permission and supporting me along the hallway. "You're welcome."

I push him away when I reach my bed, leveraging myself onto it. He lets me go, but only for a second, taking the medical kit from William as soon as he hurries into the room. Cain pulls out a pair of scissors and brandishes them at me. "Do you love this shirt or can I cut it?"

"I'm not stripping off for you." I've already done that once today. Not again.

"Then I'm cutting it off."

"No, you are not cutting—"

Rip.

He snips the bottom of the shirt and tears it up to the neckline in two seconds flat.

I grit my teeth at him. "You're lucky I'm too tired to punch your lights out, Cain Carter."

He doesn't respond, lifting the patches away, staring at the wounds beneath with widening eyes. His expression quickly darkens and he appears genuinely upset.

"Hunter, why weren't these stitched? You can't throw patches over wounds like these and expect them to heal."

It's a good thing he's not Slade or I'd have to answer his question.

I meet William's eyes across the top of Cain's head. William's worry hits me hard. He knows that I shouldn't need stitches. My wounds have never opened up before. I've always healed quickly. Mom never needed stitches.

I can only put it down to taking the death blow yesterday. It must have sapped my power more than I thought.

Cain produces a needle and thread with a stony expression. "Slade and I are going to have a serious disagreement if he thinks he can send you home with a shoddy patch-up job like this."

I grab Cain's arm, putting more strength into it than I can afford. "It wasn't Slade's fault. I wasn't exactly a willing patient."

"Hmm."

I fixate on the ceiling again. "I'm not used to people

helping me, Cain. And I'm not good at accepting help. You can't blame Slade for that."

His expression softens. "Hunter Cassidy, if you were my woman, you wouldn't think of it as 'help.' Loving someone is not about obligation."

I blink at the ceiling. There's a speck in my eye. A hot, watery speck. *Damn, he's going to make some woman very happy one day.*

He squeezes my shoulder. "Alright, then. Do you want to do this with painkillers or without?"

I've had enough of toughing it out. "With, please."

"Good choice."

Half an hour later, my body is dotted with clean patches, I have a new shirt on, and I'm in a very happy state of mind. "Those are great painkillers."

Cain finishes cleaning up. The sound of repairs floats up to us from downstairs. William is down there instructing the repair team and so far he seems happy with what they're doing. He has popped up to check on me several times.

"You need food." Cain disappears and reappears with the brown paper bag he was carrying earlier, along with plates and cutlery. He props me up against my pillow so I can sit.

I peer inside the bag. It's not the usual mass-produced takeaway. Multiple clear containers are filled to the brim with what look like specially-prepared meals.

He gives me a surprisingly self-conscious smile. "I wasn't sure what you like, so I asked my chef to make a variety of dishes. There's some for William, too."

I suppress the urge to raise an eyebrow at him. "Your chef?"

He shrugs his broad shoulders. He's not quite as massive as Vlad and slightly leaner than Slade. He's casually dressed in what I suspect are thousand-dollar designer pants and a long-sleeved shirt that fits his muscular physique perfectly.

As soon as I take the first bite, I can't help but moan. "Can I get a personal chef, please?"

Cain gives me a smile that would kick-start my heart if I was any other woman. "I'll bring you meals whenever you like, Hunter."

"Hah! Your girlfriend wouldn't like that much." When I bumped into Cain at the last charity event he hosted, the woman on his arm looked at me like I was gum under her shoe.

He clears his throat, suddenly serious. "There's a difference between the public persona I maintain and the life I actually lead."

I'm smart enough to know that I've hit a nerve. None of us can have a normal relationship. Especially not the Masters. I know better than anyone what it's like to reveal only a tiny portion of my true self to someone while I keep the rest hidden.

When he finishes his meal, he puts down his fork and says, "I'm not going to push you for details about what happened this morning. But I'm coming back tomorrow. You're going to tell me everything then. In the meantime, I've had an infrared security system installed outside the shop as well as at the entrance to the street. Vlad can monitor it. I'm also leaving a security team here to help out until you're back on your feet. Don't worry, they'll blend in. Nobody will notice them."

"Cain… you can't…" I swallow and stop myself before we get into another discussion about 'help.' "I'll pay for all of it. The repairs, the system—"

"I'm not taking a cent from you." He takes my plate and slides off the bed.

I hurry to stop him. "Wait, it's important. Nobody can know about this." I point to my wounds. "I walked into the Realm and I walked out of it. As far as everyone knows, the wounds were superficial. It's important they don't find out."

"I understand. You need to be indestructible." He rubs his jaw. "If anyone asks why you're not out and about, I'll tell them you're doing research. You have targets, correct?"

"Yes."

"Then that's your cover while you rest," he says. "I'll see you tomorrow."

Once he's gone, I slide under the blankets. I've never been physically vulnerable and I... *really* don't like it.

I close my eyes, telling myself I will rest for a moment and then I'll get up.

Before I know it, I'm asleep.

CHAPTER TWENTY-FIVE

I wake to sunlight and a growling stomach. Also voices coming from the kitchen.

I peel up the corner of a patch to check my wounds, disappointed to find that they aren't completely healed, but they're close. I check my power and my senses, seeking my wings inside my mind. They are strong again and ready to release if I need them.

All in all, I might need one more day of rest and I'll be okay.

I dress and emerge into the kitchen. Three people are huddled around the table: William, Briar, and… Ridley.

"Dad."

Ridley rises to his feet and crosses the distance between us but stops before he hugs me. "I'd wrap you up in hugs if you weren't already wrapped in bandages. I don't want to hurt you—"

I throw my arms around him and drop my head to his shoulder. He relaxes into it, gently sliding an arm around my back, pressing lightly. "That's the second time you've scared the life out of me, Hunter."

"I'm sorry."

He sighs. "It won't be the last. Don't apologize for doing your job." He pulls back to look at me. "Well… you're standing up so that's a good sign."

"I'm okay. Really. Much better today. I'm happy you're here."

"I can't stay long," Ridley says. "I needed to see for myself that you're okay. And I brought these." He gestures to the two large trunks sitting at the side of the room. One of them I've never seen before but the other is my trunk from the safe house.

Ridley explains, "That box contains your clothes from the Realm. The second is from Vlad. Apparently it's yours."

The trunk from the safe house contains the last of my clothing and belongings, including Mom's ledger. It feels right to have it back here in the bookshop.

"Thank you." I pause. "I'll tell Vlad myself but… can you thank Slade for me?"

"Of course." Ridley nods and clears his throat. "Uh… that dojo at the end of Saber Lane… will you train there?"

"As soon as I'm recovered. Why?"

"Would you mind if I join you?" He shrugs self-consciously. "Next year's intake of Novices isn't for another five months. I need something to do with myself. And… it would be nice to spend time with you."

The last comes out in a rush. The breath in his chest stops as he holds it, waiting for my answer.

"I'd like that."

"Good. See you in a few days, then."

He spins and strides down the stairs without another

word. I guess that was as much emotion as he was prepared to share today. Ridley is used to expressing his feelings with his fists, his approval taking the form of a stern order to 'get up and try again.'

Briar's gentle question interrupts my thoughts. She rounds the table to ask, "What do you need my help with right now, Milady?"

I've been debating whether or not to ask for Briar's help locating the Keres girl. I can't do it alone and I'm not sure how much assistance Slade will give me.

I exchange a cautious glance with William as I say, "I have an impossible task for you, Briar. I need you to locate a woman for me. She could be in Boston. She could be anywhere in the world actually, but I need to start small and then cast the net wider."

A smile breaks out on Briar's face. She tugs her beanie over her ears. "I like challenges, Milady. Tell me what you know about her."

"Only two things: she's twenty years old and she has violet flecks in her eyes."

Briar waits, expecting more. When I give her an apologetic smile, she asks, "Is she a target?"

"No. The opposite. I need to protect her."

Wow, I never thought I would say that about any Keres. I don't know if it's actually true. The baby that Mom saved twenty years ago may have grown into my worst enemy.

"I'll do my best," she says.

"Thank you, Briar."

Later, Cain arrives as promised, carrying another paper bag. As soon as he steps foot in the kitchen, I glare at him, freezing him in my sights. "Cain Carter, you didn't ask my permission to enter Saber Lane yesterday. Or today."

He breaks into a charismatic smile, making it very difficult to remain mad at him as he raises his bare hand to show me that he isn't wearing his assassin's ring. "I wasn't here as an assassin yesterday. Or today for that matter. I'm a customer."

I narrow my eyes at him suspiciously but he simply passes me the paper bag. "You look much better today."

I peer into it. My mouth is already watering. "I don't know, Cain. I don't feel so good. I think you should bring me lunch for another few days just to be sure."

He gives me a sly smile and dishes out the meal, but he levels his gaze with me when we begin to eat. "Tell me about the ambush yesterday. What happened?"

I give him the details of the attack on the Guardian as well as what happened in the shop, although I omit any parts that involve my wings.

I also give him brief details about what Lady Tirelli wants —the feather that I stole and the books.

He remembers the feather from the dinner with Gareth while I was still a Novice.

I take the chance to tell him that the feather supposedly reveals a weapon, but I don't tell him the long history of the Clave, about my mother's death, or about the Keres girl. That information is too dangerous for anyone else to know.

"What worries me most is that Lady Tirelli was brazen enough to attack the Guardian in broad daylight," I say. "Coming here is one thing, but sending her thugs into a hotel? Slade is safe in the Realm, but you aren't, Cain. You can't assume she won't come after you, too."

He tilts his head at me with a quizzical look, his green eyes filling with secrets. "Aside from all the security around my home… you don't read the tabloids, do you?"

I snort. "Not at all. Why?"

Cain quietly clears up the plates and stacks them in the sink. Then he says, "Are you up for a stroll along the street? There's something you've been missing."

"I think I can manage that."

Outside, I ask him, "Where are we going?"

He smiles, maintaining a casual stride beside me. "To the grocery store. Or, more specifically…"

As we reach it, Cain points at the wide newsstand positioned on the footpath at the front of Christopher James's store. The stand rests directly beneath the window that is painted with the replica of my tattoo.

Neat rows of bright magazines vie for attention, blaring one sensationalist headline after the next.

The one Cain points to reads:

Millionaire playboy acquires majority shareholding in mining company.

The next one shouts: *Cain Carter broke my heart!* Beneath which is a picture of the woman he was with at the last charity event.

I swing from one to the next. Cain's image is on all of them. "You're everywhere."

He lifts an overconfident eyebrow at me. "The spotlight has its advantages. It's hard to kill someone who is always in the eye of the camera."

"So this keeps you safe?" I peer around the street, scrutinizing the random tourists walking up and down it. I'm suddenly wary of those taking photos. "What about now? Should I expect photographers to jump out and start rumors about you and me?"

I run my hands across the air in an exaggerated gesture. "Who is the mysterious new woman in Cain Carter's life?"

He laughs. "Don't worry, I gave the photographers the slip four streets over. Even without assassin's magic."

I'm not surprised. With or without blurring, Cain has mastered the technique of disappearing into the background. "So your status as a social figure is the perfect disguise and defense."

I meet his serious eyes and amend my statement by saying, "Except that it's all true, isn't it? Mr. Millionaire. Buying shares in mining companies and breaking hearts."

I'm not sorry he ditched that woman, if he was ever really with her to begin with. As he said, his public image is very different to his reality.

He grimaces. "My fortune has its advantages and disadvantages."

I narrow my eyes at him, taking a leaf out of Vlad's blunt book when I ask, "Did you buy yourself into the Horde Master position?"

He narrows his eyes at me, drawing himself upright, his true strength gleaming in his eyes and revealing itself in the stern cut of his jaw and the squaring of his shoulders. Whatever casual role he was playing, it's gone in an instant.

A slow smile breaks across my face. *There you are, Cain Carter. The real assassin. I missed you.*

He growls, "Don't forget who held the record for the most kills on a mission."

I grin at him, feigning surprise. "Oh, that was you? Five, was it?"

We're getting into dangerous territory now. Slade broke Cain's record with seven kills. I don't want to get onto the topic of Slade, so I quickly scan the article and change the subject. "I don't see any mention of your family."

He is deadly serious. "My half-sister's existence is not

public knowledge and I plan to keep it that way. The world thinks I'm an only child. Heir to the Carter fortune—that's on my mother's side. I didn't know about Parker until a year ago when our father died. I'm the only family Parker has left and I won't let her get dragged into this. Unfortunately, I couldn't keep her existence a secret from Gareth, so I have to assume that Lady Tirelli also knows about her."

I sigh. "Which means she could become a target. Does she know you're an assassin?"

He runs his hand through his hair. "No. Which makes protecting her much harder. The safest place is the Horde's Realm, but a Realm full of warriors will take a lot of explaining, let alone the magical nature of the Realm itself."

I suck in a sympathetic breath. "I can't imagine what that conversation looks like."

"I want you to know that I will stay in Boston for as long as I can," he says. "I won't ditch you before the charity event. But if my sister is threatened, I'll have to get her out of the city quickly, and I might not have time to get word to you. I don't want you to think I've abandoned you."

The concern in his eyes is deeper than I expected it to be. I hurry to assure him. "Of course not. You have to protect your family. At all costs. Believe me I know how important that is." I clear my throat before my emotions show, deflecting the conversation. "You said you're here as a customer but you didn't buy any books."

He remains serious as he says, "I'm here to see the Saber Lane Witch."

I'm surprised. "You came to see Tansy?"

"I need my daggers spelled and I was told she was the best."

The best, huh? I'm reminded of the way Tansy woke up the other night, powerful magic screaming through her.

I think I need to see this. "May I come with you?"

"Of course," he says. "You're the reason I need my knives spelled, remember?"

I 'hmm' at him. I had carried his dagger strapped between my breasts after an attempt was made to frame him with my murder. He had vowed to have his daggers spelled so it could never happen again.

When we reach Tansy's door, Cain takes the steps two at a time and knocks confidently. The door opens to reveal Tansy standing tall inside her home. She's wearing black heels and a long, black dress that contrasts with the highlights in her blonde hair. "Hello, Cain Carter."

Cain replies smoothly, "Blessings on your home and your power."

Tansy inclines her head toward the inside, spinning on her heels.

She didn't tell me I *couldn't* come in so I follow Cain through the hallway and into the large parlor immediately to the right.

It's light and airy, simply furnished with plush seats along the back wall and abstract blue paintings on the walls. It's calm in a way I wasn't expecting, but the crowning glory is the large book resting on the pedestal in the middle of the room.

Vlad sits quietly on a chair in the far corner, leaning forward with his elbows on his knees. He doesn't seem surprised to see me.

I take the seat next to him while Cain acknowledges Vlad with a quiet nod. The truce between the Masters seems to be holding.

Tansy wastes no time telling Cain to stand in front of the pedestal while she takes up position behind it.

She whispers something under her breath and it's only because I know she has to read spells that I can tell her focus is on the book instead of on Cain. She hides her limitations well. I have to respect that. I hide a lot, too.

As soon as Tansy speaks, four daggers rise up from various places around Cain's body—three from his pockets and one from his boot—sliding neatly out of their hiding places to hover, pointed safely downward, in the air above the book.

Cain is as startled as I am that Tansy was able to locate and remove his weapons so easily.

This is a side of Tansy I've never seen. The times I've encountered her, she's been emotional, angry, and vulnerable around me.

Inside this room, she is confident, her head held high, her power a glittering force. Cain won't be able to see her aura without his assassin's ring but Vlad and I can.

It's enthralling, multi-colored, and luminescent, reminding me of brilliant diamonds. I lean forward, mesmerized as it grows in strength, building outward from her body like layers of color being painted in the air.

She asks Cain, "Do you want me to bind these weapons to you, Cain Carter?"

He replies, "I don't want anyone else to be able to touch them."

Her golden hair cascades across one shoulder as she tilts her head with a questioning glance. "Are you sure? All magic has unexpected outcomes. If you go ahead with this, nobody else will be able to hold these four weapons. Ever."

A crease appears on his forehead. He considers her warning before he says, "I'm sure."

"Very well."

She murmurs under her breath and the knives begin rotating gently in the air. The glow in her eyes deepens and her aura changes color from a rainbow to deep, burnished gold, brightening with every word she speaks.

She lifts her hands at her sides while a force grows around her and the knives spin faster. Her hair rises around her shoulders and the power lighting her eyes suddenly sparks like electricity. At the same time, the room darkens, making the light around her sharp and palpable.

The power filling the room makes my skin tingle. It's painful, like a trapped force that is screaming to be released.

That's when I realize... Tansy has stopped reading the spell. She's lost herself in the magic and she doesn't need the book anymore.

As the darkness presses down on us, Vlad's big hand brushes my knee.

I side-eye him, trying to remain calm. It's not like him to make physical contact without a reason.

He indicates Tansy with a slow and careful tilt of his head. He won't speak his thoughts, but the way he focuses on her tells me he wants me to see her. Really see her.

I do.

I finally do.

She is far more powerful than she knows.

CHAPTER TWENTY-SIX

*T*he light dims. The knives settle to the surface of the spell book, lining up in a neat row.

Tansy blinks rapidly, shaking herself a little. She appears uncertain for a brief moment, swallowing and clearing her throat, but she hides it quickly. She lifts her chin, confident again as she says, "It is done. Do you want to test the spell?"

Cain nods. "Sure."

Tansy inclines her head at me, a glimmer of challenge lighting up her olive green eyes. "Perhaps Hunter will assist by trying to take one of the knives?"

Perhaps I can.

Curiosity compels me to leap out of my chair and sidestep Cain.

I make a grab for the hilt of the nearest knife. As soon as I touch it, the dagger zips out of my fingertips and flies toward my face.

I recoil but it follows me with every backward step until I press against the wall, the dagger's tip stopping an inch from my right eye, seconds away from impaling me.

Cain plucks the weapon out of the air and slides it safely into his pocket.

I mouth a 'thanks' to him.

His lips compress as he pockets the other weapons. I've seen that look on his face enough to know that the way the dagger reacted concerns him. He must be reconsidering the warning Tansy gave him.

He asks her, "Will these weapons kill someone who tries to take them?"

A satisfied smile rests on Tansy's lips. It occurs to me that she wanted to test how strong the spell was. If anyone could get past it, it would be me. Now she knows it's rock solid.

"Don't worry, they won't hurt anyone. But it will be a nasty shock when the dagger turns on them. The more they try to take it, the faster the knife will jab at them." She challenges me with a smile. "I wonder if Hunter will give it another try for us?"

"Not on your life." I've recovered enough from the surprise to grin at Cain. "I think you can rest assured that nobody will tuck these weapons into their bodice in the future."

He snorts and the tension eases.

When we exit Tansy's house, Cain tells me to stay safe and rest. "Lady Tirelli won't be happy that she failed yesterday. But we'll make sure she continues to fail."

I lay a hand on his arm before he can leave, sensing his muscles flex in surprise beneath my touch. There was never any romantic attraction between us, but I don't often cross this line.

I've chosen to touch him now because I need his full attention. "Cain, I know you want to help, but if your sister is threatened, promise me you'll put her first. I know what it's like to lose family. I don't want that to happen to you."

His gaze softens. "Parker is very important to me. Thank you, Hunter."

After saying goodbye, I head back to the bookshop to focus on my next steps.

Aside from resting, I have two missions now: one is to end the Tirelli brothers and the other is to find the Keres girl. Briar will help with finding the girl, and as for the brothers, three boxes of information have arrived from the Guardian filled with photographic and documentary evidence.

Some of the crime scene photos… it's difficult to look at them. I spread them out over my bed and force myself to consider the damage these three men have done since Patrick Ryan died.

I won't let their violence continue.

For the next three weeks, I become a ghost in my own city.

Every morning I get up when the sun rises, blur myself, and jog around the streets of Boston like Mom and I did when I was younger. I run at a slow pace for the first week until I'm completely healed.

No matter how hard I try to avoid it, I always end up outside the Boston Common near the Realm door that won't open for me.

Sometimes I sense Slade's presence on the other side of the wall, an increasingly powerful force.

After my run each morning, I meet Ridley at the dojo

where he and Drake take turns trying to beat me at whatever weapon they decide to focus on that day.

Ridley brings me information about what's happening inside the Legion, especially any missions that might impact on our goal of trapping Lady Tirelli. He tells me that Rowan, Brandon, and Lutz have been busy. So have Matthew and Thomas. Requests have been coming in from many who lost loved ones or whose loved ones are threatened because of the Tirelli's actions.

After breakfast each day, Briar gives me her regular report and I sense her growing frustration when finding the Keres girl proves difficult. I'm not surprised. Mom hid the baby well enough to evade Lady Tirelli. We aren't going to find her in a week.

I spend an hour each morning doing the only normal thing in my day: helping William in the shop. I actually learn how to use a cash register.

He's far better than me at interacting with the customers. I find myself constantly assessing them for threats, waiting for the scent of roses that was left by our unwelcome visitor the other day.

After lunch each day, I blur again, relentlessly tracking the movements of the Tirelli brothers. They have an efficient operation: Geno is the businessman who makes the deals, Vincent is the muscle, and Enric overseas drug production—he's just as trigger-happy with his own people as he was with me.

Vlad maintains constant security on Saber Lane and Cain was true to his word—his people blend in. There are no more attacks and after a quiet week, I ask Cain to pull his people back.

At the start of the second week, Ridley arrives at the dojo looking troubled. When I ask him what's wrong, he shakes it off, instead asking Drake whether he has a bow and arrows. It seems like Ridley is in the mood for target practice.

Drake obliges by setting up a target at one end of the dojo and telling me he doesn't mind if I hit the wall by accident. The space is only just long enough for archery, but short of practicing on the street, Ridley says it will have to do.

I've used a crossbow before but never a bow and arrows. Ridley teaches me how to place my feet, nock the arrow, and release it. My first arrows fly wide, but the next few hit closer to the middle of the target. By the tenth try, I'm hitting the center.

Ridley remains deep in thought, breaking the silence only to give me instructions. I decide to push things a little when I ask, "Did you and Mom practice together?"

He gives me a quiet smile. "The bow and arrow was the only skill she needed my help with. In every other way, she excelled during training."

I remember he told me she was a Novice in the year after him. "You were her teacher?"

"No. I was a first-year Superior then. I didn't take up teaching until a few years later."

I lower the bow for a moment. "She never taught me this. Maybe… she wanted you to teach me."

He gives me a short nod, an almost-smile, the expression in his eyes deepening. I haven't asked him much about his relationship with Mom. It seems hard for him to talk about it.

"You're a natural," he says.

I laugh. "Well, I'm glad, because she did give me the name 'Glass Arrow.'"

His eyebrows knit together. Before I can take aim, he touches my arm. "I just remembered something… She gave me a message the last time I saw her. It was when she told me you were mine. I was in shock so I didn't really hear what she said… but I remember it now."

I put down the bow. "Dad?"

"She said… 'tell Hunter that an archer needs an arrow.'" The furrow in his brow deepens. "It didn't make any sense to me at the time."

I give him a light shake of my head. *An archer needs an arrow?* It seems obvious—what good is an archer without arrows?—but also very random. "Maybe it was her way of asking you to train me."

"Maybe. Hunter… there's something else…"

He pauses and I sense that what he wants to tell me is the thing that was troubling him when he arrived. "You should start following the Legion assassins."

My eyebrows lift. "Why?"

"Just do it. It's important."

It's a cryptic suggestion, but I take it seriously.

The next day, I track Brandon Baker as he carries out a mission to kill a drug dealer. The day after that, I follow Rowan Robertson when he completes a mission to assassinate a corrupt businessman. Then I follow Lutz Logan, the brutal assassin who chooses to kill with his hands. Their weapons are all marked with the Legion's new identity: *SL*. Slade's Legion.

Each of them says the same thing to their target before they dispatch them: "Be grateful I'm not Slade."

It sends shudders down my spine.

By the time Lutz says it, I need answers.

As he walks away from his mission, I materialize in front

of him, making him jump. He's dressed in protective gear that conforms to his powerful figure. There was a time when his muscles were all for show but six months of hard training changed that. It changed a lot of things.

"Hunter?"

I raise my hand in a peaceful gesture and speak quickly. "I'm not interfering. I just want to know why you said that about Slade."

Lutz's gaze rakes over me, a glimmer of his former arrogance visible through his carefully-guarded exterior. "You aren't with him anymore, are you?"

I maintain my own blank expression, giving nothing of my emotions away. "I'm not."

"Then you should know that he's dangerous. To you and everyone else."

"Why?"

He exhales. "I don't know when it happened. Maybe the day you took all those bullets but now…" A muscle ticks in Lutz's jaw as he clenches his teeth. "Slade seeks death at every opportunity. I never thought I would say this about any assassin but he's too good at what he does."

I hide my shiver. "Explain, please."

Lutz sighs. "Do you know why I kill with my hands?"

I shake my head.

He holds his big hands up at chest height, palms down, fingers splayed. They're shaking, trembling hard, but he doesn't try to hide it.

"I kill with my hands because when I take a life, I need it to be the hardest thing I've ever done. I don't want it to be easy. A cold bullet, even a sharp dagger is too easy to dismiss."

"Lutz…"

He squeezes his hands into fists. "Slade is like you now."

My voice diminishes to a whisper. "What do you mean?"

"Slade is a cold killer," he says. "He never stops. Barely sleeps. Four kills yesterday and three today. Me? I'm going to huddle over a strong drink and try to remember why I wanted to do this in the first place. There's no glory in this. Even if my target is the scum of the earth."

Before he turns away, I grab his closed fist, sensing the tremble stop within my strong grasp. I lift up on my tip-toes and plant a kiss on his cheek. "I'm glad I didn't rip off your balls, Lutz Logan."

A glimmer of a smile touches his lips. A touch of charisma returns. He considers my lips for a moment, but he makes no move toward me. "Me too, Hunter."

I watch him walk away before I blur again, my heart as cold as Slade's kills.

At the end of the second week, I locate the secret warehouse where the Tirelli brothers conduct their business.

Snippets of conversation from each of them over the course of the week tell me that the brothers have a situation they need to deal with on Friday of the third week. All three of them will be at the warehouse at the same time.

That day, I visit Tansy when I know Vlad is out, taking my protective suit to her. Without speaking, I point to the shoulders at the back of the suit. I can't cut through the material myself but I need my wings to be able to emerge from it.

Her gaze follows the line of my finger up to my face, scrutinizing me. Finally, she gives me a single nod and tells me to come back later.

The same day, an invitation arrives from Cain for the charity ball. The event is set for the evening on the same day that the Tirelli brothers will be at the warehouse.

It's perfect timing.

I will end the brothers.

And then I will end the Lady.

CHAPTER TWENTY-SEVEN

I slip on my glass ring in front of the mirror in my room.

I'm wearing my modified protective gear, including a mask that is attached to the suit and rests at the back of my neck. I can pull it forward over my face to hide my identity. I'm also wearing gloves so I won't leave fingerprints.

A black evening dress hangs at the front of the closet behind me, a reminder of the ball tonight. The gold-embossed invitation from Cain sits on top of the chest of drawers right next to the photo of Mom.

My hands remain steady as I step through my plan inside my mind. I intend to use all of the power at my disposal to kill the Tirelli brothers this morning.

I stride from the room, surprised to find William sitting at the kitchen table. It's barely sunrise and the way his head rests on his hands, eyes half-closed, tells me he didn't go to bed.

He raises his bleary eyes from the two books spread out

in front of him. The Coda and the Vade are both open to the identical illustrations of the woman holding the babies. Scattered pages of scribbled notes surround the books, evidence of William's continuing efforts to decode the image.

He blinks at me in the dim light. "I've discovered something, Hunter, but I don't know what it means. Do you have time to talk?"

I've given myself plenty of time to get to the warehouse. "I do."

"Do you remember when Tansy first met you and she was afraid? She quoted a passage from the Keres Coda that reads: *Where the Valkyrie walks, darkness grows, paving the way for death with every step.*"

Tansy was terrified of me that day. "It's hard for me to forget."

He makes an apologetic noise. "That phrase is repeated here—do you see the words in the folds of the woman's dress? It also occurs in other parts of Coda and Vade, but it refers to *the* Valkyrie, which I previously interpreted to mean the Valkyrie race generally." His forehead creases. "In this section it is more specific. It refers to *a* Valkyrie. Which makes me think… what if the phrase is about a particular Valkyrie, not about your race."

He runs his finger along a specific fold of the woman's clothing. "I now believe it is referring to a Valkyrie who has lost her way."

A shiver runs through me. It could easily be talking about me. It is too easy to lose my way. I've stepped toward that edge time and time again. Only Mom's last words have kept me from leaping off it. *I can overcome it.*

I push aside my fears as I lean forward to brush the page.

The gold and silver draws me closer. "Have you figured out who this woman is?"

"I believe she is Nyx."

"The mother of death?"

"According to the old tales. And these are her children: one Keres and one Valkyrie. Sisters." He points to the feathers on either side of the babies. "I've also discovered a message written in each of the birth feathers. It says: *Trust is shared.*"

"What does that mean?"

"I'm not sure yet, but I'm slowly piecing together parts of the message written along the woman's arms. So far I have a lot of scattered words: riddle, royalty, adversary, a healer and more references to death and darkness… There's even mention of a Realm in here. I don't know how they fit together yet."

He rubs his eyes, sighing through his fingers. "It's taken me all week to decipher that much. But I'm close to understanding it. Maybe today…"

I place a gentle hand on his shoulder. "You need to rest. I'm sorry I can't help out in the shop this morning, but I can ask Tansy to come by."

William reaches for me before I turn away. "Wait, Hunter. I need to tell you something else."

His hand shakes on my arm. I feel it all the way through my protective suit. "What is it? What's wrong?"

He pauses. "Anna didn't burn your birth feather."

I blink at him. Then I drag out a chair to take a seat, mostly because my legs don't want to hold me up. "She told me that she did."

He counters, "But not right away. She asked Tansy's grandmother to help her first."

My heart rate speeds up and I don't like it. I can kill three men and not feel fear, but finding out about my past is like drinking poison. "This is what you argued about, isn't it?"

He nods. "I told you that she did everything she could to make sure you don't have the same weakness she did."

I stare at my hands, unable to stand the pity in his eyes. "My wings didn't reveal themselves when I bonded."

"It's because she bound your birth feather with a spell that put a lock on your wings during bonding," he says. "Then she burned your feather so there was no way to reverse the spell. I didn't agree with her decision to do that. The same way I didn't agree with her alliance with Patrick Ryan or her protection of his son, Archer. Over time, those disagreements festered between us. I lost Anna from my life because I couldn't agree with her choices. But the consequences are worse for you, Hunter."

I try to breathe. "Worse than not revealing my wings?"

His hand rattles against my arm. I slide my own over his to steady him.

"You can never fully bond," he says. "It's why you were able to separate from Slade when you did. If you had fully bonded, you would not have been able to fly away."

Everything stops around me. "You're telling me that I... *can't...* bond."

"Not completely," he says.

I shake my head. "You're wrong. I bonded. I did. I had to tell Slade the truth and it *hurt* when I left. It ripped me apart."

"*Because you love him.*" He grips both my hands. "You partially bonded, which means you can't lie to him, but it was your heart that did the rest."

I try to pull away from William, but he's surprisingly strong when he wants to be.

Unable to escape, I ask, "Why are you telling me this now?"

"Because you left part of yourself on that mountain and I can't stand to see you in pain. I made a mistake when I told Slade he didn't deserve you. I pushed him further away from you. I can't make up for that, but I can help you see the truth. You believe that you love Slade because you bonded with him. You think the choice was taken away from you. But the opposite is true. You bonded with him *because* you love him. Love came first."

I always saw bonding as an involuntary burden, something to be feared. That was Mom's experience and she passed that fear on to me. In a big way. But if William is telling the truth…

I inhale and it's like a breath of freedom.

I chose Slade.

I really chose him.

But what does that mean now that he doesn't want to be part of my life?

William says, "Your mother's experiences are not yours. Her fears don't have to be your fears. You can show Slade how you feel. That's the only way to reach him. Because… Hunter… what if Slade is the Valkyrie who loses his path?"

I jolt. "No, Slade wouldn't… He's…." *Angry. Cold. Seeks death at every opportunity.*

And he is growing more powerful every day. I sensed it when I stood outside the Realm all those mornings. He called to my deathly power like nothing ever has.

He is on the precipice.

William won't let me go. "You have to make sure he doesn't step over the edge."

"I don't know if I can."

I'm scared of how I feel. I'm scared of what Slade is becoming. I feel like a little girl right now, small and consumed by fear. Slade asked me if I loved him the night I flew away and I said 'yes.' But I didn't say the words, not willingly, not with my whole heart.

William pulls me close. "The things worth fighting for are the ones that terrify us."

Ridley might be my father—even if he is slowly coming to terms with that role—but William is like a father and brother rolled into one. I don't know what I would do without him.

"I believe in you, Hunter," he says. "You're a determined, strong woman."

I pull away from him before I turn into an emotional mess. "Thank you, William."

He taps the book in front of him. "I'll keep working on this." He stifles a powerful yawn. "But maybe after I've had a nap."

I leave the shop, feeling as if one weight has lifted from my shoulders only to be replaced with another.

Dean warned me that Slade could become a sledgehammer in my life. In fact, Vlad, Ridley, and even Lutz have been trying to warn me. I can't believe Slade would ever lose his path like that. But if he does…

I won't let him.

Determination settles inside me as I blur and release my wings, muted silver in the pre-dawn glow. They slide right through the slits Tansy created in my suit.

It takes me twenty minutes to fly to the warehouse, the chill morning air rushing against me.

Remaining blurred when I get there, I soar over the top of the rusted rooftop, noting the positions of the seven guards situated at strategic points around it. I'll have to move quickly to tranquilize each of them without raising the alarm.

Then I will deal with the brothers inside.

I don't plan on putting away my wings for this. Death can't come soon enough for these men.

CHAPTER TWENTY-EIGHT

Swooping toward the rusted rooftop, I target the guard with the sniper rifle positioned there, grabbing him from behind and dragging him into my blur so that his shout of alarm doesn't extend beyond us.

The tip of a tranquilizer meets his neck and he's out within seconds. I relocate him to the back of the building, propping him up against the wall.

Minutes later, I've snatched and deposited the remainder of the guards, positioning them in a neat row beside the first.

Most of them are older men, but some aren't much more than teenagers. Their chins rest on their chests, peaceful as I fly back to the front door. Willow promised me they will be out for hours with the potion she created for me.

Silence follows me inside the warehouse, along with the crisp morning air. There is no warmth in this place. The building is open and barren inside, a large space with a single chair in the middle of it.

Its rusted walls and wooden planks barely keep the whole structure upright. Cracked windows high above allow the new dawn's light to filter across the three brothers as they stand around a figure tied to the chair.

They are all armed with guns, although Enric is the only one dressed in combat gear. He's also the only one holding his silenced weapon pointed and ready while the other two have left their weapons in holsters at their waists.

Geno is dressed in a crisp suit, his lip curled in distaste as he stares down at his captive. Vincent is the most casual in jeans and a t-shirt, his arms crossed, tapping the blade of a dagger against his thigh, a brutal furrow in his brow.

Blood smears the knife.

Their captive is blindfolded and gagged. His ankles and wrists are zip-tied to the legs and arms of the chair. He's dressed in regular clothes and it's impossible to tell who he is.

I pause to reconsider my plan, tucking my wings into my sides. I wasn't expecting a hostage. This must be the 'situation' that they have gathered to deal with.

The third rule of the Assassin's Code makes collateral damage unacceptable. If the captive is killed, I will be stripped of my status.

Even without the rule, collateral damage is not acceptable to me on any level. My Valkyrie nature is primed to punish, but never the undeserving.

I am here to kill the brothers. Nobody else.

I was going to snatch the nearest brother into my blur and kill him with my power, then do the same with the other two, but they will open fire and aim wherever they think I am located. That didn't bother me before but now the hostage is in the way. Random bullets are not a good idea.

A cold kill is what I need now.

Vincent leans down to the captive, tapping the flat side of

the blade across the guy's chest. "You should not have made our Lady angry."

The captive shouts around his gag, the sound distorted by the material, but the brothers don't remove it. They are clearly disinterested in what he has to say.

Vincent continues, "We're going to make an example out of you."

I tuck away my wings but maintain my blur, creeping up behind Enric. I carefully position myself behind and to his right, maintaining the smallest distance between our bodies as I reach around him, mimicking his stance, my right arm outstretched, my palm curved at the same angle as his.

The hostage doesn't have long.

I take a deep breath. Focus.

I harness my power and speed so that I will move faster than Enric or his brothers can follow.

The hostage screams. He's out of time.

With rapid movements, I materialize, fold my hand over the gun, and yank Enric's arm to the right.

I pull the trigger and force his arm left. I pull the trigger again.

His brothers drop to the grimy floor without a sound, both clean shots.

Enric's reflexes kick in. He shouts, wrenching away from me, but I hold on tight enough that he breaks his own wrist, leaving the gun in my hand. My left has already closed around the spare firearm he keeps tucked in his waistband, sliding the handgun out as he moves.

The bullet from that weapon hits his lung.

I aim the gun with my left hand as he crashes to the floor. I'm not prepared to let him suffer despite everything he's done.

He stares up at me, gasping for breath. "Lady Tirelli will end you. You won't know you're trapped… until it's too late."

My jaw clenches. The weapon is steady in my hand. The trigger requires a gentle squeeze, and then it's done.

I drop both weapons to the floor and back away, checking my gloved hands, waiting to see if they tremble.

I am calm. My heart rate is even.

I'm built to kill. It's why I exist. Sudden tears burn behind my eyes. *Is killing all I'm good at?*

I swipe at my cheeks and try to focus on my next steps.

I need to free the prisoner and then get out of here. All three Tirelli brothers are dead. Lady Tirelli vowed to come after me, but now her wrath will rain down on me. I don't want to be here when she discovers them. I want her to come to me tonight when I have Vlad, Cain, and Slade for backup.

That is… if Slade is still willing to be my backup.

The guy in the blindfold shouts around his gag, struggling against his bindings.

I shush him, making sure my face mask is in place before I pull off his blindfold. If he sees what I'm doing he won't be afraid that I'm going to kill him. Especially since I need to use my blade to cut the ties.

"You're okay now," I say.

His gaze snaps to the dead bodies around us. He yanks at the zip-ties, struggling and snarling against his gag. I pull it off and bend to release one of his feet.

He hisses, "Hurry up and untie me."

I slow down, not quite cutting the tie from his ankle. I made sure this guy didn't end up as collateral damage but I have no idea why he's here. I assumed he was a victim like so many others but the cold expression in his eyes doesn't fit with innocence.

He's shaking but he isn't terrified… he's angry.

"I said hurry up!"

Hmm.

I keep my voice low, maintaining the appearance of working at the binding around his ankle as I ask, "Why were they holding you?"

His lips twist. "Lady Tirelli doesn't like ground glass in the drugs. She doesn't understand that it keeps profits high."

"It can also kill people, can't it?" I ask.

He snarls, "Get me out of here before she turns up."

I sigh inwardly. He is not an innocent victim after all.

I rise to my feet, leaving him where he is while I consider the technicalities of the collateral damage rule.

I didn't tie him up so… it can't count as collateral damage if I do nothing to free him. Especially if I'm long gone by the time Lady Tirelli arrives. If the police get to him first, he'll be lucky.

He shouts as I back away. "Hey! You're not going to leave me here, are you?"

"Actually, I am—"

My skin prickles a mere second before the air shifts beside me.

Thump.

The guy's head whips backward. Then he slowly tips forward, revealing the dagger lodged neatly in his forehead.

Shock forces me backward.

The weapon came out of nowhere!

I spin, but there's nobody there, nobody near me, no lingering aura, not even the outline of a blurred figure. I don't smell roses so it can't be the presence from the shop.

I brace, ready to take cover… until I see what's engraved on the dagger's hilt.

It's just like Cain's. Except that the stylized initials are not.

SB.

Slade Baines.

A cold kill...

Slade materializes beside me, his presence like a thud to the air and a quiet breeze at the same time.

I can't believe his blur is as good as mine. I had no idea he was standing there. None at all. Even the blurred presence in the shop, whose invisibility was the most complete that I've come across, was no comparison to this.

He retrieves his dagger before I have time to take a breath. He is focused, cold, the need to kill radiating off him in waves with such power that I hardly recognize him.

I shiver at how quiet he is, my skin tingling as his power reaches out to me. It's a mirror to my own darkness, the force that can draw life from a person. It hits me so hard that my wings almost unfold in reaction to the call.

I rip off my face mask, trying not to shout, trying harder to quell my inner nature. He just killed a bystander and I have no idea what the consequences will be.

I whisper-shout, "I wasn't in danger. You didn't have to do that."

Slade pockets the blade, but his focus remains on the dead man. His voice doesn't sound like his own, making me tremble at the deep tones that sing through me.

"Don't worry, Hunter. He isn't collateral damage. He was my mission: a sanctioned kill. I didn't want to interrupt you or I would have broken the sixth rule."

That's the rule about assassins interfering in assassinations. To break it means that the aggrieved Master is entitled to draw blood from the other. If he had interrupted me, I would have been entitled to fight him. It was why Mom gave her katana to Ridley all that time ago.

"I waited for you to end your targets," he says. "I haven't broken any rules."

The energy around him is darker than I've sensed before. It is cold, hard, unfeeling, *inhuman*.

It is all Valkyrie.

Now my hands are shaking.

He spins without looking at me and I sense him drawing on his blur, ready to disappear again. He hasn't looked at me, has barely acknowledged me.

This is not Slade.

It confirms the warnings I've been given: Slade is losing himself. The man standing in front of me—this cold assassin —is not the man I fell in love with and I won't let that man slip away.

Dean told me I didn't really try before. Well… now I'm going to give it everything I've got.

"No!" My back shifts and my wings shoot out, powerful and strong, piercing the air. My right wing strikes across the space in front of Slade, stopping his forward step.

He always did everything he could to avoid fighting me.

I'm changing that. Right now.

He stares at the glittering mass of my wings before he turns to me, slow and dangerous. "No?"

He finally looks at me, the lights from my wings reflected in his eyes, which are gleaming and cold.

I snarl, "I wasn't finished here. You broke the sixth rule. You will fight me, Slade. I demand it."

A smile breaks across his face as he meets my eyes. His are full of silver, glowing like a predator's in the night. His gaze tracks from my face to my silvery wings. Then back to my lips. His own curve and soften while his pupils darken.

Oh, damn.

The way his gaze caresses me turns my legs to liquid. He takes a step toward me, his voice a husky growl as he says, "You have beautiful wings."

He shivers. Power rips through him and a shimmering, silver mass appears before my eyes, shooting outward from his shoulders, cutting across the space on either side of us.

A scream grows in my throat, strangling within me.

Wings!

He has wings.

Glowing, silver, transparent, not-quite there, made up of streaks of Valkyrie power like electrical currents running through the air. Not solid like mine. Not metallic like mine. But… wings.

"Hunter Cassidy," he says. "I accept the challenge."

CHAPTER TWENTY-NINE

My heart has stopped and I can't breathe, but he doesn't wait for me to recover, coming straight at me.

My instincts fire and I evade the fist Slade aims at my face as well as the next he aims for my shoulder and then my side. I step, duck, and side-step again, my wings tucked tight to my sides, my arms shooting up between us to block each blow.

I press against him as he presses forward, our forearms locked against each other while he scrutinizes me through the gap between our limbs.

He's testing my strength and reflexes, as well as his own. He comes at me faster and this time I retaliate, my fists blurring, connecting, crashing into his side and chest.

He takes the blows, absorbs them, and keeps coming. We crash into the side of the building, cracking one of the supports.

Ducking his fist as it smacks into the broken wood, I switch to attack mode, tucking my head down and barreling into him, spreading my wings at the same time. I catch him and soar upward, powerful beats taking us higher.

His wings curve, upsetting my flight arc, forcing us into a somersault. Tumbling through the air, we spin upward and hit the ceiling.

Rusty metal sheeting busts at the seams, groaning under the force of the impact. Slade ends up with his back against it, my body pressed up against his in an effort to pin him there.

There's only one way I'm going to get through to him, to get past his power, and it involves placing my hands on his face.

He struggles, the ceiling creaks, and I use everything at my disposal—arms, legs, shoulders—to keep him in place as I slide a hand toward his temple.

Unfortunately, I don't succeed in pinning his arms. He wraps them around me, expands his wings against the ceiling and uses them to push off it.

Suddenly, I'm the one who is captive.

I hurry to let go and fly backward, trying to pull out of the closing circle of his arms. He follows my every move, blocking the fist I aim squarely at his jaw and the next I aim for his stomach.

We're evenly matched. We always were. Even before I gave him my power, he could detect my weaknesses, my strengths, and match me.

There's only one thing I can do.

I rapidly switch approach and dart forward, wrap my arms around him, and spin, using my wings to propel us around so fast that it takes him a moment to recalibrate.

His wings become his enemy as they pull him off balance. He tries to tuck them into his sides, but it's too late.

As we spin, I propel us upward, bending one arm to protect my head and brace for impact.

We break through the roof, the metal sheeting ripping apart, nails popping as we spiral upward. He draws breath, landing a hit to my side in an effort to free himself. The air whooshes out of my lungs at the power behind his fist, but I'm not done, not by a long shot.

As soon as we clear the roof, I beat my wings, force us forward, and then... *down*.

We crash back through the metal sheeting, iron and wood splitting and cracking, debris falling around us as I propel us straight at the floor.

At the last moment, I wrap my wings around him, cocooning him.

We hit the ground.

The impact shudders through me. Cracks in the floor shatter out from us. Only my wings prevent us from breaking every bone in our bodies.

Slade's wings disappear on impact.

He roars and his power strikes through me in a protective instinct, the killing force burning agony through my arms, chest, and legs, but I won't let him go.

He's lying on my wings, his body weight trapping himself within them. For now.

I have seconds before he breaks free of my grasp. Seconds to make the connection. The power shrieking through him is building, screaming through us both but I won't release him.

I will never let him push me away again.

I slap my hand against his temple. *"You will come back to me!"*

Diving deep into his mind, I seize control of his emotions and memories, sensing him tense and freeze where he lies half beside me, half under me, the breath hitching in his lungs, his big chest rising and falling beneath mine.

He struggles but I have control now. Just like I took control of Fallon. Just like Mom took control of me when I was little and I couldn't regulate my power by myself—when I was a danger to myself and everyone around me.

Everything depends on the connection I make now, on the memories I find. I need a memory strong enough to calm his power... but as I dive deeper, a cry grows inside my throat.

I wasn't prepared for this.

His mind is filled with painful turmoil. Images swarm around me—hot, burning memories that cut me like razors.

Go, Hunter. Don't look back.

You don't deserve her.

Nothing good happens when you're near me.

Is it possible that you're my match?

Not wings. Please not wings.

What am I?

Then rage. Pure rage.

I force myself beneath the turmoil to the memory driving his anger—a memory so shattered that only shards remain, like the pieces of a broken mirror.

Slade has tried to destroy what he remembers about his brother's death with every kill, every powerful blow of fist on skin, every turn of a dagger, and every shot from a gun.

The images settle and pull together, watery but perceptible.

His brother stands in the middle of a kitchen, one fist clenched around a knife. He's dressed in black, an arsenal of weapons strapped around his waist and chest.

I know right away that it's Slade's home. The kitchen

smells like cinnamon. Floral dish towels hang across the oven door and a child's drawings decorate the front of the refrigerator. It's dark outside the far window. The lights inside the room are dimmed.

I'm looking at it from a child's height through a crack in a door—through Slade's eyes. His breathing is sharp, on edge. He should be asleep but voices woke him.

His brother looks about eighteen. He has the same blue eyes as Slade, the same physique, but he's beautiful in a way that Slade is not, as if he got all the perfect angles while Slade got all the harsh ones.

His brother snaps, "Don't deny our purpose!"

The image swings to the woman pressed up against the sink. Tears streak down her cheeks. "We don't want this for you. We left it behind to give you a better life."

"You can't change what we are, Mom! This is what I was born to do. I will prove myself."

She propels herself off the sink. She moves so fast that I can hardly follow the movements. Her hand strikes out, twists, and within seconds she has disarmed him.

He stumbles backward, but rights himself with an angry glare at her.

She hisses, "What you're up against is faster than I am, Foster." She pitches the knife into the top of the kitchen table where it sticks and quivers. "You won't survive. She will kill you. Please. *Don't do this.*"

His lips compress into an ugly line. "You can't stop me."

He spins and strides from the room, leaving the knife where it is.

"No, Foster!" She darts after him but then her gaze lands on the door. "Slade?" Her eyes widen. "No… Slade!"

The image spins. Slade darts backward, taking me with

him, and then he's running. He's fast at ten years of age. Faster than his mom.

"Slade!" Her voice fades into the background as the images blur and become tangled… the back door… grass… a fence he scales easily, chasing after his brother, running to catch the darkened figure who sprints like a panther through the streets, never tiring, never stopping.

The images crack and shift, disjointed again, splitting and trying to pull apart. I fight to force them together so I can see what he saw…

It's an alley, dark and dirty.

Two figures struggle inside it—his brother and a woman. I try to see her face, but it's too dark. She uses every available space to fight back but always remains in the shadows.

Slade takes a step forward. A shout sticks in his throat. He wants to fight, to help his brother.

The image wobbles as he darts along the alley toward them, but a dagger thuds into the wall in front of him, the gleaming blade right at his eye level.

An inch to the left and Slade would have died. The breath stops in his lungs and my own burn with him.

The woman screams, a sound of terrible pain. Her back arches. A flash of light brightens the alley and at the same time, her silhouette changes. Her wings shoot outward, glowing so brightly that Slade shields his eyes.

Smoke fills my lungs, stinging like acid.

The image cracks again. There are pieces missing. I search for them but Slade has ground them into dust, granules that scatter at the base of the next image.

The woman is gone. His brother groans on the ground. Slade's young voice tears at my heart. "Foster!"

Blood bubbles up through his brother's lips. Foster grabs

Slade and pulls him closer, pressing something into Slade's hand.

The image splits again. Nothing is clear now, only a single feeling: the cold thing that Foster gave him slips out of Slade's hand. He lets it fall. He doesn't want it.

His cry spirals into the night.

I've seen all there is to see. Slade has obliterated the missing pieces, crushing them at every opportunity. I turn away from them, seeking the memory that will counter the darkness.

I find one—a memory from a year before his brother's death. It's inside his family's bakery, when Slade felt safe, sunlight streaming over freshly baked apple muffins, his brother laughing and eating them when he shouldn't while their mom shoos the boys away…

Even with all his rage, Slade still smells like cinnamon.

I draw out the warmth and comfort in that memory and use it to flood his mind now, pushing back against the need to kill. I know it's working when Slade thumps the ground with his fist.

I risk a glance. He has torn his hand against my wings, leaving a bloody smudge on them.

He roars into the echoing space around us as parts of the ceiling continue to fall. "I didn't want this power!"

Some of the silver has disappeared from his eyes, but not all of it. He's still in danger, but for the first time this morning, it seems that he actually sees me.

He lifts both his hands to cup my face. "Hunter. I didn't want this."

I'm hesitant as I ask, "Slade?"

"I need your help. I can't control it."

It was my fault this happened. I made a choice, I gave him

my feather, and then I didn't stay with him to protect him from the consequences.

I should have stayed. "You have me. Always."

Slowly, I test the strength of the memory from his childhood by removing my fingertips from his temple, but the second I disconnect, the power inside him surges and his eyes flood with silver again.

"No!" I can't let it take over again.

I quickly press my fingers back to his temple, diving into his consciousness, but this time I need a stronger memory. One that will give him the power to overcome the darkness.

I'm surprised when the whirl of images slows and pinpoints something I wasn't expecting...

We're lying on a bed together, him and me. He's stroking my hair, his fingertips brushing my neck. His lips press gently against my forehead. It's the briefest moment in time, but it's enough that when I check his eyes again, they're clear blue, stronger than before, but filled with confusion and dread.

"I don't know what I am now," he says.

I leave my fingertips where they are, gently brushing his temple, not disconnecting, holding the memory at the forefront of his mind so we can talk.

"You're Slade Baines, Master of the Legion," I say. "You're the man I bonded with."

He shifts his bleeding hand to stroke the hair from my face. "I thought that if I stayed away from you, I could control this power. I thought that being around you would make it worse. Even though I wanted to be with you with every shred of my soul."

"Slade..." I dare to press my cheek to his, holding my

breath in case he pulls away, but he doesn't. His breathing is slow and even.

"You have Valkyrie power now, but you can control it," I say. "The same way I control it."

He nods against my cheek, a day's growth of fine stubble grazing my skin. "I need you to show me how."

I draw back a little, but not far. I need to show him all the things that Mom taught me from the day I was born: how to control my power, how to subdue it, when to use it, when *not* to use it.

My voice falters. "I can teach you. But learning control means trusting me. Can you do that?"

I hold my breath. He can already blur like me, kill like me, hunt like me. If he chooses to, he could give in to the power's seductive nature and then he would become a monster.

Even though I can't kill him, but the Keres ring can. It would shatter what's left of my heart to use it.

His response is to very carefully, very slowly, cover my hand with his, pressing it closer to his temple. His palm is even more calloused than the last time he touched me. I picture him beating his open palms against wooden planks, trying to rid himself of the Valkyrie rage that has slowly taken over his mind.

His assassin's ring glows for a moment and I tense as a wash of colors spills across the air above us, as if what remains of the ceiling is descending and changing, the walls closing in and morphing into something else.

At first I'm afraid that the building is finally collapsing but the sudden quiet says otherwise.

My breath trembles between my lips. "What are you doing?"

"Please, don't be afraid," he says. "I need a place without death in it."

A blue sky forms above us, cool and crisp. A warm beach takes shape. Pristine sand stretches in both directions, crystal clear water lapping gently a few paces away while the hush of the ocean fills my ears.

I quickly carry out a visual check of our new surroundings. We're still in a lying position. His back rests against my wings, which in turn are cushioned in sand. His dark hair is a charcoal smudge against the white grains.

I gasp. "This is a Realm."

It's not a sub-Realm, not a small creation, but an entire expanse stretching out in every direction, its peaceful calm washing over us. "How did you create this?"

"The Guardian gave me the most powerful assassin's ring, formed from the feather of the Valkyrie Queen herself," he says. "According to the records, this ring was used to create the three Realms. Other assassins can create sub-realms within a Realm. But I can create a whole Realm from nothing."

The Guardian had offered me the ring that Slade now wears, telling me that I could accomplish magic never before seen. The power in that ring calls to me, a reflection of the Valkyrie Queen's soul. I wish I knew what became of her—and all the other Valkyrie who perished before my time.

Slade slips an arm around my lower back beneath my wings, but he isn't trying to push me away this time. He leverages us onto our sides, careful to ensure that my fingertips never leave his temple, before he draws us upright without breaking the connection.

I fold away my wings.

His gaze is piercing. "I don't want to become something I'm not. Please, tell me what to do."

CHAPTER THIRTY

I let out the breath I was holding. "I need you to close your eyes and see what I see, even if it hurts you to remember…"

His arms remain around me, pulling me close. He shuts his eyes and I sense him relax, allowing me to immerse myself in his mind again.

It's the same process that I used when he was unconscious in the men's shower room on our first night in the Realm. Mom did this for me over and over when I was a child, calming me whenever I was out of control. Now that I'm an adult, I can repeat the process for myself, just like Slade will be able to do once he knows how.

I dive beneath the turmoil, past the greatest dark, steering clear of the memory of his brother's death this time. I seek only the brightest memories… the bakery… the day he stroked my hair… and finally… the brightest and strongest…

The first day at the Realm.

He is stripped nearly naked, cold, colder than he's ever been before. Rain drips down his chest, washing away the pain and sweat as he holds that damn plank of wood above his shoulders.

Pain strikes through him, wracking every inch of his arms and back. He wants to break the record but he doesn't know how much longer he can keep holding it.

In the present, I'm confused because I don't understand how this is a source of light in his life. I was drawn to this memory by its brightness, its ability to banish the dark, but nothing I see here resembles happiness.

Then his focus shifts inside the memory. I see what he saw.

Me.

I stand in the rain, my mahogany hair plastered down my back, the heavy log gripped and elevated above my shoulders higher than the other Novices held it, my muscles straining, trembling. I refuse to let go. Refuse to show any pain as Master Gareth goads me and insults me with his every breath.

I stand upright, and no matter what Gareth says, his abuse washes off me with the raindrops.

Slade's voice is a husky whisper in the present. "You didn't break."

I open my eyes to find him looking at me now with his own eyes. There is no silver light in them, no deadly power. It is all gone. He is completely in control.

He sees me.

He sees me now the same way he saw me on that first day.

I search for any sign of Valkyrie power, opening my senses to detect any hint of an uncontrolled surge that might rise and overwhelm him again.

I don't want to lose him to that power. Never again. I won't disconnect until I'm sure he can control it himself.

I whisper as the ocean laps at the sand, "Do you *feel* that memory?"

His response is hoarse. "Yes."

"You need to draw on that feeling whenever the Valkyrie power surges. The memory will calm the power so you can control it."

He waits for me to say more. "That's it?"

"That's all you have to do. Try it."

I dive with him toward the brightness of that moment, the flood of calm that comes with it, the moment when I entered his life.

Slowly, I draw away from it, leaving him submerged in the memory. I very carefully remove my fingertips from his face, giving him the chance to control it by himself.

He remains calm. He opens his eyes again, focused on me.

The sound of the waves lapping at the sand is all that breaks the silence.

"Remember that you're always in control," I say. "The power doesn't control you. It can't take over again. Not while you remember that moment. You are not a monster, Slade, and you never will be."

His lips press together. "The Furies called me an abomination. You know I could become something terrible, Hunter."

"So could I. Do you understand? But I won't become that person and neither will you." My voice breaks. "Promise me you believe me?"

He doesn't answer. Our bodies are pressed together, our chests and thighs smashed against each other.

Now that the danger is over, I'm suddenly aware of how

close we're standing to each other. His arms remain around me. Not tight. I could pull away if I wanted to, but I… don't… want to.

His voice breaks. "You flew away."

I suck in a breath. He's talking about the night on the mountain.

I try to remain still. "You told me to go."

He searches my eyes. "You were afraid to stay."

"I didn't want to hurt you," I say. "I didn't want to remind you of what you lost."

He doesn't move away from me. "It hurt more when you left."

Neither of us moves.

Quietly, he says, "I need to ask you something."

My jaw clenches. I try to stop the fear striking through me, but I can't stop how trapped I feel about telling him the truth. "You know I have to answer you honestly."

He winces, a moment of pain strikes through his expression, but he asks, "I need to know… how old you are."

That's all he wants to know?

"I'm twenty years old. The same as you."

He exhales heavily, as if he was holding his breath. His shoulders sink and his eyes close. Whatever I just said, it's had a big impact on him and I have no idea why.

"What does my age have to do with anything?"

He pauses. "It means you didn't kill my brother."

"You thought *what*?" My shocked exclamation escapes my lips before I can stop it. Indignation rises fast inside me.

I pull back but he doesn't let me go, holding me tight now.

I grip both his shoulders with a cry, "How could you think that I could look you in the eyes, *sleep beside you*, if I'd done that? I didn't know anything about your brother until you told me."

His emotions rise to meet mine. He doesn't try to justify his fears and I hate that I see the logic in them. Valkyrie women live longer than humans and we don't lose our youthful appearance. If I was pretending to be the same age as him, then I could have killed his brother ten years ago and I could still appear to be twenty years old now.

Sharp pain suddenly rips into my heart. If that's what he was thinking when he told me to go... that it might have been *me* who tore his life apart...

His response to my indignation is raw and painful but it's not what I expect.

"How could you think I'd take the Keres ring and kill you?"

Shock shoots through me. I'd offered the ring to him freely. I told him he could kill me with it. My intention was to make sure he knew he didn't have to be afraid of me, but it was only when I did that, that the mask fell over his face. Not before. Not even when he thought I might have killed his brother.

The corners of his mouth turn down. "When you handed me that ring, you broke my heart."

I inhale sharply. My own heart is breaking all over again.

The tension in his hand, the way he tugs me, pulling me closer, tells me he wants to ask me something else. He knows that I will have to answer truthfully but the storm of emotions in his eyes tells me he doesn't want to know the answer.

He asks, "Did you really think that I could kill you?"

He holds his breath, waiting for me to confirm or deny my feelings.

My fears.

I can't stop the truth. The single reply rips out of me. "Yes."

He flinches as if I crushed him. He recoils from me, sucking in a sharp breath, dropping my hand, and removing his arms.

The mask falls over his features again.

He takes slow steps away from me, one foot after the other, placing deliberate distance between us until he reaches the edge of the water. It laps at his boots, washing them clean with every swipe in the same way I want my past wiped clean.

My heart sinks as I witness the impact of my confession on him. It's taken me far too long to realize that the trigger for his emotional shield is not anger—because he's never been afraid to show rage—and it's not the absence of emotions, it's not coldness toward me.

It's *pain*.

It's why the Valkyrie power took hold of him so easily. It feeds on pain. He's fighting it hard now. He closes his eyes for a moment, taking deep breaths until he's calm again.

He's remembering me that first day. Not as I am now.

His eyes flash open. "Trust goes both ways, Hunter. I can trust you all I want, but you have to trust me, too."

My heart hurts. My chest burns. "I want to, but I can't."

I thought I could learn to trust him. For a long time, I told myself I did. I told Cain that I trusted Slade with my life. I insisted to William that giving Slade my feather was a risk I wouldn't regret.

But then Slade told me about his brother. He showed me that his greatest fear... is *me*.

What I have to admit is that he is my greatest fear, too.

Loving him is the most dangerous thing I have ever done.

He is quiet now, resigned, shoulders slumped. "Why can't you trust me, Hunter?"

No!

I clutch my stomach, trying to fight the answer—the whole terrible mess of it. I'm wired to respond to him no matter what. Whatever partial bond I have with him forces me to speak.

His head shoots up, eyes wide, but it's too late for him to take it back.

The truth is a burning knife in my throat. "Because Mom bonded with Gareth and he killed her. He said he loved her, but he stepped over her dying body and stole the Keres feather from her."

I gasp a painful breath. "He forced her to kill herself. All because she was trying to protect the Keres girl. She protected that girl instead of protecting me, instead of staying alive for me, and I'm angry at her because she betrayed my trust, too."

I'm shaking but I can't stop. "Now I have to tell you the truth and you'll kill me just like Gareth killed Mom. No matter what I do. No matter what I want. So why not make it quick? Why not give you the ring so you can make it less painful for both of us when the time comes…"

I fight to breathe. Grip my stomach.

I double over. Hot tears stream down my cheeks.

I scream out the pain, emptying my lungs into the silence, my cry washing out with the waves.

He knows the truth now and so do I, all of it ripped out of me so that I have to face it.

I sob, "Please… please… don't ask me any more questions."

He is suddenly right in front of me, reaching out for me, pulling me upright, pressing me against his chest. He strokes my hair as our feet sink into the sand, calming movements as my head nestles into the crook of his neck and my tears drip against his throat.

I need to stop crying. I can't lose control more than I already have. He's okay now. He's in control of his power. And this is when I have to fly away again…

He trails gentle kisses down the side of my face, drawing back to brush his thumb across my cheek, smoothing away my tears. I gasp as shivers race through me, tingling down my spine. His assassin's ring rests against my cheekbone. It glows from the corner of my eye, soft silver like the highlights that have returned to Slade's eyes.

The pull toward him is so strong. When he brushes his lips across my forehead, the burn in my back becomes agony. He has barely touched me but it's enough to ignite the partial bond I formed with him.

His voice is a hoarse whisper. "You tried to talk to me after the Guardian was attacked and I wouldn't let you because I was afraid of what I wanted. You told me once that you want me in your life. I want you in my life, too, Hunter."

A shiver rocks me so hard that I shudder against him. I can't allow myself to connect with him again, because if I do, it will shred me into tiny pieces when he pushes me away.

I can't stop the moan of pain escaping my lips. I clamp my hand over my mouth to smother the sound.

He drops another kiss on the back of my hand where it rests against my mouth before coaxing my fingers away from my face.

"Stop fighting it, Hunter. I understand now why you were

afraid. We pushed each other away before. I won't let that happen again."

I squeeze my eyes closed, fighting everything I want. "There are no halfway measures for me. I can't turn this off again. It hurt too much the first time—"

My eyes fly open as his lips brush mine, the barest, tingling touch, a gentle question planted on my mouth.

"You're the reason I'm alive," he says. "You're the reason I have a memory to cling to." A slow smile lifts one corner of his mouth. "And it's not even my favorite one."

My heart skips a beat. I shake my head at him. "You…"

I lean forward, my lips unbearably close to his. Our lower halves are still pushed together but I know he'll let me go if I ask him to.

I press the lightest kiss against the corner of his mouth, sensing him shiver, before I whisper, "I need to tell you something."

He nuzzles my cheek with his. "Hmm?"

"I love you, Slade Baines."

I hold my breath, not sure of his reaction. He almost told me he loved me at the Fury's cabin, but I have no reason to believe he will reciprocate now after everything that has happened. I have to accept that he might not. It's his choice. The same way it's my choice to say what I'm feeling now.

He is suddenly reserved. "Because you bonded to me."

I pull back, gripping his shoulders. "No. That's different."

He must think I love him because I'm compelled to. The same way I believed I was forced into bonding. "Mom bonded with Gareth, but she didn't love him. That's not the way it is for me with you."

I sigh and press another kiss to his lips. "I love you. Not because I have to. Not because I bonded with you. But because you're my match and I'll be there for you whenever you need me."

His gaze has softened. He is open to me, perhaps for the very first time.

His voice binds me to the spot. "I tried so hard, for so long, not to hurt you. But what I should have done... is love you."

His lips curve into a smile. He doesn't kiss me again. Instead, he separates us but holds out his hand to me. "Will you come with me? I want to give you something."

I answer him by wrapping my fingers around his and following him from the beach.

CHAPTER THIRTY-ONE

We pass the tree line where the nature of our surroundings changes, the palm tree fronds spreading high above us to form a canopy that drops us into cool shadow.

The ground beneath our feet transforms from sand to soft moss. The cool breeze wafts around us, ruffling the strands of my hair that have come loose.

Up ahead, I make out the shape of a shaded wooden gazebo.

Slade adjusts the environment as we walk, as if he's still perfecting it, creating new trees and a pathway and, as we approach, a curling vine that grows rapidly up the mahogany beams that form the gazebo.

Flowers spring to life along the vines, dripping down the structure's sides in a rainbow of colors. Wild tulips sprout beside the path, mingling with lilacs, white lilies, daffodils, and orchids.

He pauses to scoop up a bunch of gardenias, handing

them to me before he stops further along the path in front of the structure.

The gazebo bursts with flowers and the scent in the air is heavenly.

He stands uncertainly in front of the blooming structure, a killing machine surrounded by impossible beauty of his own creation. "This is for you."

I press the gardenias to my lips, inhaling the wild scent. "I… Nobody has ever… This is…" *Amazing. Beautiful. Kind.*

He takes a deep breath. "The memory that shaped my life is a violent one. You grapple with nightmares, too. We are both assassins. Both Masters. I want to give you more than that."

My heart swells. *Is this what being loved feels like?*

I swallow. "Can you make me new clothes? I don't want to stand here in this." Not with the blood of my enemies staining my assassin's suit. Violence doesn't belong in this place.

The corner of his mouth rises, a smile growing on his lips. "Sure, but you have to take those off first."

I break into an answering smile, ready to do as he asks without any hesitation, but as soon as I tug on the suit, he turns his back to give me privacy.

I peel off the protective layer, bumps rising across my arms and legs in the cool breeze. Dropping the suit to the ground, I stand in my underwear the same as the day he first saw me.

He hears the material drop and turns around, but keeps his eyes closed. His features relax and his powerful arms rest at his sides.

I whisper, "Don't you need to see me?"

He smiles with his eyes closed. "I remember everything about you."

A shiver runs through me as a swath of delicate white material appears in the air, gliding in the breeze to layer itself across my shoulders and torso. It falls in a caress across my hips and outer thighs, shifting and conforming to my shape, the lightest whisper against my skin.

I gasp as a ripple runs through the material down my spine, as if he ran both his hands from my shoulders to my hips. My breathing quickens, but he continues to concentrate, shaping the dress around me.

A sash winds carefully around my waist, trailing in a motion that reminds me of his fingertips stroking my stomach until it settles into place. Then the edges of material tuck in around my torso to form a bodice, the lightest brush of material across my collarbone and between my breasts sending shivers to my toes.

I check his expression but he's doing it again… that thing where he doesn't realize he's touching me while he works. He is fully immersed in his task.

The dress lengthens around my legs, the folds brushing my knees and calves. Still, he's not done. Gauzy material takes the shape of white lilies, appearing one by one across the sash at my waist and down my left leg. They form with excruciating care one at a time, each one pressed momentarily against the sensitive skin of my stomach, then my lower hip bone, my upper thigh and then just a little too close to...

I gasp.

He freezes, his shoulders tensing as if he came back to himself. "Sorry."

What is there to be sorry about? I'm thrumming. Tremors

and tingles scatter across my body where the silken material whispers in the breeze as if he's running his fingertips through every fold. "Slade?"

"Yes?"

"Open your eyes."

He does as I ask, standing quietly for a moment, drinking me in before he says, "But I'm not finished."

He runs his hand downward in the air and flowers appear in a wash all the way to the base of the dress, the sensation of that many forming at once leaving me gasping.

He holds out his hand again with a satisfied smile. "Will you walk with me, Hunter? I want to show you everything."

I close the gap, curling my palm around his big hand and pulling his arm around my waist, crushing the silken flowers between us. "There will be no walking."

I press my lips against his, sensing his indrawn breath before he claims my lips and kisses me back with a ferocity of his own.

His movements while he created the dress might have been unconscious but now every move he makes is aware and deliberate. A fire ignites between us as he runs his hands into my hair, tugging it free to flow down my back.

His hands mimic what I felt when he dressed me, running from my shoulder blades to my hips, his thumbs grazing across my sensitive curves, rising to rest around my ribs while he continues to kiss me.

He lifts me off my feet, dropping kisses on every inch of my face as he walks us off the path into the wildflowers. A thick bed of petals form across the ground and he carefully lowers us into a kneeling position onto them, our bodies pressed together.

I tip my head back as he kisses my neck and nuzzles my

ear. The flowers are soft beneath my knees, the dress a gauzy pool floating across the ground. It has no clasps, no way to remove it.

I pull back with a hopeful smile, but only for a moment before I kiss him again, drawing breath to whisper, "Dress?"

He smiles against my lips. "I created it. I can remove it."

A delicious shiver runs through me but he immediately becomes serious, his palms pausing against my back. Even that pressure is unbearable, igniting my need for more.

He growls, "But I'm not sure I want to. I didn't create this place so I could be with you. I made it *for* you. As a gift."

I press my cheek against his, soaking in all the hard lines of his face as well as his perfectly sculpted chest beneath my hands, sensing his pounding heart.

"Also, I didn't come prepared," he murmurs.

I smother a smile. "No surprises in your boot?"

He shakes his head.

"Then you should know that diseases don't survive in our bodies," I say. "Valkyrie don't get sick. And… since I can't lie to you, I want you to know that I've taken measures to make sure there are no unexpected bundles of joy either."

My cheeks flame. Talking about contraception is harder than I expected. Somehow harder than telling him I love him.

All of this seems to be a revelation to him. "So… all those times I stayed away from you…" He brushes his smiling lips against mine, before he becomes serious again. "I'm not sorry we waited so long. And I won't be sorry to wait again."

I wrap my arms around him in a fierce hug. "I love this place. It's the most beautiful gift anyone has ever given me." I meet his eyes, just as serious as he is. "I can't think of anything I want to do more than be with you here."

I press my lips to his. Whatever reservations he had, however much he was holding back, his guard seems to disappear, the intensity of his kiss leaving me breathless.

I respond with a need of my own, tugging at his protective suit. His strength and power have called to me ever since I returned to Boston. Staying away from him is torture. Waiting for him to let me into his life has been torture.

We're still kneeling on the flowers, a perfumed cushion beneath my knees. I peel the protective suit off his arms and torso, but I force myself to take it slow, keeping my breathing even, leaving the suit pooled at his waist so I can explore his chest and shoulders, the muscles in his forearms and biceps. All the way to his fingertips and the callouses on his palms, which I kiss one by one.

I inhale the scent of his skin, dropping kisses along the curve of his neck, tracing his jaw to his lips.

He shivers.

I pause, my lips so close to his.

I raise my eyes, discovering that I am his sole focus, his gaze pinpoint.

His lips part as if he's about to speak, but then he smiles instead and sweeps us upward to our feet, peeling the suit all the way off. My underwear follows, his fingertips grazing my legs.

He leaves the dress where it is, taking his time kissing me everywhere through the diaphanous material, his lips whispering across my skin until I'm burning.

I arch against him, needing the material off. He gives me another smile that sends my heart into overdrive as the sash around my waist slides across my skin, unwinding, but this time he follows it with his fingertips, the lightest touches.

The bodice gently splits at the sides, leaving my breasts covered, but parting to allow him to kiss and stroke the curve at the top of my hips. One shoulder strap finally separates beneath his touch, the material falling as he follows the curves of my body all the way to my waist.

As soon as the next one falls, I press my naked chest against his, needing more.

I whisper against his lips, "Slade?"

"Hmm?"

He is still so much in control, taking our movements one moment at a time, but I'm already lost.

I can't voice my thoughts—that I need him, want him, not just like this, but in my life.

I kiss him instead, drawing my hands through his hair the same way he tangles his fingers in mine. My hands descend to his shoulders, his shoulder blades, and the places on either side of his back where his wings can emerge.

I taste his sudden inhale, the charge that runs through him, as if my power touched his. I draw back to meet his eyes, exhaling quietly, challenging his control before I kiss him again.

He groans against my mouth and the dress finally separates as he deftly lowers us to the ground. He positions my legs around him so I'm straddling his hips, but he remains sitting, his chest pressed against mine.

Our bodies swiftly join.

He holds my gaze as I spiral, my heart barely in one piece.

Silver highlights glow in his eyes, his power reaching out to me, our strength matched as we move together.

I gasp against the force rising inside me, responding to both his human and Valkyrie sides.

He's breathing rapidly but controlling it, his hands flexing against my back. The silver lights in his eyes grow brighter. The environment around us shivers, a ripple flowing through the flowers, transforming the rainbow of colors into silvery white, as if we're sitting on a bed made of a million stars.

My back burns. So badly. But my wings won't release. I know that now, even though knowing and feeling are two different things. I arch against him, drowning in the need to bond, to give all of myself to him, trying to anchor myself somehow.

He senses my need and places both his hands over mine, planting my palms firmly against his chest, one covering his pounding heart.

His eyes meet mine. He inhales. Closes his eyes. Gives over control of our movements to me, letting me take charge.

As soon as I move against him, a glimmer grows around his shoulders, stronger than the light in his eyes, taking shape as the force between us becomes unbearable.

He exhales.

I sense a force ripple through him and then…

His wings burst from his back.

The glittering mass extends across the field of flowers. A thousand petals break free around us, disturbed by the electrical force, floating upward, dazzling in the air.

His wings…

His wings released…

It's too much. So much. His heartbeat becomes mine. My movements become his.

I cry as I crash. He follows me and everything shatters between us, my sense of time and space expand, the Realm contracts, and nothing else exists.

I descend into his arms. My heart pounds as I wrap my arms around him. He holds me close, stroking my back, soothing my shoulders, easing the burn in them as if he senses it.

His wings close around me, a protective force, and instantly, I'm grounded inside the safest place I've found in years—a place he gave me.

He kisses my cheeks, my forehead, and then my lips, only drawing back when I press my hand to his heart. The deep rhythm thrums through me, speeding up at my touch. When I brush my lips against his, his heart kicks in his chest, a rapid *thud-thud*.

He gives me a small smile, vulnerable despite his ferocity. "I bonded with you, didn't I?"

Tears burn at the back of my eyes, escaping when I close them. He bonded with me in a way that I can never bond with him.

He brushes the tears away from my cheeks, kissing them carefully.

"I meant it when I said your wings are beautiful," he says. "I wasn't in control of anything else when we were fighting, but that part was me."

I curl into him and we stay like that for a long time. Then he helps me stand, retrieves his clothing and the sash that remains of the dress, and draws me inside the gazebo.

He pulls me gently down onto the large pillows there, urging me close again. My upper leg curls over his as he strokes my hair, fanning it out over the soft surface.

I don't want to break this moment, but I don't want secrets or misunderstandings between us anymore. Truth is hard, but I need to speak it. "I need to tell you... I don't know who killed your brother."

He continues to drop gentle kisses on my face and neck. "I know."

"But I'm afraid that it could have been my mother."

"I know that, too," he says.

I try to banish the worry rising inside me. "I can't read her ledger to know for sure. Or... it could have been someone else. I used to believe that I was the last Valkyrie, that the Keres were extinct, but they aren't." I squeeze my eyes shut for a moment. "I wish I had answers for you."

Slade is quiet, stroking my arm in a soothing gesture. "It wasn't your Mom."

My lips part in surprise. "How do you know?"

"I don't remember much about that night," he says. "I've tried to obliterate the memory, but my brother went out to kill that woman. Not the other way around. Your mother was an honorable assassin. She only killed when it was sanctioned. I had the chance to ask the Guardian when she started staying in the Realm. She didn't want to tell me anything, but I wouldn't let it go. She confirmed that my brother was never a target."

A world of relief floods me. "I was so afraid..."

His gaze fills with regret. "I wanted to tell you but I wasn't in control after that day."

I ask, gently, "Why did your brother go out that night?"

Slade shakes his head. "None of it makes sense to me. He was eighteen. He wasn't an assassin. I tried talking to my parents about it but they refuse to tell me anything. They tried very hard to make everything normal. Including me." He gives a humorless laugh. "That didn't work."

I study his eyes, lifting myself to kiss his cheeks. "I love who you are. Especially your eyes."

He raises an eyebrow. "What about them?"

"They have silver flecks in them when you access your Valkyrie power. I don't think mine do that."

He becomes serious again. "You gave me a powerful memory to hold onto, Hunter. I promise I won't lose myself again."

"I trust you." I inhale as I realize what I said, knowing that it's the truth.

Snuggling into him, my eyelids droop. I murmur as my limbs grow heavy. "This is the safest I've ever felt."

Despite my best intentions, I fall asleep.

I jolt awake, a sense of alarm shooting through me.

I'm still lying next to Slade, curled into him. The dress has transformed into a silken blanket over us, leaving me in my underwear, but I'm not cold. Slade's breathing is deep and even, but it hitches as soon as I shift beside him.

His eyes fly open. "Hunter?"

I try to shake it off. "I don't know... I felt something..."

A worried crease forms across his forehead. Then he winces, pressing his fist to his temple. He jolts upright, the blanket sliding away from his bare chest. "Something's wrong in the Legion. I can feel it."

"We need to get back there." I reach for my assassin's suit, pulling it on as quickly as I can, but I stop Slade before he pulls the upper half of his suit up. "How long is the beach?"

"It reaches all the way back to the Legion. Why?"

"We should use the cover of this Realm to fly back," I say. "It will be faster."

We race to the beach, but Slade takes my hand before I spread my wings.

"I have to dismantle this Realm as soon as we get back to the Legion," he says. "I can't leave a world this large stretching across the city. I'm sorry. I didn't want to leave like this."

I kiss him, gently. "I understand. I loved it here, Slade. I wish we could stay longer."

His power thuds the air and his wings shoot out on either side of his body. My own release, spreading wide.

We race each other across the sand, taking flight together. Soaring through the clear blue sky, we follow the path of the twisting, turning beach below us, until Slade finally points downward.

We alight onto the end of the beach, knees bent, folding our wings away and striding toward the memorial leading into the Realm as soon as it becomes visible in front of us.

The beach Realm fades away, taking all my peace and security with it.

Slade pulls up his suit, sliding it over his muscled chest and arms as he hurries to open the door into the Legion, pulling me inside with him.

The screams chill my heart.

CHAPTER THIRTY-TWO

can't take it in. Can't process what my eyes are telling me.

The Guardian kneels on the grass, her dress bloodied, her caramel hair hanging loose. She rocks back and forth, weeping. An assassin lies across her knees, his head cradled in her lap.

Bodies are strewn all around her. Ten… twenty bodies.

They aren't moving.

A cry of horror rips out of me.

Slade runs to her. I'm close behind. "Guardian!"

The Guardian's face is splattered with blood. "She came for Gareth… She killed everyone who got in her way. They're all… dead."

The man she holds is Superior Lincoln, the poisons teacher. He is lifeless in her arms, a shotgun dropped mere paces away, the barrel bent.

My heart plummets. *They're all dead?* But Ridley's here too… *Dad…*

I search the faces of the fallen men, terrified that I'll see Ridley among them.

Slade's focus is sharp, pinpointed, rage thrumming through him. "Was it Lady Tirelli?"

His stern demand breaks through the Guardian's shock. She shakes her head rapidly. "I don't know. She was wearing a suit. Her face was covered. I'm sorry..."

She tries to wipe her tears, her hands trembling. "But the smell..." She gags, her hand flying over her mouth. "Roses. Rotten roses."

She continues rocking, choking back her sobs.

I press my hand against her shoulder, demanding that she focus on me, asking urgently, "Is she still here?"

The Guardian shakes her head. "She sensed you were coming back, Hunter. It's the only reason she left me alive. She didn't have time to kill me."

Fear is a vice around my heart. I try to hold myself together. I push away my dread for my father, whispering to Slade, "The Guardian is in shock. We need to get her to the medical wing. We need to... check the dead."

I pause. "Slade?"

He is frozen beside me. "Roses..." His expression changes as he scans the bodies, desperation mixing with rage. "My people..."

His focus snaps back into place. "This is not the entire Legion. Where are the others?"

The Guardian points a shaking arm toward the Cathedral. Three figures sprint from that direction. It's Lutz, Rowan, and Brandon, their legs pounding the ground.

Relief floods me when I see that Ridley is close behind them.

Rowan reaches us first. "Master! We tried to stop her, but she took Gareth."

They are all beaten and bruising, their clothing cut and torn as if they stepped out of a war zone.

Brandon wipes blood out of his eyes. "We tried the tranquilizers. Then we emptied whole clips at her, but she was wearing a protective suit. Nothing touched her."

Ridley reaches my side, checking me over. Compared to him I am as pristine as the beach I just left. I throw my arms around him in a fierce hug. "Dad."

I can't say anything else. My fears have clamped my throat tight. I can't lose him like I lost Mom.

He returns the hug, holding me tight. "It's okay. I'm okay."

Slade is still searching the faces of the dead. "What about Thomas and Matthew?"

Ridley answers quickly, lifting his head as I shift beside him, not quite letting him go. "They're out in the city on reconnaissance. They're safe."

Now that he knows his cousin is alive, Slade's anger rises and so does his power. "How the hell did she get in here? The Realm is protected."

Lutz presses a hand to a wound on his arm. "She walked right in and then… she took them all down."

I stare at the fallen men. "By herself?"

Rowan nods. "She was like lightning. Faster than anyone I've ever seen. They never had a chance. We were further back and were able to take cover."

The Guardian tugs on my hand, demanding my attention. "She must have access to an assassin's ring—a powerful one that I don't know about. There were always rumors of more rings… The ringmakers had rogues too…" She's mumbling now, barely making sense.

As Rowan helps the Guardian to stand, I say, "It has to be Lady Tirelli. I can't think of anyone else who would free Gareth."

Slade asks, "But why now? She's obviously powerful. What can he do for her that she can't do herself?"

I close my eyes as the answer hits me. "Gareth knows how to decode the books."

There must be something hidden in them that I don't know about. William used the Keres Coda to find out how to remove the resin from the Clave. He was close to discovering other secrets when I left this morning... before I killed the Tirelli brothers.

I've struck at the heart of Lady Tirelli's organization. I've killed her men. If she is the Realm's attacker then she's on the rampage now.

Slade brow furrows. "But you have the books."

Fear rakes through me.

I pull away from Ridley. "I have to get back to Saber Lane right away. Everyone there is in danger."

Slade spins. "I'm coming with you."

I'm at war inside myself. He needs to stay here and look after his Legion. There are so many dead. But his bond with me will control his movements now. I try to find a way to tell him he doesn't have to come with me, to ease the force of the bond so he can make a free choice.

He glares at me, all the harsh lines returning to his features. He knows exactly what I'm thinking. "I *want* to come with you, Hunter. I'm not letting you fight her alone."

Brandon speaks up. "Go, Master. We will take care of the Guardian and the wounded."

Rowan nods beside him. "We'll call back all of the

assassins who are out in the city. We need to regroup and protect the Realm from another attack."

Lutz has been quiet, contemplating Slade and me. He told me that Slade was becoming a ruthless killer. Despite the horror around him, he looks relieved to see that Slade is himself again.

Lutz says, "Master, I'm coming with you. You need backup."

Ridley also speaks up, "I'm not letting you out of my sight, Hunter. Not while that woman is still alive. Whether or not she is Lady Tirelli, she's dangerous."

I glance at Slade, hoping he will hear what I'm *not* saying. "I intend to blur. If you want to help, meet me at Saber Lane as fast as you can."

Slade immediately spins to Rowan. "Tranquilizers! Now!" He catches the tranquilizer belt that Rowan throws him right before I break into a run.

My heart is in my throat as I disappear into a blur, release my wings, and take to the sky. A whoosh behind me tells me that Slade has blurred and followed, rising into the air with me. I'm relieved to know that he understood my unspoken intention to fly to Saber Lane.

I push myself faster than ever before, cold fear gripping my heart. There were so many dead assassins in the Realm and they were trained fighters. Other than Drake who owns the dojo, the people of Saber Lane are peaceful. They are not trained to fight.

As I near my home, men dressed in combat gear become visible converging on the entrance to Saber Lane, at least twenty of them. Gareth and Fallon stride at their head, but there is no sign of Lady Tirelli, no awful scent of roses wafting through the air.

Fallon told me that Lady Tirelli knows what I am.

My lip curls. She has sent them to do her work for her.

I land in the middle of the street so hard that the pebbles crack. I emerge from my blur facing the attackers and stand my ground.

A second later, another crack appears on the street and Slade emerges, his expression stony. He is controlling the Valkyrie power but he will unleash it if he has to.

As Gareth, Fallon, and their men pause at the entrance to the street, taking note of our arrival, Briar races out from the Diner. She's carrying my katana, her lanky legs a blur as she sprints across the distance. "Dean sensed them coming. Vlad and Tansy have taken everyone back to the dojo where Drake is standing guard. Vlad will join you soon."

I ask, "Is William safe?"

"He's in the dojo." She lowers her voice. "He took the books with him."

"Thank you, Briar. You should head back to the dojo, too."

She gives me a firm shake of her head. "My place is here beside you, Milady."

I spin to her. "Briar, no. Slade and I are both wearing protective suits. You aren't. Seek shelter now, please. I won't lose another friend to this monster."

She places her hand on my shoulder. "I love you, Hunter. But I will do as I please. I'm not leaving you."

She shocks me by hitching up her dress and drawing a dagger from a surprising arsenal of blades strapped to her thigh. She winks at me. "That's just one leg."

There's something etched in the dagger's handle, but she quickly covers it with her hand.

I pick up my jaw. "You know how to use that?"

She grins and I've never seen such a light of vehemence in her eyes. "I've been waiting for the chance."

Vlad sprints up behind us, his boots pounding the cobbles, and I'm relieved to see that he is in full combat gear.

"Everyone is safe at the back of the street," he says. "I'm glad you're here. As much as I rate my skills, I wasn't looking forward to defending Saber Lane alone."

Briar clears her throat and Vlad quickly adjusts his statement, "Alone with Briar, that is."

Vlad hands me a belt of tranquilizers. He's wearing one himself—along with a handgun and a cloak of rage. He's a towering inferno glaring at Gareth and Fallon as they dare to approach. The twenty men behind them crowd into the street in rows of five, weapons raised and ready.

I murmur, "Those are submachine guns. We need to protect bystanders. And people on neighboring streets. Our friends in the dojo aren't safe either."

Bullets travel far and fast. Gareth won't care who gets killed in the crossfire.

Slade places a hand on my arm, his determined gaze meeting my own. "I can help with that."

As he speaks, a brick wall sprouts out of nothing on our left and right hand sides directly in front of the shop fronts. Bricks layer on top of each other, rising high enough to protect the buildings on Saber Lane as well as the neighboring streets. The wall grows behind us, forming a barrier in front of the dojo and, much to our attacker's surprise, it forms behind them too, blocking off their retreat. The back row of men jumps forward, shouting, clearly not liking this new trap.

Vlad stares at Slade. Alarm is etched on Vlad's imposing features. "What are you doing?"

Slade shrugs. "I've created a partial Realm. It will appear as an illusion to anyone walking past the street—they will only see Saber Lane as it's meant to be. But the wall will absorb any stray bullets. It looks like brick, but it's spongy. If I could, I would pull all of those men into a full Realm where we could fight them without any risk of collateral damage, but that would require grabbing them and pulling them in one by one. This will have to do for now."

Vlad gives the walls a wary once-over. "We'll have to grow wings to get out of here."

Slade grins, catching my eye for a moment. "Don't worry, I'll take it down when the threat is gone."

Vlad gives him a stern look, indicating Slade's assassin's ring as he says, "That ring is dangerous in your hands, my friend."

Slade doesn't deny it. "The disadvantage is that we're boxed in."

Like fighters in a cage.

My teeth grind together.

Bring it on.

CHAPTER THIRTY-THREE

Gareth, Fallon, and their men continue to advance, stopping ten paces away from us.

I shout, "You've invaded my territory without permission, Gareth."

He smiles, cold and cruel. He has grown a short beard during his time of imprisonment, but he is not weakened, his gaze gleaming with vengeance.

If only he was still a Master; he would have broken the seventh rule like Vlad did, and I would be entitled to kill him.

He snarls, "You've seen what Lady Tirelli can do. She destroyed the Legion. You will hand over the feather, the verdan, and the books, before more of your friends die."

I scoff, "Who says you killed my friends? I hated those assholes in the Legion. Especially Superior Lincoln."

Oh, how cruelly the lies slip from my tongue. Superior Lincoln was the kindest teacher in the entire Realm. He even pulled Lutz into line on the first day. Even Ridley, who knew I was his daughter, was relentlessly harsh and never went easy on me, but Lincoln was always fair.

Gareth's expression hardens when his taunt washes off me.

Fallon twitches, and a creeping sensation slithers up my spine. His earthy brown eyes shimmer with power. He is already trying to get inside our minds, but his eyebrows draw down in a frustrated expression and a hiss emits from his lips when it's clear he can't get inside Slade's mind this time. Nor Vlad's for that matter.

Vlad glares at Fallon. "I warned you never to come back here. You will not leave with the use of your limbs this time."

Gareth barks, "Last chance, Hunter. You can't kill us but we don't obey the Code anymore. We will kill anyone who gets in our way. Give me the feather! Or Lady Tirelli will tear down your world."

I take a step toward him, tightening my grip on my sword. "If she wants it, she can fight me for it!"

Gareth's expression darkens. The energy around him is like the dead of night, making me shudder.

He snaps, "She will reveal herself at a time and place of her choosing."

My eyes narrow. It had better be tonight. I can't go another day knowing that woman is alive. "Then she's a coward."

He flexes his fingers. He's wearing his old assassin's ring on the forefinger of his right hand, since there is a conspicuous gap where I removed the forefinger of his left.

His declaration is cold and clear. "You've brought a world of pain down on yourself—and everyone you love."

I stride toward him, unsheathing my katana. "I don't fear you."

I swing the sword, knowing full well that he will use his power to deflect it, but that's exactly what I want him to do.

As soon as his focus shifts to my sword, I blur to disorient him, grab a tranquilizer, and aim it for his neck.

Gareth is already shouting to his men, "Shoot them!"

A storm of bullets forces me to jump out of my previous position before I can tranquilize him.

Slade goes straight for Gareth in my absence and Vlad confronts Fallon. They're smart—as long as they stay near the assassins, the men won't shoot at them. Nobody will risk blurring for fear of being accidentally shot.

Well, nobody but me.

I take a moment to assess where I'm needed.

Fallon darts to the side, slinging lines of icy flame at Vlad, but Vlad retaliates with his own power, his assassin's magic taking the form of ebony needles that spear the air like darts, forcing Fallon to flee as the darts track his path.

Briar dashes around a path of bullets, slides on her knees, and slams a tranquilizer into the leg of one of our attackers before racing out of the line of fire again. The man takes a step, wobbles, and thuds to the ground. Willow wasn't mucking around with the meds.

Nearby, Slade's body is lit with silver, his movements a blur as he lands blow after blow on Gareth. Gareth doesn't have the Keres ring this time but he is agile, darting back and forth, his power colliding with Slade's. The impact of their fight cracks the pavement, unsettling the men with guns and forcing them to stay clear.

While Slade and Vlad keep Gareth and Fallon busy, I focus on the rest of the men. I quickly sheath my sword, remain blurred, and release my wings, swooping on the men while they can't see me.

I succeed in tranquilizing two of them before a barrage of bullets sweeps my way. I have far more room to maneuver than I did when I confronted Enric Tirelli in the hotel corridor and I easily evade the projectiles, but these guys are coordinated and skilled. They group themselves in a protective circle, facing outward, ready for me to come at them from any direction.

As soon as I jab one of them, they know where to shoot. Subduing them one by one is taking too long.

I need some sort of crossbow or…

Just then, Ridley and Lutz appear, running straight through the brick wall. As soon as they pass through it, they spin and stare at it. It's only visible from our side so it will have taken them by surprise.

They recover quickly, pulling protective face masks over their heads. Only their eyes are visible now. To my surprise, the Guardian is with them, her features drawn and tense. Her hair is pulled back into a tight ponytail and she is wearing protective gear.

She isn't shaking anymore. In fact, quite the opposite. As she tugs on her face mask, she races right at the huddled men.

She has a crossbow.

I grin as she drops beneath a spray of bullets and aims it at the man firing at Lutz, tranquilizing the guy cleanly in the chest.

Lutz zigzags along the street with Ridley, both men moving at a lithe blur. They seem to have some sort of silent communication going on because they both run straight for the huddle of invaders, barreling into the men at full speed, shooting tranquilizer darts as they go.

I spin and check the fighting behind me. Vlad has raced away from Fallon to intercept a handful of men who have taken the knife fight to Briar. She spins and whirls, deflecting their weapons, but she's outnumbered. I hear the crunches as Vlad breaks arms and legs in powerful strokes.

Slade is keeping Gareth busy, but the older man evades Slade's every attempt to tranquilize him, using his power to absorb the impact of Slade's fists. Even so, Slade predicts every move Gareth makes and the older man is visibly tiring. He won't last much longer against Slade.

As I materialize again, Slade shouts, "Hunter! Get Fallon!"

I spin to locate the oily assassin. He creeps along the street toward the vicinity of the bookshop.

He must think the books and feather are there and that he can steal them during the fight. He presses against the brick wall as he proceeds as if he's looking for a weakness.

I grab a tranquilizer and race toward him.

As soon as Fallon sees me, he flings fire at me, narrowly missing my face.

My aim is quicker, the dart sailing through the air. It flies right through his arm... and emerges out the other side. It hits the brick wall.

What?

Fallon's image flickers before my eyes.

Cold fear shoots through me, freezing the blood in my veins.

I reach for my sword as I close the gap. It glints as I swing it straight through Fallon's torso, a blow that would finish him...

If he was really standing in front of me.

Fallon's laughter echoes around me. "Oh, dear. You figured it out."

He's not really here.

He was never here.

Gareth and Fallon came for the feather and the books.

They don't know that the feather doesn't exist anymore, but they do know that William has the books.

I spin to the fight between Gareth and Slade. Every move Gareth makes is defensive. He isn't attacking. He's keeping Slade busy. He's… stalling.

If Fallon was never in front of us, then he was here *before* Slade put up the wall. Which means he could have the books already.

His threats about hurting my friends are like a dagger in my heart.

I have to get to William!

I race toward the end of the street, slamming a fist into the nearest man, knocking him out of my way. My feet pound the pavement. My heart is in my throat. Reaching the end of the lane, I thud against the brick wall in front of the dojo, kicking it and smashing my fists against it.

I put all my power into the blows, trying to get through, but it doesn't budge. Slade made it strong.

I scream, "Slade! The wall!" My fists are bleeding, my fear unbearable. "Take it down! *Slade!*"

"Hunter!" He shouts my name and a second later, the wall disappears.

I stumble forward, swiftly taking the stairs up to the porch.

The dojo doors are wide open in front of me.

Blood spatters the floor. Tansy lies half across the porch, half inside the room, a gash on her forehead. The rise and fall of her chest tells me she's alive, but barely.

Drake's prone body rests further inside the room but he's facing away from me and I can't tell if he's alive or dead. All of my friends, including Willow and Christopher James, are herded into the back of the room, huddled on their knees, their arms and legs tied with ropes made from assassin's magic.

Their faces are pale with shock and fear.

In the center of the room, Fallon grips William by the throat. He has forced William to his knees, binding him with ropes of flaming light that pull his hands behind his back. The ropes extend to William's ankles, immobilizing him.

With one hand, Fallon digs his fingernails into William's windpipe.

With the other, he presses a gun to William's temple.

They're seven paces away. Seven steps too far. A tranquilizer won't work fast enough to stop Fallon pulling the trigger.

"We warned you, Hunter," he says.

No. Please.

My ears buzz. My focus narrows. Every breath stretches out, the seconds far too short, the beat of my heart too loud.

William tries to speak against the pressure around his throat. He captures my gaze, insistent, needing me to hear him. "Remember… Just because you're born into darkness…"

I burst into action, racing across the distance.

I will stop Fallon. I will take the gun. I will stop—

A deafening sound splits my hearing as I slam into Fallon, flinging him across the room. He thuds against the wall, winded, falling in a heap on the floor, his dark hair lank across his eyes, but he's laughing…

A cry rises in my throat as William slips to the side.

Fear screams through me. "No, William!"

I catch him before he hits the floor. His body is heavy, limp, folding in my arms as the ropes disappear. There's so much blood. So much on the floor and on my hands. I try to hold him upright, try to see his face, try to help him stand, pulling at him even though he slips in my arms... until I realize...

He's already gone.

I scream, shock and grief building like a tornado inside me. William was a father to me. A friend. A guiding light. I can't lose him.

"No, please. *William! Wake up!*"

I pull him upright. I have to... he has to stand up. He has to open his eyes.

I drop to my knees, holding him against me, willing him to be alive, trying to support his torso, his head... screaming while Fallon draws to his feet, pushing the strands of his hair out of his eyes.

He's still laughing, snarling, "You should have given us the feather. I will keep killing your friends until you give us what we want."

Fallon.

Cold like winter washes through me, numbing every cell in my body. The blood reminds me of Mom. William's final words remind me of Mom. Fallon laughed about Mom, too.

Fallon who is afraid of enclosed spaces, who grew up in darkness and never overcame it.

Someone shouts my name. "Hunter!"

It's Slade. I sense his presence approaching fast. He's running toward me but he won't reach me in time to stop me.

I lay William gently on the floor and rise to my feet, the sobs dying in my throat, my focus narrowing until it is pinpoint. Silence falls around me and everything fades into the background. I narrow my eyes and lower my head. My power shrieks through me and my back shifts, preparing to release my wings.

I restrain it.

I am in control.

My heart burns with ice, my hands burn with fire, liquid rage pulses through me, pumping inside me like a hammer beating hard. I take one deliberate step in front of the other.

Fallon hiccups and swallows, scrambling backward, pressing against the wall as he scoots along it. "You won't kill me. You're not allowed to."

I am not afraid. I am not sad.

I'm *angry*.

The space darkens around me, my power absorbs the light around us, and my killing energy crackles through my hands. "You will end today."

I wrap one hand around his throat, drawing him upright, squeezing, calling on my power as he struggles against me. He thumps at my chest, kicks at my legs, releases all of his assassin's magic into me. Sapphire flames curl around me as he conjures them, but I don't feel a thing.

Another voice shouts behind me but I barely hear it. "No, Hunter!"

I don't care about the Code. I don't care about the rules. Let them hunt me down. Let them come for me.

Fallon will not breathe another second of air on this earth.

CHAPTER THIRTY-FOUR

There's a whoosh beside me, followed by another. *Thud-thud.*

I inhale with a jolt. My hand slides from Fallon's throat but he remains where he is, his eyes wide and vacant. He's pinned to the wall by the dagger in his shoulder, killed by the dagger to his forehead.

I stumble backward.

The initials on the two daggers are not Slade's.

I spin as everything speeds up around me.

Briar stands behind me, her chest heaving, her hands shaking.

She whispers, "He had to die. But not by your hand."

Slade is a powerful blur as he races across the porch, sliding to a halt beside me, taking in the bloody scene within seconds. His gaze lands on William and his face pales. "Hunter…"

My chest is heaving and my power ripples around me. Slade knows better than to try to take me in his arms right now. He doesn't try to soothe me with words or actions.

Instead he growls with deep threat, "Lady Tirelli will pay."

A shriek from the floor snaps my attention to Tansy.

"William?" She drags herself to William's body as the wound on her forehead heals rapidly now that she's awake. "William? No... please, no!"

She lifts his head into her hands, her lips parting, a shriek growing on her lips. *"William!"*

Everyone huddled in the back of the dojo is sobbing and clinging to each other.

Tansy's gaze sweeps over them before she inhales, her breath shrieking into her lungs, her ferocious gaze landing on Fallon.

He is already dead. There is no vengeance for her.

An oppressive force grows around Tansy, a darkness beyond anything I've felt before. It is a power so immense that it beats into me like a fist, driving Slade and I backward as she strides across the porch and down the stairs where the fighting continues.

Vlad shouts her name but she doesn't respond.

She stops on the pavement, screaming, "This is my street. *This is my home.*"

She lifts her hands, a wild wind growing around her, the air crackling with her magic. It builds so fast that it's a tidal wave rushing around me, an enormous force that she lets loose, shrieking, "You will not step foot here again!"

Air streams around her, whistling and weaving around the attackers, picking them up and forcing them backward. They dig their heels in and try to cling to anything they can, but the storm picks them up like trash, flinging them away from us, slamming them into Slade's brick wall.

Crunch. They shout and scream against the force that

presses into their lungs, threatening to snap their bones. The unconscious men we tranquilized fly with them.

Slade's wide eyes meet mine. With a flicker of his assassin's magic, he removes the final walls of the sub-Realm he created.

Gareth tumbles out with the others, ending up clinging to a lamp post before the force halts, allowing him to get back to his feet.

He rages forward, hitting an invisible wall and bouncing off it. He tries again in another spot, but the shield Tansy created stretches from one side of the entrance to the other.

No matter how much magic Gareth throws at it, he can't get through. He slams his fist against the barrier one last time before he seems to realize that he's not invisible to the outside world anymore.

With a frustrated gesture for the men to follow, he strides away. The conscious men pick up their sleeping comrades and hurry after him.

Only Vlad, Lutz, Ridley, and the Guardian remain inside the lane.

I've never seen magic like this, never felt it before. It lingers in the air around me as Tansy drops her arms to her sides, her shoulders slumping, her legs wobbling.

Vlad runs to her, wrapping his big arms around her. "Tansy?"

She tips her head back to see him, her hair falling across his arms. She's tall, but Vlad is a giant.

Her movements are wooden, her voice mechanical. "I've placed a permanent protective shield around Saber Lane. Nobody with ill intentions will ever step foot here again."

"But are you okay?"

"No… I'm not…" Her knees give way but Vlad holds her

tightly, pulling her close. He meets my eyes over the top of her head.

I stumble over to the porch railing, gripping it hard as Slade murmurs, "Who killed Fallon? Please tell me it wasn't you."

He must be terrified that I will be hunted now. Fear is etched in every tense line of his face and the desperate angle of his shoulders as if he's ready to jump in front of me if he has to.

Briar steps into the light. "It was me."

The Guardian, Lutz, and Ridley gather at the dojo's steps while Vlad helps Tansy walk to our position. Inside the room, the occupants of Saber Lane have gathered around William now that their bindings have disappeared. Some kneel, others stand.

Dean holds William's hand. Dean's eyes are closed, his lips nearly blue with pain. Willow wraps an arm around him, rubbing his arms to try to warm him. Drake has recovered but he and Christopher James are in shock, standing back from the others, staring at nothing.

I want to get them all out of here, tell them they're safe now, but the tension in the Guardian's posture tells me I shouldn't make a move.

She climbs the stairs to examine the knife that killed Fallon. I'm not sure how she can stand to look at him. I refuse to.

Her movements are slow and considered, her face paler than pale. "Briar, this is your weapon."

Briar remains tall and emotionless. "It is."

The Guardian's voice shakes, her hands folding over and over in front of her, wringing themselves. "Then, under the

Assassin's Code, you are charged with killing an assassin for which the penalty is death."

I jump away from the railing. "What are you saying? Briar isn't bound by the Code. She isn't an assassin."

Tears fill the Guardian's eyes. "You don't understand. Briar is a Horde assassin. In fact, she was once second in command."

I shake my head. "No, that's not true. Briar is my friend. She's loyal to me. She's… homeless for goodness sake! Look at her. She isn't an assassin…"

"Hunter." Slade reaches for me but I dodge him.

"No." I step in front of Briar, pulling her behind me. They're wrong. She's too frail to be an assassin. "This is a mistake."

The Guardian doesn't try to move me. Nobody tries to touch me.

Briar speaks softly as she slides her hand into mine. "I'm sorry I never told you. I left the Horde many years ago. I was lucky to find your mother and she gave me a new purpose in life: protecting you. I've watched over you since you were a baby. It's been my honor to serve you."

My eyes burn. I can't look at her or acknowledge what she said because that will make it true. "I've lost William. I can't lose you, too."

She squeezes my hand. "I broke the first rule. That means death." She turns to the Guardian with a clear declaration. "I would do it again."

My fear and grief turn to rage.

I scream at the others, "Which one of you will do it? Which one of you will dare lay a hand on her?"

There is silence. Slade doesn't move. Neither does Vlad.

Standing off to the side, Ridley's worry hits me hard.

The Guardian turns to them. "Someone must. If Briar's actions are allowed to go unpunished, then none of you is safe from the others. You are all trained to kill. If there are no consequences for killing each other then you can expect a bloodbath."

Her shoulders sag. Tears drip down her cheeks. "I'm begging you. One of you… please…"

Lutz breaks the silence with a low murmur. "I will do it."

He meets my eyes. He told me that he kills with his hands because he never wants it to be easy. Of all the assassins here, I never expected him to take on this burden.

He speaks directly to me when he says, "I can be the bad guy you need me to be."

He's doing it so I won't have to hate someone I love. I won't have to hate Slade, Vlad, Ridley, or even Cain. But I don't want to hate Lutz either. I cover my mouth with my hand, unable to cry or scream.

The Guardian whispers, "Sanctioned."

Lutz growls at Briar, "You have until tomorrow morning, old lady. Put your affairs in order. Say your goodbyes. I will find you then."

He spins on his heel and strides away up the street. He knows I won't want to look at him again.

I swing to her. "Briar, please, run. Go somewhere safe. You can go back to the Horde. They will protect you—"

"No, Milady. The death of an assassin is a matter for all. I would rather die at the hands of one who will regret it." She takes my face in both her hands, forcing me to listen to her. "Lutz Logan will remember me always. There are those in the Horde who would not kill me so kindly."

She presses her forehead to mine, a fierce final gesture. "I have watched you grow up, Hunter. Your mother was so proud of you. Always choosing your own path, paving your own way in this world. I will be with you in spirit. Always. As will William."

She releases me, striding away before I can stop her.

I don't know where to turn. The foundations of my world have shifted irreversibly and now I have none. I don't know what I'm standing on or where I fit. With the assassins gathered in front of me? With Slade and my father? Or with the people—my people—mourning William behind me?

"Hunter?" Tansy's quiet voice breaks through.

She holds out her hand to me as she reaches the porch, a gesture I never expected her to make.

I place my hand in hers and follow her to William's side, dropping to my knees beside him. I am unable to move any longer. Every part of my body has frozen like old, rusted joints.

Tansy's arm brushes against mine as we lean into each other. He was a father to both of us and now we've lost him.

She whispers, "I would like to bury him in witch's fire tonight. Please, will you agree?"

I ask, "What is witch's fire?"

"It's a pyre but it doesn't burn like ordinary flames. It is only for the most honorable, the most beloved..." Her voice cracks. She squeezes her eyes closed, tears escaping down her cheeks.

I whisper, "You don't need my permission."

The assassins gather behind us, quiet and strong. Ridley and Vlad give me the space I need, lending me their quiet presence. The Guardian bends her head, praying quietly.

Slade meets my eyes for a moment before he lowers his own, but not before I see the fire in them.

Lady Tirelli will die.

CHAPTER THIRTY-FIVE

*S*lade takes charge of the clean-up, including dealing with Fallon's body.

He creates another partial Realm, a fake illusion of the Lane to shield us from the outside world while the Legion's clean-up crew quietly sets to work removing all signs of the battle. The men and women in the crew look tired. They've just come from the Realm where many assassins died.

Vlad brings Tansy her spellbook and she takes a moment to place a spell on Dean to stop his pain and cause him to enter a deep sleep the moment he gets home.

She also uses her magic to tend lovingly to William's body, removing all signs of his wound and cleaning up the space around us.

Then, she reveals the Coda and the Vade, telling me she hid them using her magic as soon as Fallon appeared in the room. It was why he hit her and knocked her out.

She and I remain with William, unable to leave him, while Slade and the others come and go.

It's quiet inside the dojo, even with the wide doors left open. The breeze inside the Lane is no longer freezing cold. Not so warm that a bystander would think the seasons had shifted from winter to spring, but warm enough that our breath doesn't frost as we wait for the sun to lower.

At one point, Tansy tells me that to summon the witch's fire she needs to stay by William's side until night falls.

"You have to get ready for tonight," she says. "I'll understand if you can't stay."

"I'm not going anywhere." I curl my knees to my chest and lean against the nearest wooden support.

She gives me a nod and that is all.

Later, Slade brings us food and hot drinks. It's a simple but thoughtful gesture, this ferocious assassin taking care of me. He hands a mug to Tansy who surprises me when she takes hold of his hand before he can leave.

His eyes grow wide at the contact—they were never friends—but she doesn't let go.

"Vlad told me that Lady Tirelli breached your Realm," she says.

He sighs. "She did."

She asks, "Does that mean she could attack again?"

"Unfortunately, yes. We have to assume she can breach any Realm. We aren't safe like we thought."

He meets her steady gaze, his expression weighted with the knowledge that he can't protect his people.

Tansy considers Slade for a moment. "Then you should bring your men here."

He is surprised. "To Saber Lane?"

"The protective shield I've placed around Saber Lane is not Realm magic and it's not assassin's magic," she says. "It's my magic. Lady Tirelli will never breach it. Bring your men here where they will be safe until you can end her tonight."

"I… that would be…" Slade clears his throat and gives her a deep nod. "I would be grateful. Thank you."

Tansy returns to her former brusqueness as she follows up with a pointed finger. "But only for one night. You'd better finish that woman because I'm sending all your people back where they belong tomorrow. I won't have my home overrun with assassins."

"Of course."

I say to Slade, "Thank you for the coffee," but I mean so much more than that. Thank you for being here. Thank you for helping protect *my* people.

When he heads back out to the street, Tansy says, "Assassins are unusual creatures." She flicks me a glance. "They kill and yet they love."

Her eyes lower. "I finally figured out what 'Solnyshka' means."

It's the name Vlad calls Tansy. I give a quiet, "Hmm?"

"It means 'little sun.'" Her forehead puckers and she appears perplexed. "I think it might be because of my hair."

I hide a smile. "Are you and Vlad…?"

Her eyes widen. "No. Of course not. He sleeps in the spare room. He's ferocious, violent, and—" She deflates. "Unexpectedly kind."

I murmur, "All of the above."

When the sun finally sinks below the horizon and the cold creeps back into the air, a glow builds around Tansy. It might have been there all day and I just couldn't see it. It's stronger than her aura, like the beginning of a burning ember.

As the last ray of light descends, she says to me, "This is a time of truth."

She falters, folding her hands in her lap. "William wanted me to tell you… why I am the way I am."

I stay very still. "You don't have to explain yourself to me."

"But I need to," she says. "I need to tell you that when I first met you, I was angry. But what I couldn't admit was that I was angry with myself. Seeing you after all that time reminded me of how much I hate myself."

I shake my head, keeping my response to a whisper. "Why?"

"Because it's my fault that my mother died."

I tilt my head. "You were three years old. You can't be responsible for that."

"But I am." She tucks her skirt beneath her knees as she twists toward me. "It was believed within my mother's coven and beyond, that I had been born with incredible power. My aunt wanted my power so badly that she killed ten other witches to make herself strong enough to take it. She wasn't after my mother. She was after me."

I consider Tansy carefully. "That was her choice, not yours."

She studies her hands. "But it was my power that killed my mother. My aunt was holding me in her arms, sucking my power from me. My mother tried to stop her so my aunt directed my power toward my mother to kill her. That's when your mother arrived."

She raises her compelling, green eyes to mine, speaking softly, "Anna had a choice: the only way to save my mother was to kill me to reverse the spell already cast. She chose to kill my aunt instead, leaving my mother to die. She chose *my* life."

I remain quiet while Tansy continues, "So I hate myself. I hate my power. I was damaged after what my aunt did to me, but my true power remains beneath the surface. I can only access it in moments of extreme emotion. Otherwise, I have to read from a book, as you know."

She reaches out to me, lifting her hand into the air between us, waiting for me to take it.

She blinks away her tears, pressing her lips together, trying to speak. "I don't want to hate myself anymore."

I uncurl from my position and lean forward to take her hand, allowing her to lean on me as she clambers to her feet.

She holds on tight as the glow around her brightens, faint, flickering flames growing, dimming, and then rising again. I'm not afraid of them. Or of her. She lifts her other hand and William's body rises off the floor, floating ahead of us as we turn and follow his body down the stairs and out onto the street.

The others have gathered at a spot outside the bookshop, waiting for us. Slade has brought all of the remaining assassins here. Some are wounded, others are helping the wounded, but they all wait quietly.

Tansy says, "William was a father to me."

She trickles flames through the air. They lap at William's body, curling around him, covering him completely until the glow is too bright to watch.

I turn aside, the light playing at the edge of my vision. Tansy is the only one who doesn't take her eyes off him. Her eyes glow with the same fiery light.

When the fire around William recedes, only a single flame remains burning in the air where his body used to be. Finally, it also flickers out.

The light in her eyes dies. "He will rest in peace."

She turns to me as the dark of evening grows around us. "It's time for you to get ready."

Vlad steps out from behind Tansy. "Hunter, I will write in your ledger now."

I nod and lead him to the bookshop while Slade, the Guardian, and Ridley follow close behind. The others stay out on the street.

Inside the shop, I inhale the comforting scent of books. William isn't gone. He's here, inside the pages of all the books he touched and the knowledge he left behind.

Vlad takes up my pen and swiftly fills out my ledger. In the section for the target's name, he writes:

The woman known as Lady Tirelli.

And in the reasons section, he writes:

For the future.

But he pauses at the section for offered payment. This is the tricky part. He already offered me a favor—which I don't intend to ask him for. He is a Master. For him to owe another Master a debt creates a very delicate situation.

He rumbles in his deep voice, "When my former Master wrote Lady Tirelli's name in my ledger, he wrote in this part… *'Your life.'*" Vlad grips the pen hard. "He meant that he was offering me his allegiance. Many former Masters seek to undermine the new Master in any way they can. At the same time, new Masters often seek to have their former Master killed—in ways that don't break the Code. That's why Briar came here."

He swallows. "This is what I'm offering you, Hunter."

He writes: *Peace.*

I acknowledge his offer. "Thank you, Vlad."

"When I failed to kill Lady Tirelli, it wasn't because she

was stronger or faster than me," he says. "It was because she blindsided me. She isn't what you expect. Don't be fooled by her appearance. You need to strike, and strike hard."

He steps back from the ledger.

The Guardian presses her ring to the page and her sanction glows golden across it.

Lady Tirelli is now my target.

Before I go upstairs to get ready, Slade sends a message to Cain about what happened on Saber Lane but reassures him that our plan for the evening still holds. Cain sends a swift response in the form of a sleek, armored vehicle to transport us safely to the event.

I block out my surroundings while I dress, ignoring every reminder of William—his scribbled notes on the kitchen table, his partly open bedroom door—focusing on showering, dressing, finding my heels…

But I hit a wall when it comes to doing my hair and makeup. Such stupid things to struggle with. I grip the bathroom sink, frozen, until a tentative knock on the door jolts me upright.

Tansy is pale when I open it, but she reaches for my hairbrush, pulling it through my hair. "When my grandmother died, I felt like it was wrong to care about the way I looked, like it was vanity. But William helped me see that caring for myself is important. It's not selfish."

She sprays my hair and then painstakingly curls the ends until it's tamed and silky, cascading down my back. "You don't normally need makeup but tonight, you need a face."

She sets to work and when she's done, the woman staring back at me in the mirror is both vulnerable and untouchable —dark lashes, full lips, and fierce emerald eyes.

Tansy has certainly worked some magic on me.

When I *tap-tap* my way to the bottom of the stairs in my heels, I find both Vlad and Slade waiting. Cain is already at the gala, but nobody else is coming with us.

After a lot of objections, we finally convince Ridley that he needs to stay here where it's safe. I look him in the eye and tell him that I won't lose him, too. He hugs me and lets me go.

Slade and Vlad are both dressed in black tie attire, their suits tailored to perfection. Their clothing is made out of protective material with numerous hidden pockets. My dress, on the other hand, was made for taking off, not protecting me. I carry a single, short blade tucked down my front beneath the scaffolding provided by my push-up bra.

My dress is black with a fitted V-neck bodice that is beaded provocatively across the bust and flares at the waist. The folds of material stop above my knees and are lined with deep purple material that is visible from the front. It allows for full movement of my arms and legs and it's the perfect color for my task tonight.

Slade takes my hand as we walk up the street toward the waiting vehicle.

He leans in to me, his voice a soothing whisper. "I know you need to do this. But you just lost William. Remember you're not alone."

I haven't cried since the witch's fire. If I give in to grief, I'll stop functioning.

For the second time in a month, I tell myself: *I am a machine.*

"I promise I'll deal with the pain," I say. "But I'll do it tomorrow. Tonight I have only one focus."

He gives me a nod but his own expression is open to me.

He's worried. He knows what it's like to lose himself to pain. It's written all over his face that he doesn't want to lose me to it, too.

I push the last of my emotions away and let my Valkyrie power rise. Tonight I need the killer, not the human.

Tonight I will wear the assassin's mask.

CHAPTER THIRTY-SIX

It takes less than ten minutes to drive to the grand hotel on St. James Avenue where the ball is being held.

The front entrance is lit up with golden lights. A valet opens the car door for us. The foyer is decorated with soft blue lights and the vast ballroom with glittering chandeliers.

Slade stays at my elbow, a protective presence. Vlad also sticks with me for now, but he will soon break off to find a strategic position to keep watch.

Our plan is to meet with Cain, drawing as much attention as we can, and then separate to different corners of the room. That way, Lady Tirelli will be forced to choose her target.

More than a few women eye Slade from beneath their lashes, but several others aren't so subtle about it.

On any other night, I would appreciate the way the black suit hugs his muscular form and brings out the dark rims around his blue eyes. I might even take note that I'm drawing a little attention myself.

Actually, more than a little attention when Cain heads directly toward me. Like the other men, he's dressed in black tie. He is an equally imposing figure, but minus a socialite on his arm tonight.

In my heels, I'm eye height with both him and Slade. It would take a miracle to elevate me to eye height with Vlad but that's okay with me.

Cain draws gasps from nearby guests when he presses a gentle kiss to my cheek. He ignores them, murmuring, "I'm so sorry, Hunter. William was a good man."

The sincerity in his voice is almost my undoing. While Slade's determined presence holds me together, Cain's compassion threatens to split me into emotional shards.

Before I can break down, multiple cameras flash. A pretty young woman wearing a press badge wedges herself into the space beside me. "How long have you known Cain Carter, Miss…?"

I glare at her, but before I can tell her where to shove her question, Slade edges in front of me with a smile that would make any woman's knees go weak. "Can I help you?"

She looks him up and down, blinking rapidly, a blush growing on her cheeks. "Whoa, bodyguard."

His eyes crinkle with dangerous humor. "Boyfriend, actually. And friend of the host."

Before she can pick up her jaw, he turns and shakes Cain's hand. The two men draw forward in a warrior's grip to clap each other on the back.

More cameras flash.

Cain speaks clearly for anyone listening, "It's good to see you again, Hunter and Slade. I appreciate your support of the fund for children's scholarships. I hope you enjoy the night."

He drops another kiss on my cheek, giving my shoulder a

gentle squeeze before he turns away. Now that we've made our presence known, we'll separate and wait for the Lady to find us.

Two kisses from Cain Carter is definitely enough to draw attention. Vlad steps in to intercept the young reporter before she can demand my attention again.

She drops her phone with a shriek at his sudden appearance. I guess he was doing that thing where he blends into the background before making his presence known.

He grins down at her from his great height. "*I'm* the bodyguard. You might like to give my friends some space tonight."

She scoops up her phone and immediately backs off. "Yes, sir."

A single glare from Vlad at a couple of men wearing press badges is enough to make them hastily retreat.

Slade whisks me away to the bar and orders us both a strong drink. Neither of us plans on drinking, but it helps to hold it in my hands. I'd rather grip a dagger right now but *that* would certainly cause a commotion.

Even here, we can't escape scrutiny.

A man with the aura of a vampire who sits at the end of the bar flicks glances in our direction, gripping his drink as if it's his liquid of choice. He identifies our assassin's rings and quickly finds an opportunity to disappear.

The back of my neck prickles as others walk past—a wolf shifter out for a good time and several human men who pause briefly at my back before Slade narrows his eyes at them.

I square my shoulders. There is only one pair of eyes I want to find tonight and unfortunately, their owner knows what I look like and not the other way around.

"Hunter." Slade breaks into my thoughts with a light graze of his thumb across my shoulder. Even in my grief, he can trail a path of fire across my skin with a single touch.

It has the welcome effect of refocusing me. "Yes?"

"There wasn't a good time to tell you this afternoon, but I remembered something about the night my brother died. It's what he gave me." His forehead crinkles. "I don't understand but—"

Roses.

The scent invades the space around us with treacherous speed.

Slade's eyes snap to mine. "She's here."

I search the crowd for the source of the scent. My gaze lands on a woman standing alone in the middle of the dance floor while couples dance around her.

She's much younger-looking than I expected, late twenties at most, with lustrous hazel eyes and masses of dark brown hair piled high on her head, wisps resting across her pale shoulders.

She's wearing a strapless ball gown that hugs her curves. She could be anyone's girlfriend, a small slip of a woman, petite and fragile, the kind of woman who would make men want to protect her.

She continues to capture my attention, a faint smile on her delicate lips. Her age is disconcerting, making me second-guess my instincts. Lots of people are watching me. Cain's kisses did that. It doesn't mean this woman is my target.

Only her scent will tell me. "I have to get closer."

Slade has also spotted her. "I'll be ready if you need me."

I slide off the bar stool and glide in her direction. As soon as she sees me coming, she skips to the side, maintaining eye contact with me. She moves off the dance floor and darts toward an open door at the side of the ballroom, slipping through it.

I catch Vlad's eye as well as Cain's before I hurry after her. They are both alert to my movements and quickly disengage from the people around them to follow after me.

I regain sight of the woman when I exit the ballroom. She waits for me in the foyer, craning her neck as if waiting for the exact moment that I appear around the corner.

Then, she dashes down a quiet hallway and into a nearby room, leaving the door open behind her. It's one of the smaller meeting rooms. According to the layout of this building, there's only one door in and out of it.

I guess she isn't trying to escape.

Slade has stayed on my heels, but he backs off a little. "I'll keep my distance, but I won't let you out of my sight. Be careful, Hunter."

Cain and Vlad also take up position in the hallway outside the room. I plan to remain within their line of sight through the open door as long as I can.

Two steps inside the smaller space, the scent of roses is overpowering. The woman leans against the center table, her dress crushed against it, one pale hand planted on its glossy surface as if she's not strong enough to hold herself upright.

Her presence is as confusing as when she came to the bookshop.

She's... slight and vulnerable but at the same time commanding and dominant, ferocity lurking beneath the surface of her delicate features.

There is a war of life and death around her, bright as sunlight but dark as decay. Her presence is a deep contradiction that sends my senses into a spin.

Her voice is like honey. "You have a beautiful ledger, Hunter Cassidy. I wanted to buy it, but of course, it wasn't for sale."

I grit my teeth. She was the woman who touched my ledger and asked William if she could buy it. That's how she got into the shop that day without breaking the door—she must have blurred and never left.

Her scent is as strong now as it was then.

I try to shake off the confusing input I'm receiving from her.

She speaks in a sympathetic melody. "It's hard to process, isn't it? What you sense but can't identify."

Vlad warned me not to be deceived. This woman is not going to fool me into believing she is harmless, no matter how innocent she looks.

I narrow my eyes at her, drawing on my power to clear my head. I banish the sensory contradictions to the back of my mind, using my power to stay focused.

My head clears.

I plant my feet, ready to attack if I wish. My demand is crisp. "You will tell me your name."

All I need is confirmation that she is Lady Tirelli. Then she is mine to kill.

She draws a short breath at my sharp tone, her posture shifting upright, a trickle of ice bleeding into her expression. "My true name is Amalia Avery. But most people know me as Lady Tirelli."

"Good." I draw on my power as I descend on her, quick strides closing the gap. I've moved out of Slade's sight but it's a risk I'm willing to take.

It also means that Cain and Vlad can't see me. Which means I can release my wings and end this woman.

She backs up, her palms lifted. "You don't want to kill me."

Rage simmers through me. "You're the reason William died."

She snaps, "And you're the reason my boys died."

I snarl, "They weren't your sons."

"They were the closest I'll ever have." She stops retreating, angling her body defensively. "I gave you every chance to come to me, Hunter. You chose not to. *That* is why William died."

Her expression shifts again, eyes narrowing. For the briefest moment, I glimpse her true nature—a woman with a will of iron.

She barely moves. A slight turn of her hand. Then the floor shifts.

I pull up sharp, registering the movement beneath my feet. That's... definitely not normal. I reassess my surroundings: four walls, one door, a table, and random, scattered chairs. It looks exactly like a meeting room should, except...

From the corner of my eye, a glimmer of light flickers, extinguished by the time I turn my head. At the same moment, a subtle vibration, almost imperceptible, shudders through the wall to my left.

"What have you done to this room?" I ask.

She replies, "What I can."

I quickly check her hands. The Guardian thought Lady Tirelli might have an assassin's ring that let her invade the Legion's Realm. The Guardian also said something about rumors of rogue ringmakers.

But Lady Tirelli doesn't wear a ring.

Or rather... *Amalia* doesn't wear a ring. For some reason,

she chose to tell me her real name and so far… she hasn't lied to me. I'm not sure how I know she's telling the truth, but every time she speaks, my senses hum.

She follows my gaze to her hands. She lowers her voice. "I'm not an assassin."

I inhale a calming breath and use my power to reach out to my surroundings. The room is no longer a room.

It's a space dressed up to look the way Amalia wants it to. It's layered with magic and has the potential to become… anything she wants it to be.

I stay very still. "This is a Realm."

I walked right into a Realm—one of her making. Enric Tirelli warned me before he died that I would walk into her trap and wouldn't know until it was too late.

She smiles, but her radiance fades when the wall vibrates again, harder this time. It makes a soft *thud*. Then another. The way she flinches tells me it isn't her doing.

"Your friends are trying to get in." She tilts her head as if she's sensing what's happening outside the room. "Slade Baines is desperate right now. He just dislocated his shoulder trying to break down the barrier. Don't worry, the big one will fix his arm for him."

I slowly and carefully remove my heels without taking my eyes off her, stating aloud everything that I know about her, "You don't wear a ring. You're not an assassin. You're a cold-blooded killer… a manipulator of hearts and minds… and you aren't human… but you don't have an aura…"

I place both shoes neatly on the table. Then I reach into my bodice for my dagger, sliding it out and flicking off the cover to reveal the sharp blade. I place that on the table next to the shoes. After all, a blade won't work on this woman.

I once told Slade that I would recognize a Ker if she stood in front of me.

It turns out I was wrong.

It's taken me far too long to catch up.

But there's one thing I know about Amalia: she's afraid of me.

She should be.

CHAPTER THIRTY-SEVEN

I never found out what extra powers the Keres have.

William was trying to help by decoding the Coda. I don't know for sure what I'm up against.

So far, it seems that Amalia can breach Realms as well as create them. And of course, she can take life the same way I can.

It's time to find out what else she can do.

I don't wait for her to alter our surroundings again.

I cross the distance in two strides and land a hit to her perfect nose. Her head snaps back under the blow, but she responds quickly, blocking my follow up kick with a quick downward thrust of her palm. I land another hit with my left fist but she blocks my next, gripping my arm and using my momentum against me.

She swings me bodily and throws me against the wall.

Oomph.

I guess that makes her as strong as me.

I drop to the ground, landing on my back and taking a

second too long to get up. Long enough for her to stomp her heeled foot straight down at my chest.

My protective reflexes kick in and I block with both forearms against the sole of her shoe, the stiletto heel pressing into my ribcage but not breaking skin.

I push upward, throwing her off balance, flicking my foot up in a kick to her chin that does the rest. It's her turn to kiss the floor.

She tumbles, tangling in her dress as she crashes against one of the wooden chairs. She snatches up a broken chair leg, brandishing it. "You should rethink your present course of action, Hunter."

So far I've ascertained that she can fight. And fight dirty, too. I removed my heels but she was willing to use hers. In every other way, she fights like I do. So far she hasn't exhibited any unusual traits. Of course, that doesn't mean she doesn't have them.

She blocks my next fist and answers by swinging the chair leg, thumping my cheek so hard that it breaks skin.

I ignore the pain and return the favor, whacking her cheek and then her stomach so hard that it propels her down the room. I snatch up my shoe from the table as I follow after her. Gripping it heel out, I quickly slash once, then twice at her face.

She is agile, gliding backward and then to the side to avoid both swings, blocking the next with the chair leg. I swing the heel hard enough to lodge it in the wood. She wrenches it out of my grip, forcing me to duck when she swings the shoe-lodged weapon at my head.

On my way down, I thump a fist onto her bent knee.

She shrieks and crumples more easily than I expected her to, which tells me that her legs are weaker than her arms. Come to think of it, I can't see them at all under her dress.

I use my location to quickly sweep my leg across hers, toppling her backward. She gasps again.

Her legs are definitely her weakness.

I've had enough of testing her.

My power sizzles through my fingertips as I launch myself forward. My back burns. I'm two seconds away from releasing my wings and I'm surprised she hasn't used hers.

Keres or not, I'm here to end her.

I press one knee into her stomach as my hands close around her arm and shoulder, gripping her bare skin.

She screams, "I'm not what you think I am!"

I shout, "You're Keres."

She chokes, "I'm not."

I falter.

Is she lying? What else could she be?

"But you're afraid of me," I say.

"Yes."

Rage thrums through me. She can create Realms. Breach them. She sent Gareth and Fallon to attack Saber Lane and take the books and the feather. She sent the Dominion Master to kill a Keres woman twenty years ago so she could get her hands on a Keres baby.

But now she says she isn't Keres and the hum in my senses tells me it's the truth.

I'm missing something—the piece that ties them all together...

I press my knee harder into her ribs, maintaining my dominant position despite her violent struggle to throw me off.

I demand an answer. "Then tell me what you are!"

She tries again to knock me off balance, but I absorb every blow she lands to my chest and shoulders. Her eyes widen at the way my fingers dig deeper around her arm no matter what she does. She knows I can release my power at any moment.

I'm surprised she hasn't used hers.

She begs, "Let me go and I'll show you."

It's a ploy. It has to be. There's steel behind her vulnerable act. She is as hard as knives beneath her exterior. "First tell me why you want the Keres girl."

Amalia gasps. "You know about her… You used the verdan on the feather."

"Of course I did."

She is suddenly excited, thrumming within my grasp, the change in her expression so rapid that I do a double-take.

She bubbles with excitement. "Then you know what she looks like. You can locate her?"

"I know what she looks like," I say. "I've burned the feather so nobody else will ever know."

It's mostly the truth. I know what she looked like as a baby. I know she has violet eyes. But I have no idea what she looks like now. She could be blonde, brunette, tall, short, or anywhere in between. I have no clues about her whereabouts. Briar turned up nothing and no amount of racking my brain has triggered any memory that might give me a sign.

Now William is gone and the secrets of the Coda and Vade are gone with him.

"Why do you need her?"

Amalia struggles again. "Because she can open a door that is locked to me."

I growl, "Stop speaking half-truths!"

She chokes on her sudden laughter. "That's hypocrisy coming from you, Hunter. You are the most competent liar I've ever met."

I squeeze her arms tighter, trickling my power into my fingertips, making her laughter die.

She snarls, "I can't tell you. I have to show you."

Do I want to know so badly that I'm willing to let her get up? I could kill her right now and this would be over.

Her eyes flicker with violence. "I'm afraid of you, Hunter. But it's because you can hurt me. Not because you can kill me. If you allow me to get up, I will show you why."

She says I can't kill her but I can kill anything. Only Slade is safe from me.

Still, my senses hum. There is enough truth in what she said to make me pause. If she isn't Keres after all, then I need to know what she is. Very carefully, I slide my knee off her chest, sensing her deep inhalation now that she can breathe properly.

I quickly release her from my grasp, leaping away from her, ready for anything.

Amalia rushes to her feet, backing away from me, one hand raised, ready to defend herself. I've proven that I can beat her in a fight and I know her weakness is in her legs. I will take her down again if I have to.

"Don't react," she says.

There's a creak like the branches of a tree groaning against each other. She hunches her shoulders and presses her lips together, her forehead crinkling.

Wings spread out at either side of her, unfolding in painfully slow increments. Her feathers are clumped together in places, damaged in others. In some sections, they are layered over the top of each other. They are metallic like mine but…

One of them is missing, and of the ones that remain, some are silver and some are… copper.

She has both Valkyrie and Keres feathers.

My heart stops beating. "How is this possible?"

She contemplates her wings. Her eyes close briefly as she passes over the spot where her feather is missing. "I stole the Keres feathers and placed them over my own."

I can't breathe. If the copper feathers aren't hers, then that means…

"You're Valkyrie."

She was telling the truth: I can't use my power to kill her. In fact, I can't kill her at all. I don't even know if the Keres ring could harm her. As far as I can see, she has assimilated with the Keres feathers.

"I am Valkyrie." She ruffles her feathers. They grate and creak against each other, the copper feathers grinding against the silver ones.

I exhale my shock. "Who are you to me? Are we related?" She looks so young, not even a decade older than me, but the person she is beneath her outer façade tells me she's much older. I remember Slade's fear that I was pretending to be the same age as him…

She sighs. "Open your senses, Hunter. Dig beneath the perfume I use to hide the cruel reality. Tell me what you sense."

My forehead creases. I allow the scent to invade my senses again. The odor of decay follows hard on its heels.

My eyes widen. "You're dying."

She nods. "A long and painful death. I've been dying for… oh… five hundred years to be exact."

Five hundred years ago, the first rings were made. The Valkyrie were hunted and their feathers ripped out. Just like her missing feather…

I stumble backward. My senses scream at me with everything that I've been ignoring, everything I've been pushing away because I didn't understand it. Her immense power. Her commanding presence…

I choke on the realization. "You're…"

"I am Amalia Avery, the last Valkyrie Queen."

CHAPTER THIRTY-EIGHT

She is my Queen.

The Queen whose feather gives Slade his power to create Realms. That's how she walked straight into the Legion's Realm.

After all, her feather was used to make it. It must also be how she hijacks the ledgers. Her power is the pure Valkyrie power from which assassin's magic was created.

But as the answers become clear to me, anger boils to the surface.

Her feather may have been stolen, but she has perpetrated that evil act herself. She has caused so much pain and violence on top of it.

The Keres feathers she wears are not soft birth feathers; they are fully grown feathers that had to be ripped out. "You took feathers from Keres women! Why?"

She snaps, "It was justice for their betrayal! The Keres Queen was my friend. I protected her. But when the first ringmakers captured her, she sold out *my* people in exchange for her freedom.

"The ringmakers raided my home, dragged my ladies from their beds in the middle of the night. They took my daughter. Ripped out her feathers. All because of the Keres Queen's betrayal. That's when we became enemies."

I flinch at the pain in her voice, the deep agony of watching her people suffer. Of her own suffering. But there are at least thirty copper feathers attached to her wings. She committed the same atrocity.

"How do you wear them without dying?"

A sly smile appears on her face, replacing her pain. "Because I took them when their owners were unaware of my intentions. The Keres power is only dangerous to us when it is activated. A Ker could hug you and not kill you unless she wants to."

I cry, "But the Keres ring hurts when I touch it!"

"Because the rings are in a constant state of active power." She contemplates me, her gaze open and guileless, her innocent façade making me ill. She must have tricked each one of those Keres women into trusting her.

I spit in disgust, "You took the feathers for revenge! You're no better than the ringmakers."

She hisses, "I took the feathers to stay alive! You don't understand—"

A massive *thud* against the wall snaps my attention to the left.

Amalia gasps, her wings folding to her side with a *crack*. She suddenly appears terrified, her chest rising and falling rapidly. "He's breaking through... But that's not possible... Not even using my ring..."

The wall splits up the middle, a neat parting, to reveal Slade standing on the other side. He is full of fury, hands clenched at his sides, a haze of power swirling around him.

He has removed his jacket and tie, unbuttoned his shirt at the neck, and rolled up his sleeves.

He storms through the gap, his blazing eyes meeting mine as it closes behind him.

The connection between us is instant, his power leaping out to me, his quick assessment taking in everything at once: me, Amalia… and her multi-colored wings.

His eyes widen. His protective instincts are already high, silver highlights flooding his eyes. Now his anger accelerates. His voice is an urgent demand. "Hunter! Are you okay?"

Before I can respond, Amalia lowers her center of gravity and hunches her shoulders, her entire body tense. Her lips draw back in a snarl as she spreads her wings, extending them to their full extent. They're massive, larger than mine.

Her power thuds through her so hard that it forces me to take a step backward. The force growing around her beats at me in waves, hot and unbearable.

Fear grows in my stomach. There's a reason she is the Valkyrie Queen. She is the strongest, the most dominant, a woman with many faces.

She spits, "Slade Baines, descendant of Josiah Baines who murdered innocent women. You will die today."

She leaps toward him but I ram myself into the space between them, bracing for impact, both of my fists connecting with her chest. "No! You won't touch him."

She stumbles backward, hissing, "You don't know what he is."

She hits back at me, trying to force me out of her way, her fist like iron, so much harder than before. Pain explodes through my cheek, radiating down my neck.

She let me believe I could beat her. She's stronger than she allowed me to think.

I grit my teeth, harness my power, and crash into her, lifting her off her feet. At the same time, I release my wings. They cut the air like pure silver blades.

I beat them and carry her up toward the ceiling. The roof elevates as we soar toward it—she's changing it so I can't push her into it.

She tries to beat her wings, but her ability to soar out of my hold is abysmal. As I suspected, she has no balance in the air. Her mismatched feathers make sure of that.

It doesn't stop her.

She hits my left wing, right where it connects with my shoulder. The impact sends me spinning, forcing me to let her go. She plummets clumsily to the floor, landing in a heap of material, her legs buckling, but she regains her balance within seconds.

The table vanishes, allowing her to storm straight toward Slade.

He's ready for her, darting forward to dodge her grasping hands and exchange quick blows back and forth between them. He holds his own against her, but I'm terrified of what she could do to him.

I don't know if she can harness the Keres power through the feathers she stole. She seems reluctant to kill me but she has made it clear that she has no reservations about harming Slade.

I angle my wings and spear toward them, grabbing her wings and wrenching her away from him. Swinging her around, I fling her at the wall. It transforms when she hits it, becoming spongy instead of cracking. It cushions the impact and allows her to drop neatly to her feet.

The environment changes rapidly around us. The ceiling opens up and brilliant sunlight glares down into the room.

The walls dissolve and searing heat beats around us. My feet sink into sand, but this is not a beautiful beach like the one Slade created.

We're suddenly standing in the middle of a desert. The air is so hot that it burns my lungs. Sand swirls around my legs, biting my skin. Slade stands two steps apart from me, ankle-deep in it.

Amalia quickly creates a stone platform for herself so she can move freely. It shifts and remains under her feet with every step she takes. I try to move but I only slide deeper into the grit.

She shouts, "You should not protect him, Hunter. He is a ringmaker!"

Slade freezes, eyes wide with shock.

I spin back to Amalia. "What are you talking about?"

She wears a cruel twist on her lips. "Slade Baines is descended from a long line of warriors bred for their strength and speed. Their sole purpose is to hunt us for our feathers. His parents left the Order, but his brother was seduced by the hunt."

The breath drags in and out of Slade's lungs. "You killed Foster."

"I should have killed you, too." Her expression cycles from rage to disbelief. "But you let go of the feather he tried to give you."

Slade's breathing calms. He was about to tell me about it when Amalia appeared in the ballroom; about what he remembered.

"It was one of the copper feathers," he says. "I picked it up and I gave it back to you."

The sunlight plays in Amalia's eyes, highlighting the weight of darkness that has consumed her. "I let you live because you did that. I thought I could control you. But now you've grown more powerful than I ever dreamed."

Her shoulders hunch protectively and her features contort with rage, her emotions cycling back to anger. "You will never take my feathers!"

He replies, simply, "I don't want them."

She narrows her eyes at him; she can't understand why he gave her feather back, but Slade is different. He always was. I know him like I know myself. He is his own person. He found his own way. Even if he is descended from ringmakers, it doesn't define him.

He is not the Valkyrie who lost his way.

Amalia is.

The only way I'm going to fight her now is to fly. Slade has the same thought, spreading his wings at the exact moment that I do. The electrical current thrumming through his wings crackles in the air. Our feet suck out of the ground as we rise in unison.

I'm about to soar toward her when Amalia screams, stumbling backward, missing a step and ending up in the sand.

I pull up sharp as her perfect features contort in horror. She points at Slade's wings. "What did you do?"

I hover above the sand, carefully beating my wings. "I gave him my feather."

She clambers to her feet, finally searching my wings. Her focus zeros in on the gap—my missing feather.

There's a moment when she freezes. Then her face drains pale. "Why would you do that to yourself?"

I expected her to be surprised, shocked, maybe even afraid, but she looks like she's going to be sick. Her reaction is so intense that I'm not sure what to make of it.

She demands, "Did he force you?"

I stare at her, baffled. "I did it willingly."

Is she afraid of him? Or me? Or something else?

She shakes her head. "Our feathers are our life, Hunter. Literally."

She struggles to her feet as she gestures at the gap in her own wing where her feather was taken. "*This* is why I'm dying. The moment the ringmakers took my feather, they triggered my death."

Everything slows down around me as her meaning sinks in.

"You've killed yourself," she says.

CHAPTER THIRTY-NINE

My wings fail me. I drop to the sand, numb and unable to speak.

I remember how much trouble I've had healing; how long the bullet wounds took to close and how weak I was after the fight to save the Guardian.

I thought it was because of restraining Slade the day before.

My focus shoots to Slade. He falls to the sand, his wings crumpling around him. The gorgeous electrical current disappears as rapidly as his feet descend into the sand.

His fists clench and unclench and a mask takes over his features. It's the mask he uses to conceal his pain. "Hunter… no…"

I spin back to Amalia. "You're lying! There are only two ways to kill us—"

"There are three! Foolish humans don't realize because it doesn't happen straight away. You won't die today. Not even next week. Maybe not for months. But you won't live another year. Your mother should have warned you but... perhaps she didn't know."

There were lots of things Mom didn't know. It was the dangerous side-effect of being the last of our kind, of all the knowledge that was lost over time.

I was always worried about the information that wasn't given to her and therefore she couldn't pass on to me. She didn't know that the assassin's rings were made of feathers and why she felt sick wearing one.

What Amalia just told me goes hand in hand with that information. It's a gaping hole in what Mom could teach me.

I shake my head, backing up to Slade, needing him to know that I don't believe it. Despite everything, I refuse to consider it. I bump into him, his warmth searing my back, his nearness a comfort that I need right now.

I glare at Amalia. "If what you say is true, then how are you still alive?"

She sweeps a hand through her copper feathers. "I'm alive because of these. The Keres are like us. They can take life. But they have an additional power: they can return a soul to a dying body. Imagine how awful that is on the battlefield, to return life to a tortured, broken person, extending their pain. But it's how I'm still alive."

The feathers glisten in the increasing heat as she continues speaking. "These copper feathers keep my soul in my dying body. Unfortunately, their effect doesn't last forever. I need a new one every thirty years or so."

"That's why you want the Keres girl."

"No, actually," she says. "She can lead me to a place where I can be healed forever. Where I can replace my lost feather with a much more powerful one and—"

She sucks in a sharp breath, as if she never intended to

tell me so much. She shakes her head, her hair falling loose around her shoulders. "It is a Queen's burden to speak the truth to her people. It's why I stayed away from you for so long. But now… you will obey me."

I am resolute. "I will not."

Her lip curls. "You are my soldier. Mine! You will do what I want!"

A laugh tears out of me. "I belong to myself. I fight the darkness. You embraced it."

Amalia's expression turns to stone. "Then you will die."

I've avoided meeting Slade's eyes because I'm afraid of what I'll see. The intensity in his expression now breaks my heart.

"I can't lose you, Hunter."

I shake my head. "You won't."

Amalia screams at us, "You think you love each other, but you don't. You're connected because he is a ringmaker, because that's how they trap us. The ringmakers are the strongest, the worthiest match. That's how they lure us. He doesn't love you. Nobody loves us!"

She throws her hands into the air and a windstorm billows up into the air, wild and sudden. Sand flicks into my eyes, tearing around me, grating my skin. I snap my wings closed before the gust lifts me off my feet.

The change in the environment is too rapid for me to scream or shout. There is no warning and no way to hold onto Slade. A thick wall of sand rises between us. It is so dense that it forces me away from him. I inhale the gritty substance, trying not to choke. I can't even scream his name.

Slade!

The sandstorm shrieks in my ears, blocking out all other sound. I can barely open my eyes, shielding my face with one arm and pushing through the storm with the other. The granules shred my skin, razor sharp pain slicing through me. I can't see my legs but they hurt, too.

I push on through the sandstorm.

Where is he? He was right here a moment ago.

I trip over something. A foot. Slade's boot. I drop and grip it, feeling my way upward toward his torso. His arms close around me and then...

The windstorm dies.

The sand plummets in a sheet toward the dunes.

It's suddenly very quiet.

Slade falls to his knees in the circle of my arms, bumping against me. I drop with him, my knees connecting with the sharp sand, holding tight to his chest.

His head drops to my shoulder, resting there, a heavy weight.

"Slade?"

Amalia looms behind him, her hand on the back of his neck.

Her power is a violent hum through my senses, but it's not the Valkyrie power that I'm familiar with. The power she is using now is foreign and terrifying.

"I hold his soul in my hands, Hunter," she says. "If you love him, you will do what I ask."

Fear invades my whole body, making me cold despite the hot sun. Slade sags against me. His arms skim my sides. He hasn't answered me. The only thing that stops me losing control and tearing Amalia apart is the shallow rise and fall of his chest.

He's breathing. Barely.

She has used the Keres power to take his soul. Now she can decide whether to give it back.

I've lost so much already… Mom, William, and soon Briar. I can't lose Slade. Not this man whose anger matches my own, who fights his inner darkness like I do, who is as damaged and as imperfect as I am.

I already know what Amalia wants.

Wretched and powerless, I make myself speak. "I will bring you the last Ker."

She smiles. "Good girl."

She slides her hand up into Slade's hair, the triumph in her eyes making me ill. The Keres power thrums again, an icy blast in the air, before she releases him.

Slade sucks in a sharp breath, his arms becoming rigid as he jerks to the side, coughing out the sand he inhaled.

I shudder with relief, frantically checking him over, but Amalia bends to stroke my cheek, her soft fingers demanding my attention.

"I have an insurance policy, Hunter. I know what his soul tastes like now. It is deliciously angry, relentlessly fierce, and incredibly in love with you. If you don't fulfill your promise, I will take his soul away when you least expect it."

I snap away from her, holding Slade as he coughs out sand that would have killed him if he wasn't Valkyrie. "Stay the hell away from us!"

She smiles at my anger and takes a step back.

Our surroundings shift again. The dunes dissolve into bright specks and fragments of light, the nature of our surroundings morphing into grays and blues, objects obscured by a growing white mist.

Amalia backs away through the thick haze. "I'm your Queen, Hunter. You can never escape me."

Her voice fades as she disappears into the swirling fog.

I hold tight to Slade as the walls, chairs, and the table

reappear around us. The carpet is soft under my bruised knees. My arms are grazed and bleeding. Slade's lip is bleeding, too, while a cut above his eye swells. I sense that the boundary around the room hasn't lifted yet. We have a few minutes until Cain and Vlad break through.

"Slade?"

He groans, still leaning forward on his knees, eyes pressed closed. I wrap my arms around his chest from the side and he responds by reaching for me, pulling me close, our thighs pressed together, his big arms folding around me, one hand tangling in my hair.

We survived our encounter with Lady Tirelli, but now we have to face the truth: I've signed my own death warrant and I've agreed to hand over the girl Mom died to protect.

The depth of Slade's emotion is impossible to ignore. "I… won't… lose you."

I press my forehead to his, fighting the tears that burn behind my eyes. "I would save you again, Slade. Even knowing the consequences. A single day with you is worth more than a lifetime of being alone."

Pain burns through me but it's not physical. It's taken me a long time to understand that having Slade in my life is not weakness. Loving someone is not a liability. It's a strength.

His Valkyrie power is already healing his wounds. His bruises are slowly fading.

Mine are not.

"I finally understand why Mom gave up everything to protect that girl," I say. "It's because it will take both of us to beat the Queen. Both of our powers are needed."

I take Slade's worried face in my hands, making a promise to him and myself. "I will find that girl, no matter what it takes. And with our two powers combined, we will end Amalia. Then, finally, our war will be over."

My heart hurts, my soul hurts, and every painful move I make, every sting of my wounds, reminds me that I'm dying.

But I make a vow I intend to keep. "I will end it."

Find out what happens next, and meet the violet-eyed woman, in Assassin's Menace.

ASSASSIN'S MENACE

(ASSASSIN'S MAGIC BOOK 3)

**I am a villain's daughter. Trying to escape my past.
Love can never be mine.**

I've mastered the art of hiding in plain sight.

My only goal is to bury the violent secrets of my past. A past
that was forced on me, not chosen.

But my fate is turned when I unwittingly step between an
assassin and his prey, an act that provokes the fury of the
Assassin's Legion.

Now, my only ally is a stranger. Cain Carter. A man whose
touch heats my body and soul.

I literally fall into his arms, and he is…

Kind. Compassionate. Terrifyingly sexy.

He offers me everything I've never had: pleasure, safety, and hope.

Until I discover that he has violent secrets too.

That's when I'm forced to make a choice.

A choice that will destroy my heart.

Content information: Assassin's Menace is dark urban fantasy romance, the third in the Assassin's Magic series. Recommended reading age is 17+ for sex scenes, mature themes, and violence. Ends on a cliffhanger.

ASSASSIN'S MAZE

(ASSASSIN'S MAGIC BOOK 4)

**I am a rogue assassin. Determined to protect my family.
Love is worth dying for.**

My true enemy has been exposed, but so has the terrible
truth about my life.

With my time running out, my only hope is an alliance with
my mortal enemy—a warrior whose power could destroy me
and everyone I love.

Including Slade Baines.

My bond with Slade can't be rejected.

Our connection is forged from desire so strong that it will
lead us along a path of danger and sacrifice.

Together, we must find the final Realm, the deadly maze that
holds the secret to saving us and ending our enemies.

But the maze has secrets of its own.

Magical creatures of myth and legend and a labyrinth of traps that will force me to make fatal choices.

To save my future, I must give my whole heart.

Content information: Assassin's Maze is dark urban fantasy romance, the fourth in the Assassin's Magic series. Recommended reading age is 17+ for sex scenes, mature themes, and violence. Ends on a cliffhanger.

ALSO BY EVERLY FROST

ASSASSIN'S MAGIC - COMPLETE

(Dark Urban Fantasy Romance)

1. Assassin's Magic

2. Assassin's Mask

3. Assassin's Menace

4. Assassin's Maze

5. Rebels

6. Revenge

7. Rogue

8. Assassin's Match

SOUL BITTEN SHIFTER - COMPLETE

(Dark Urban Fantasy Romance)

1. This Dark Wolf

2. This Broken Wolf

3. This Caged Wolf

4. This Cruel Blood

SUPERNATURAL LEGACY - COMPLETE

(Angels and Dragon Shifters)

1. Hunt the Night

2. Chase the Shadows

3. Slay the Dawn

4. Claim the Light

DARK MAGIC SHIFTERS

(Dark Urban Fantasy Romance)

1. Wolf of Ashes

2. Bond of Flames

3. Crown of Fate

KINGDOM OF BETRAYAL

(Fantasy Romance)

1. A Sky Like Blood

2. A Sin Like Fire

3. A Storm Like Iron

4. A Soul Like Glass

BRIGHT WICKED - COMPLETE

(Fantasy Romance)

1. Bright Wicked

2. Radiant Fierce

3. Infernal Dark

STORM PRINCESS - COMPLETE

(Fantasy Romance)

1. Book 1

2. Book 2

3. Book 3

DEMON PACK - COMPLETE

(Dark Paranormal Romance)

1. Demon Pack

2. Demon Pack: Elimination

3. Demon Pack: Eternal

MORTALITY - COMPLETE

(Science-Fantasy Romance)

Mortality Complete Set: Books 1 to 4

1. Beyond the Ever Reach

2. Beneath the Guarding Stars

3. By the Icy Wild

4. Before the Raging Lion

<u>Stand-alone fiction - dark romance</u>

Corrupt Me: Immortal Vices and Virtues

ABOUT THE AUTHOR

Everly Frost is the USA Today Bestselling author of fantasy romance, urban fantasy and paranormal romance novels. She spent her childhood dreaming of other worlds and scribbling stories on the leftover blank pages at the back of school notebooks. She lives in Brisbane, Australia with her husband and two children.

amazon.com/author/everlyfrost
facebook.com/everlyfrost
instagram.com/everlyfrost
bookbub.com/authors/everly-frost
goodreads.com/everlyfrost